Fly By Night

Fly By Night

Texas Hawthorne Legacy

Kelly Cain

TULE
PUBLISHING

Dedication

To the beloved readers who have stuck with me this far.

And to Diamond and Kamryn, always my reasons.

Readers Note

Thank you so much for picking up the first book of my Texas Hawthorne Legacy series. This was such an amazing book to research and apply knowledge from my elder family members who were around during this time, but please remember this is just my fictional take on the Airmen.

To make you aware, I'm listing some content that you may want to know about: previous death of a sibling's spouse (off page background), light profanity, heavy misogyny, and sex on the page.

CHAPTER ONE

Margaret—Meet-Cute, Bye

I STRUGGLED WITH the age-old question: *Do I indulge in what I love or toe the family line and engage with what's expected of me?*

After flying for over a decade and Daddy's expected retirement from the family business naming me his successor, I still didn't have an answer.

That question wouldn't be answered anytime soon, so I reviewed the theater ticket I'd been lucky enough to purchase while I waited on the shepherd's pie I'd just ordered. This was my treat after a long flight over the Atlantic and simmering anxieties back home in Texas. Okay, maybe avoidance of going home too, but since I didn't need to be back at work until next week, taking a little holiday sounded like a great idea. All of my family problems could wait until I returned. They'd still be there no matter how many shows I caught in the West End.

I still had a couple of hours before the show started, so I'd stopped in this gastropub near the theater, giving me somewhere to kill the time but also allow the opportunity for me to update the family tree I'd been working on. Somehow—maybe it was simply my birth order as eldest—I inherited the historian moniker for the Hawthorne family from my late grandmother. She'd laid out the basics of the tree, but all handwritten. I'd digitized it and began adding missing pieces. Honestly, I loved our rich history so much, it wasn't a burden in the least.

After placing my order, I sat my extra-large purse on the chair next to me, relieved to be rid of the heavy bag carrying my laptop, Kindle, and a couple of hardcover backup books just in case my electronics failed me somehow. I pulled out my tablet to pick up where I left off on the tree.

A shadow moved close to me, catching my attention. "Excuse me, sorry—is anyone sitting here?" The Englishman with the velvety voice asking the question moved toward the chair holding my purse like my property wasn't even there.

I glared at the man. "Um, yes, excuse me. My bag is sitting there actually." I didn't care how smooth his brown skin was or sparkly his green eyes appeared. He didn't actually give the impression of being sorry at all. Matter of fact, he seemed rather rude. I bet he thought those penetrating eyes gave him a free pass.

He tilted his head and knitted his brows. "I beg your pardon."

Since he didn't phrase it as a question, I took it as an apology but dragged the chair closer to me, his hand still attached to the chair's back. That was probably generous because he trained those piercing eyes on me, perhaps to intimidate. Something I was intimately familiar with from a lot of men. Not every man, but too many.

Resisting intimidation was my superpower.

It had to be in both my career choice and my opinionated family.

I set my tablet down and turned my chin up, giving him my full attention—and the intensity of my glare—until he released the back of the chair. He gave me a small grin. One side of his mouth quirked up, but the other side remained turned down. "My mistake." Then he walked off, presumably to rob another person's chair.

"Indeed it was," I mumbled under my breath then went back to my task, adding more details on my two-times great-grandfather, Samuel Hawthorne, who founded our branch of the family, and his Tuskegee Airmen sons, James and Harrison. Together, they established the aviation compound my kinfolk and I called home in Autumn, Texas, a suburb of Houston.

I crossed my legs and shifted in my seat as I scanned the records on the screen, settling on one name in particular. Great-Uncle Harrison was proving to be elusive. I rubbed my temples. A frustrated sigh rushed out.

My research placed him as a founder of the Hawthorne Family Flying Eagles company, but I couldn't find whether he'd ever been married or had children. There was an Alabama death certificate that put him in his fifties and documentation of his service in the war but little else. My great-uncle was a bit of a mystery. I often wondered why there was a statue at our compound of Great-Granddaddy James but not his brother. Granddaddy Isaac was of no help, which frustrated me to no end, but I'd become accustomed to his indifference. Although sharp as a tack, his memory became very fuzzy when it came to his uncle for some reason.

I sighed and shook my head.

I'd love to find out why.

Frustrated, I tore my gaze away from the tablet and stared straight ahead without truly focusing on the other patrons. Until I noticed a familiar face—the posh man who tried unsuccessfully to steal my chair. My attention lingered, roaming over his facial features. A shadow of stubble. Full lips. And that smooth golden-brown skin. Now that he wasn't trying to steal my chair, I could appreciate his looks from a distance. He'd settled across from another man, equal in skin color and features from their profiles. If I had to guess, probably his brother. He must have lifted a chair from some other unsuspecting soul.

Rudeness aside, he wasn't bad to look at, as Mama would say. My gaze lingered on his lips, full even in profile.

A steaming plate of delectable fluffy goodness, browned to perfection, appeared on the table in front of me out of nowhere, hitting my nose with savory meat and potatoes. I'd been so wrapped up in checking out Mr. Posh, I'd somehow missed the waitress coming and going. That was unlike me, to get so distracted by checking out a man.

One more glance couldn't hurt.

As if pulled by invisible strings, my gaze sought those green eyes once more. And found them staring directly at me.

He drew a bottle of beer to his lips and took a long, deep drag, watching me the entire time. He leaned back, and I noticed how the deep brown button-down he wore really complemented the sultry eyes trained on me.

If he wasn't dining with someone, I would've marched right over there and propositioned him. To meet up after the play, of course. A last-minute ticket had cost me a grip.

He lowered the beer and turned his attention back to his companion as though he hadn't just stared me down and undressed me with his gaze, and the spell was broken.

I frowned and picked up my fork, disappointed. The play would be my only source of entertainment this evening after all.

CHAPTER TWO

Lewis—Putting London in the rearview

I DRAGGED MY gaze back to my brother, unable to read the expression on the face of the beautiful American woman. I thought maybe she checked me out, but then she just stared, not altering her manner.

Charlie smiled knowingly. "Lewis, did you know that woman?" My brother released his Cheshire cat grin. He probably figured the woman was a stranger to me but had also captured my regard. He'd watched me while I watched her.

Not that it seemed like she wanted my attention.

"Cheeky. You know I don't."

He raised his brows and glanced back over at the woman across the room. "She sure seems like your type. Rich brown skin, curly, natural hair, light brown eyes…"

"They're more deep brown actually. Wait, how can you tell her eye color from here?" I gave him the most severe smirk I could manage, pulling one side of my mouth down low.

Charlie burst out with laughter. "So they're deep brown, are they? Just your type." Charlie sat back in his chair, grinning. "Ask her out."

My body leaned as if to get up, unbidden, and I took

hold of my involuntary movement. Tempting, but we had a play to get to soon. "What's the point? Plus she's American." Even though I preferred casual, I didn't make it a habit of hitting on American tourists. They romanticized Europe too much, and I hated to disappoint.

Charlie tilted his head, a sly smile creeping onto his lips. "All the better. You're moving there temporarily. You can hook up."

"You realize America is a big country, right?" My little brother had traveled as widely as I, so I knew he was just being cheeky.

Although speaking to my brother, I couldn't help my gaze sliding back to the American for another eyeful. She'd shifted her concentration to the food in front of her, spooning a mouthful of what looked to be shepherd's pie, then picking up a small tablet before her eyes flashed my way. I would have missed it had I not been looking so intently.

I removed the hand sanitizer I carried in my trouser pocket and rubbed some onto my hands before forking the steak-and-kidney pie the waitress just sat before me. Then I raised the nibble to my nose to ensure the aroma matched the appearance. It smelled delicious as the warm steam hit my nose.

"You don't need to worry about picking up anyone the way you smell your food before you taste it every single time. It's so annoying." My brother dug into his own meal with relish.

"Leave me alone, Charlie."

I wasn't worried about picking up someone. I'd only just finished packing up my flat before heading out to this going-away party of Charlie's. I'd call my parents from the airport tomorrow whilst I waited on my flight. They didn't understand nor approve of my choices—it wasn't every day you turned your back on family money.

Or deep connections.

But that had been the problem, hadn't it? My mouth settled into a deep frown.

Charlie caught my gaze. "What's that look for, brother? Having second thoughts?"

"Decidedly no. I'm looking forward to a new start and the exciting job awaiting me."

"Exciting job away from Dad and Mum, me thinks."

I couldn't hold back a grin. He was right. "That too. I'll look forward to making it on my own. America is a good place to start over where no one knows me. And more importantly, no one has expectations of our family connections." The last name of Watson-Grosvenor would mean nothing in the States.

My brother's gaze softened. "Everyone isn't like Sheila, Lewis."

The bitter laugh that escaped my throat was loud and unexpected. I glanced around, but thankfully our surroundings were loud enough not to draw attention. "As your older brother, I feel it's my duty to inform you that everyone has an agenda. Best you find out now, from me, than discover it on your own."

I'd had a series of one-night stands since I realized what Sheila was really after, and I didn't expect that to change any time soon. Setting low expectations with a woman up front kept me focused on moving forward because I would not make that mistake again. I would not be used again.

Charlie sighed. "Poor Lewis."

I leaned in and lowered my voice. "It's best you find out now—everyone has an agenda." I pointed my fork at him and raised my brows.

Sheila had used me. And used me well.

He only shook his head. "You're way too young to be so jaded."

I sharpened my tone, saying, "And you're too old not to know better."

Charlie had been out of university for over a year now, and Dad had gleefully absorbed him into the family business. Unlike me, my little brother relished it. He used our name and connections to do more than only pick up women.

"I'm going to miss you, Lewis."

My posture relaxed a bit. "Me too, Charlie. Me too."

CHAPTER THREE

Margaret—Are these seats taken?

THE WEST END was so different from Houston's theater district with its disjointed buildings in the same general area but not connected in any real way. Certainly not easy for walkability, like here. Not that I complained—we had it better than most—but this place lit up something akin to Broadway with its huge marquees and heavy foot traffic. As I walked the sidewalk, dodging other pedestrians, including many tourists like me, I took in the buildings that were older and more majestic than anything we had back home though the general feel remained the same.

After taking my seat at the beginning of a row in the theater, I checked my phone to ensure I had silenced it and noted the time. About fifteen minutes until the curtain came up. I relaxed into the comfy, plush seat and watched as people all around hurried to their seats, chatting with heads close together, readying themselves for the show to start. Back home, my lifelong best friend attended with me, but when I traveled, even to New York, taking in a Broadway show, it was normally by myself. I could enjoy the experience either way but preferred to share with someone.

I settled my big purse in the seat next to me, knowing I'd probably have to move it if someone claimed the space, and took out a book to pass the few minutes left, shutting out my surroundings. Although I was excited to take in a show—I'd been to the West End many times—the available tickets were sparse, and I wasn't able to get anything I really wanted.

The book, a fictionalized version of the Creole people on the Cane River in Louisiana where my bestie grew up, held my interest until someone cleared their throat.

"Excuse me." That silky accented voice—one I'd heard for the first time only recently—saying mostly the same words, to my surprise.

After taking a fortifying breath, I stared into the face of Mr. Posh. "I'm afraid these chairs are bolted this time."

His eyes widened. "You." The genuine surprise on his face told me he must have either been deep in conversation with his companion or not paying attention to his surroundings because no way he'd forgotten me that quickly.

"Yes, me. I don't have a chair to defend, so what is it you need this time?" His mere appearance—well, maybe more of the small rejection I'd felt back at the pub when he broke his stare—irritated me.

The unapologetic look on his face was almost comical. Very true to character, whether real or imagined by me. "It appears we're seated next to each other."

From my many flights to London, I've discovered that when an Englishman said *sorry*, which they seemed to say quite often, they were indeed not sorry at all. I preferred when people said what they meant rather than taking a subtle tact—a sharp contrast to what I was used to on the family compound.

Another face, the same man who dined with him earlier,

appeared over Mr. Posh's shoulder. Slightly taller, but much younger now that I saw him up close. He flashed a real apologetic smile and gave me a brief wave. "Sorry."

I rose, picking up my purse from his chair, and grinned back because the brother actually seemed contrite, going against my earlier thought. "Please." Then waved my hand for them to pass.

When the men were settled and I'd set my purse between my feet, balancing it so it wouldn't hit the dirty floor, Mr. Posh leaned into me. "Fancy seeing you here. Visiting from America?" The close distance between us allowed his minty breath to caress my cheek, giving me a feeling of undeserved intimacy.

I released a small smile. "What gave me away? My accent?" My Texas accent was distinctive enough.

He dipped his head and chuckled. "Vacationing alone?"

"No." I was alone, but this wasn't really a vacation, just an extended layover. Work brought me here, not that I would tell him that. When people asked me what I did, my response was normally giving the name of the airline I worked for instead of what I actually did for them.

I'd discovered people had preconceived notions of pilots: that we were all rich and promiscuous—having paramours scattered along our many travel routes—but mostly uneducated, attaining our licenses through military service. The notion that military service equaled uneducated sent my blood pressure up even though I hadn't achieved mine through that route. And as far as promiscuity went, I engaged in few one-night stands during my travels, although Mr. Posh might've been back in play for one in London.

At least I hoped that was the vibe coming from him as he leaned in closer and closer every time he spoke. Maybe I'd misjudged him back at the pub.

"No, you're not alone? Or no, you're not vacationing?"

I grinned, teasing. "You sure ask a lot of questions of a stranger. Do you live in London?" Turnabout was fair play.

He turned up the sparkle in those green eyes. "You didn't answer my question."

The lights in the theater flashed, indicating the show would begin soon. I turned off my Kindle but still held it.

We'd have to hurry this along.

Posh's response was as evasive as mine, but there was more than one way to get an answer to my question, and I was nothing if not persistent. I looked across his lap at the other man with him who had been paying close attention to our conversation, nearly sitting in Mr. Posh's lap he sat so close. "Hi. Do you live in London?"

He only laughed and shrugged, then looked at his presumed brother. "Yes?"

"Stay out of it, brother."

"But she asked me directly, Le—" The name broke off with a strong elbow to his ribs. From his brother.

Did he not want me to know his name? Or anything at all about him? Fine with me. No skin off my nose. "Am I not allowed to speak to your brother?" I gave him a quite beatific smile, the most innocent in my repertoire.

He chuckled and cocked a brow. "Not when you're mining for information."

"England is a free country, is it not? Besides, you dug first."

He huffed and opened his mouth to respond but was saved from answering when the curtain opened and the audience broke out in applause.

I put my Kindle away and clapped along with everyone else.

By halfway through, I finally came to the conclusion that I was more of a musical girlie.

I turned to my neighbor, who seemed to be enjoying the show, his gaze intent on the stage and a small smile playing at his lips.

He pressed an arm against mine but kept his attention focused on the play.

I responded with a leg to his, still staring at his handsome profile.

Both were subtle moves but broadcasted intentions.

Then he swiveled my way, peering at me with those intense eyes. The eye fucking and lip licking–slash–biting started in earnest between us.

My nipples perked in anticipation.

By the end of the play, I'd been dry flirting with my neighbor more than I should have in order to follow the plot.

When the play ended, Posh studied me a moment, then stood. "Excuse me."

His brother stood, waiting for me to vacate my seat.

Deflated over how I was so mistaken of Posh's intent, I fumbled with my belongings and exited the row as gracefully as possible, wondering how I could've been so wrong about someone wanting to get with me. In all my thirty-five years, this had never happened. Well, at least not since I'd graduated college. My stomach sank.

I made my way to the outer lobby and stood by the big window overlooking the busy street outside. The earlier pie still settled in my stomach, so dinner wasn't in the cards. I stared out the theater doors trying to make up my mind what to do next, but sometime during the play, a storm had come through and a thick sheath of rain fell, making it difficult to see much of anything other than people running past, sharing umbrellas, and fumbling down the sidewalk.

"Bit wet out there." Mr. Posh grinned, nodding toward the street.

The English never seemed bothered by the wetness of their weather. Sort of like the inhabitants of the Pacific Northwest back home. "If by a 'bit wet,' you mean a torrential downpour, I think you're on to something." I pulled my jacket tighter, schooling my expression, trying to act cool, like I wasn't completely thrilled he'd sought me out after I'd given up on him.

He laughed and leaned closer, a twinkle pronounced in his eyes.

I looked around for his companion. "Where's your brother?"

He lifted a shoulder. "Gone home."

Thrilled, my pulse quickened. "And why didn't you leave with him?" I bit my lip and allowed my eyes to smolder his way. At least I hoped that was what they conveyed.

His expression turned serious, and he leaned into me. "Do you want to get out of here?" He waggled his eyebrows, broadcasting his clear intent this time.

Very much so. "My hotel is within walking distance."

Although close enough to walk to my hotel, the rain was

too much. We had plenty of storms back home, even hurricanes, but this was cold and wet—something I wasn't used to. Instead of walking, Mr. Posh booked a rideshare on his phone.

When the appointed car drove up right outside the door, we sprinted across the passersby, dodging through the heavy foot traffic despite the weather, Posh guiding me with a hand to my back and doing his best to shield us both with his coat. We laughed when we fell into the back of the car, huddled together to maintain body heat.

Mr. Posh bent down and whispered, his warm breath against the shell of my ear doing more to raise my temperature than the car heater. "We'll be there in five minutes."

I nodded and closed my eyes, then opened them half lidded. "Can't wait."

The rideshare deposited us in front of the covered entrance to the lobby, and we sped walked past the front desk. I grabbed his hand and yanked him toward the elevator.

He pressed the button before I could, then shifted on his feet. He must have been just as impatient as I was.

The thought sent a thrill of excitement through me and brought an intoxicated smile to my lips. I leaned forward, intending to whisper something into his ear, but the elevator doors parted, revealing another couple inside. As we moved into the tight space, shifting toward the back corner, the other couple spoke to each other in an unfamiliar language.

But even if they spoke English, their words still wouldn't have registered. I was too lost in the feel of his smooth palm against mine and the depth of his green eyes. He inched closer, dipping his head into the crook of my neck.

I leaned into him, close enough to smell his floral scent. "So what's your name?"

He hesitated, then smiled. "Leon. And yours?"

His brother had started to say his name earlier, and it definitely could have been Leon. Maybe that was his real name after all. Still, although I didn't find myself in these situations regularly, when they did happen, I didn't usually give mine out. Instead of Margaret, I said, "Mary." I had sisters named Meredith and Miranda, so staying in the *M* family felt natural. My best friend, Jaymes, and I had decided on fake names when we were in high school. I was Mary and she was Stevie. I held back the laugh creeping up my throat at the many memories of us being out at the club and calling each other by those fake names.

"Mary, huh? I wouldn't have guessed." He cracked a sly smile. "Well, it's good to meet you, Mary."

"You too, Leon."

We dashed out of the elevator and made short work of the walk to my hotel room door, passing another couple in the hallway. Our hands were close together but not touching, a current running between them nonetheless evidenced by each of us stretching fingers toward the other but maintaining modesty in front of the other couple. Before I unlocked the door, when the hallway emptied, he leaned in and I met him halfway, his soft lips capturing mine, leaving me dizzy with pleasure.

When the door to my hotel room snicked shut, I dropped my purse and turned on Leon. He was ready for me, tearing at my jacket as I pushed his coat off his shoulders. He wore a long-sleeved burgundy Henley that made his green eyes pop. I didn't linger long, reaching for the hem and encouraging him to pull it off.

I pushed away from him and watched as he slowly pulled the shirt over his head, exposing defined chest and abs as well as a tattoo on his inner forearm—two hands shaking. I moved closer and ran a finger over the ink, his skin as smooth as I imagined, and only then realized that one of the hands wasn't a hand at all. It was a snake, it's fangs deep in the other hand's flesh.

After sparing a moment wondering at the unusual tattoo and its meaning, I turned my attention back to getting out of my own clothes. I didn't miss the understanding on his face though. Likely he knew I was curious. Just as likely he wouldn't tell me what the tattoo was about. No matter.

It wasn't like I would ever see him again anyway.

CHAPTER FOUR

Margaret—Family dinner, not optional

Three months later

As I PULLED into my garage, I noted the hour on the center screen. Just enough time to wheel my luggage into the laundry room, take a shower, and hoof it up to the main house. September hung on to the humidity and heat like a rediscovered lover. And since my house was the farthest away on the circular driveway from the main house, I'd likely be wet when I arrived.

My flight had only just landed back in Houston a couple of hours ago, but the time drew near for Sunday dinner. As tired as I was from my trip from Amsterdam, weekly dinners with my family weren't optional. Not even for my baby brother, Donovan, who lived in the city. Not unless there was a really good reason.

Miranda's house was just as far, directly across from mine. Although I wasn't sure what my baby sister constructed could be called a house. More like the barest cottage, but at least she could build onto it later if need be. All of us had our pilot's licenses—even Donovan; our parents had insisted—but Miranda and I were the only ones to fly commercial. She operated for about two years, but unlike me, she hated it, resigning herself back to the family compound, flitting between helping Dominick at the flight school and overseeing the plane-rental business.

Dominick had the largest house, next to the main house in size and distance, which made sense because he, a widower, had the two boys to raise and needed all the help he could get. The house had belonged to Great-Granddaddy James and had been upgraded over the years by various family members. It was the same with most of the houses on the circle.

The last house, across from Dominick's, was the property of the sister right under me in birth order, Meredith. It was a one story that my sister had built a couple of years ago and suited her simple tastes. Much to our parents' collective chagrin, she'd rather be clothed in overalls and covered in grease while working in the airplane-repair station or what we simply called the repair shop.

There were other cabins and cottages on the vast land in addition to the flight school, which was our biggest business, the plane rental next to the school, and the repair shop. The acreage boasted hiking trails, a large lake, and a small untouched forest as well. I took advantage of the trails every chance I got.

By the time I arrived at my parents', beads of sweat ran down my back. Family dinners weren't formal, but I couldn't show up in cutoffs and a tank top either. The fire-engine red sundress I wore breathed but was constructed enough to trap moisture. Especially with the heat index today.

I unlatched the back gate and rushed past the swimming pool to the sliding-glass door which led into the downstairs family room. This house had more humble beginnings back when Samuel and his sons built here, but an upstairs was added at some point over the years and the ground floor expanded as well. Daddy added the pool out back.

My house first belonged to Great-Uncle Harrison, the mystery uncle, but had been upgraded at some point as well. It still had the original wraparound porch though, which is why I claimed it as mine.

"We thought we were going to have to send a search party out for you." Mama kissed me on the cheek, then frowned. "Go get cleaned up in the bathroom."

Yeah, the sweat had definitely made itself known. "Hello to you too, Mama. Maybe y'all could turn the air up a little bit." I swiped at my face but headed to the bathroom as ordered.

When I returned, everyone was waiting for me in the dining room, Daddy at the head of the table and Mama at the other end. Granddaddy sat to Daddy's right, Aunt Deborah to Mama's. All the other seats were a free-for-all. I eased into the chair next to my bestie, Jaymes, who wasn't required, of course, but delighted in Sunday dinner. Most of us did unless there was some drama going on.

Ha! Who was I fooling? There was always some family drama, but only the big issues gave me heartburn.

I gave Jaymes a quick hug, then elbowed in the ribs my little brother, Donovan, seated on my other side, my way of saying hi.

"Ouch."

I ignored him because I barely tagged him. "Hey, everyone. Sorry I'm late. Just got in." There was no reason to say where I'd been. Everyone knew already. That was the thing with living on a family compound—no secrets.

Murmurs of greeting came my way, then everyone bowed their heads while Granddaddy gave the blessing.

Chatter exploded as we passed around platters of roast, fried catfish, mashed potatoes, collard greens, and corn bread.

Once my plate was loaded, I leaned into Jaymes and lowered my voice. "What did I miss?"

She whispered back, "Your father has some sort of announcement. He'll tell us when everyone finishes eating."

I looked into her green eyes, a sudden reminder of Mr. Posh, who I had an amazing night with three months before. Wow, I hadn't really thought about him much, but whenever he did cross my thoughts, I squeezed my legs together.

Now wasn't the time for that though. Instead I studied Jaymes to glean any additional details she might have known.

She only shrugged ever so slightly.

I looked to Meredith next, catching her gaze.

She raised her brows while I tried, unsuccessfully, to ask a question through expressions while also keeping everyone else from seeing. She narrowed her eyes in response, then shook her head.

Looks like I'd better finish my food to hear this announcement. No burden because as usual, the meal was amazing. We all pitched in on Sundays—well, whoever was available, which was usually at least three out of the five siblings, plus Mama's sister, Aunt Deborah. Granddaddy didn't cook, believing it was women's work, but Daddy usually cooked the greens. That was his specialty, although he implored someone else to do the arduous picking and cleaning. Miranda begged him to just buy the bagged greens, but he wouldn't hear of it.

I took my first bite of the roast, and the meat melted in my mouth, the rich gravy mixing well with the accompanying soft carrots. The whole catfish called my name next, and I carefully pulled the tender meat from the frame, relishing the crunchy skin. I squeezed my shoulders together at the thorough enjoyment of the taste. "Y'all outdid yourselves. Everything is delicious."

Mama took the credit. "Thank you, baby."

Donovan leaned in. "I cooked the fish."

"It's really saying something."

As I ate, thoughts of Daddy's announcement gave way to conversation and savoring the delicious meal.

Mama said, "We need to start thinking about Thanksgiving plans."

Meredith groaned. "Already? Seems like we just hosted Juneteenth."

After giving my middle sister a sharp look, Mama said, "Yes, already. This is the end of September—Thanksgiving is right around the corner. And everyone's coming in."

A collective groan sounded from around the table. It wasn't that we didn't love extended family, but there was a lot to plan for when it was our turn to host, which seemed to be more and more the last few years. Not only a lot to plan, but so much interruption to running the family businesses.

"Keep it down, y'all." Daddy always had Mama's back.

Mama would not be deterred. "Chana will be emailing everyone tasks soon, so be on the lookout."

I wasn't sure how much our house manager was paid, but whatever it was, she was underpaid. She and her son, Jaden, shared the nicest cottage on the grounds, but even that perk wasn't enough, in my opinion. She and Mama held this busy family together—no easy task.

"We'll be looking out, dear." Daddy again, but this time he put down his napkin and surveyed everyone around the table. "Now that we've finished dinner, I wanted everyone to know...and I'm sure this will be a surprise to nobody...but I'm officially retiring as CEO next September. It's time to turn over the reins."

No, it wasn't a surprise. Daddy had been hinting at this for the past several months, but heads still turned, all my siblings looking from one to the other. The truth was even though we knew this day was bound to come, none of us really wanted it. Our discussions over the years always landed on one person to take over. That person was me, and as eldest, I'd accepted my fate. Over the past few months, I'd come to embrace it and looked forward to implementing the many ideas I had, starting with upgrades to the flight school.

Since no one else seemed to want to say anything, I finally spoke up. "You deserve a well-rested retirement, Daddy." Even when Granddaddy was in charge, he relied heavily on his son. Daddy had been at this for at least forty years. I meant what I said.

"Thank you, honey. The next thing to discuss is succession."

Granddaddy Isaac whipped his head around. "What's there to discuss? Dominick is next in line. He'll take over."

"I don't want it." Dominick rocked my two-year-old

nephew on his knee. He'd only lost his wife a year ago and was in no position to take over the whole conglomerate of Hawthorne businesses. He'd made that clear and was happy to run the flight school. With Miranda's help, he had flexibility in his schedule, something needed when creating the work/life balance none of the rest of us seemed to manage. None of us had kids either though. Of course we all pitched in with their care, but Dominick took his responsibility as a father, as a single parent, deep to heart.

"Well, Donovan will have to leave his big oil-and-gas job and come back home, where he should have been to begin with." Honestly, Granddaddy had no shame.

My brother grunted next to me, not even dignifying Granddaddy's comment with a response. He ran as fast as he could and never looked back. Other than getting his pilot's license, he'd fought against the family legacy his entire life. To which I said, *Good for him*, because he excelled in business school and went after what he really wanted. Thankfully, Houston was an oil-and-gas enclave, so we still got to see him at least weekly, sometimes more.

"It should be Margaret." My siblings nearly said it in unison.

Daddy nodded, but Granddaddy's skin reddened. "No woman has ever led the Hawthorne family, and I don't plan to allow that starting now."

My blood rose. "I've taken rotations through all our businesses. I've been a pilot for over ten years. I had to fight my way through constant sexism and racism to be able to fly international flights and finally become captain. There's no reason I should face misogyny in my own family business." I constantly presented my bona fides when Granddaddy Isaac was around. Not just today, but almost every time. It was exhausting, but he was determined to ensure the women of this family knew their place.

"Of course not, Margaret." Daddy glared at his own father. "Papa, let's table this for now."

Since dinner was over, everyone got up from their chairs, but grumbles mounted all around.

Daddy walked over to me, sympathy in his gaze. "Can I talk to you in my office?"

I nodded and followed him through the house. My blood still boiled, but Daddy was reasonable.

Hopefully he had a plan.

THE QUICKEST WAY to Daddy's office, adjacent to the main house but not accessible from it, was through the back door, but for some reason, he took me through the front, the sun beaming down from above. When he walked in the direction of Great-Granddaddy James's statue, the wheels in my head turned. Apparently this detour would incorporate some family history.

"My grandfather here…" He swept his hand up, gesturing to the stone statue of our ancestor dressed in his pilot jacket, flight helmet, and goggles. "He flew escort missions all over Europe, even deep into Germany."

I nearly rolled my eyes but caught myself, obviously knowing this basic bit of family history. As the historian, I had facts like that at my fingertips. "I know, Daddy."

He nodded. "I know you know, but you may need a reminder. That didn't happen until later. In the beginning, they hunkered down in Italy, flying missions that didn't matter. Missions where the enemy hadn't been seen in months. Flying planes that barely outpace my car." He pointed in the general area of the garage.

"Right. And then they got into the action because the white escort pilots kept leaving the bombers they escorted to go after their own kills. Typically those were decoys by the Germans and then our bombers would get slaughtered." I shook my head. "A lot of arrogance."

He inclined his head and placed a hand on the statue. "Sure, some of it was hubris. But they'd also been trained to rack up the kills. Some of it was instinct and some was training."

"Sure, okay. That's generous."

He gave me a sidelong glance. "Whatever the reason, when your forefather joined the fray, he and his cohorts didn't have that option. They needed to prove themselves on that first mission, or they'd never fly another one. You know why?"

Of course I knew why. Prejudice and racism, but clearly Daddy was coming up on his point, so I figured I may as well let him make it. "Why?"

"Because most, from high up on down, believed them to be inferior, that they didn't have the coordination or intellect to fly missions." He chuckled to himself, then pushed off from the statue and restarted the pace toward his office.

I fell in line alongside him.

"And they almost stopped the program, calling the

'Tuskegee Experiment' a failure despite never actually allowing them to fly a single mission. But they didn't give up, you see. They exercised patience until they could prove everyone wrong."

And there it was. Loud and clear.

"You hear what I'm saying, Margaret."

"Yes, Daddy."

"Good. When James Hawthorne's father, Samuel, your two-times great-grandfather, wanted to set up a homestead here in Texas, everyone in the family was hesitant." He gave me a pointed look and nodded. "This was before they joined the Red Tails, mind you. But Samuel had a vision, and after the war, he made that vision come true with help from his sons. He had five—only two were Airmen."

Again, all of this I knew already. "Okay, Daddy."

He frowned and walked. "Come on."

We arrived at one of the small outbuildings, originally used for storage, but now transformed into a modern office building with three rooms and a bathroom. Daddy's space was the only official office, however we all rotated through the other two rooms as needed. I probably spent the most time there when home, learning the ins and outs of the overall business.

Dominick had his office at the flight school, but my other siblings came and went as they pleased. Meredith couldn't be tied down to an office, preferring to spend her time covered in grease, head deep in an airplane engine. Miranda split her time between the flight school and the plane rental, where there was a general office she shared with the manager—Chana's son, Jaden. We mostly only saw Donovan on

Sundays.

My red dress stuck to my back, and I relished the cold air when he unlocked the door and we stepped into the small entryway, then made the short walk to Daddy's office.

He sat behind his large wooden desk and placed his hands behind his head.

I sat on the other side. Waiting for him to say something tortured me, so I spoke up instead. Even though he'd basically told me to be patient with his background story, I don't know if it was the heat or my leftover irritation from dinner, but my blood ran hot. "I don't understand why you didn't stand up for me with Isaac."

He lifted a brow. "Isaac, is it?"

"No, sir. But I'm not feeling very generous with Granddaddy right now."

He blew out a huff of a laugh. "When have you ever?"

No lies detected. It wasn't a secret that Granddaddy got under my skin at every turn with his casual misogyny. I understood he came from a different generation, but was he not required to evolve like everyone else? "That's because I've had to overcome a lot of obstacles having to do with small-minded people like him who held my fate in their myopic little hands. Dealing with that plus the microaggressions everywhere is bad enough. Now you're asking me to over-look it here, in my home?" I placed my hands on my hips, just realizing I'd stood during that speech, then sat back down in the padded chair across from his desk.

His posture remained casual as I spoke, having heard this complaint before. "I understand, but going at Papa head-on will not get the desired outcome. He's still on the board, so we need to figure out how to sway him instead of piling on him."

"I honestly don't know what else I can do to him to convince him I'm qualified."

He sat forward then, spreading his hands on his desk. "Whenever he's in earshot, you're giving him your resume. At some point, that just became noise to him. We need to put our heads together and figure this thing out."

My skin prickled with irritation. Then another thought occurred to me, and my pulse jumped. "Daddy, do you want me to take over? You didn't say that earlier." It wasn't like we haven't discussed this in the past, but maybe he'd changed his mind.

"Of course I do."

"Do you believe in me, or is it that you know no one else wants the job?"

Now he reached out for my hands, which I placed in his. He squeezed and stared me directly in the eyes. "You are the most qualified. No one else has taken an interest in the complete operation of the Hawthorne Family Flying Eagles. Sometimes…" He chewed on his lips and glanced off to the side.

"Sometimes what, Daddy?"

He sighed and turned his attention back to me. "Sometimes I wonder if you really want it though. You love flying so much. And like you said, you've worked hard and overcome a lot to get to the position you're in with a major airline. Do you really want to give that up? Or do you feel obligated?"

You could have bought me for a penny. The air left my

lungs. "What?"

"You don't need to answer that right now. Just think about it."

None of what he just said mattered. As the eldest, I'd been preparing for this moment my entire life, and I intended to meet the moment. "I don't need to think about it. I want the job."

He withdrew his hands and steepled them in front of his nose and mouth. "Okay."

I nodded. "Okay."

It would be okay, right?

CHAPTER FIVE

Lewis—Hullo, Houston

M Y FIRST TIME at the JW Marriott in Houston was uneventful. The sun just set as I valet parked my car, as seemed to be the Houston culture, and rode the escalator up to the conference level, passing an elegant wedding reception and what looked to be a high-end sorority celebration, everyone dressed in red and white, matching the decorations.

Having given my name to the attendee at the door, I strolled into the gathering of aviation professionals. From the looks of people standing around in small groups, drinks in hand, solemn expressions on their faces, this wasn't a fun group. Then again, maybe it was early.

My first cursory review of the room yielded no one familiar. I'd memorized the scant few photos I had of Dominick Hawthorne, but no one jumped out as a match. Shawn, a mutual business associate between me and Dominick, said he'd be here, and I'd come to rely on Shawn's intel even if I didn't completely trust them. The truth was I trusted few people.

While I waited for the man to appear, I picked up an hors d'oeuvre from one of the stations and stood at an unoccupied high table, one of many set up for the reception.

I took in the room, waiting for Dominick's appearance, and ate my mini beef Wellington that wasn't half bad. I estimated about seventy to a hundred people were in attendance, mostly dressed in business attire, some more suited for the cocktail hour. Which I supposed we were technically in. This was officially an industry mixer held by the American Association of Women in Aviation, but I guessed it was only about 30 percent women. It was no secret that aviation was dominated by men, but I was surprised at the imbalance of an event put on by women.

Speaking of women, a table nearby had five women gathered around chatting. One was paying more attention my way than to her companions.

I nodded and smiled. Although my objective here tonight was clear, I wasn't adverse to meeting up with someone later after I secured my introduction to Dominick. If American women were anything like my hookup with Mary a few months prior, I might have misjudged them altogether. I'd thought them to be idealistic, but Mary had been quite pragmatic, getting straight to the business of ensuring we both got off. I'd been pleasantly surprised.

No, I wouldn't mind finding another Mary here.

That line of thought would need to wait because I caught a glimpse of who I thought was Dominick heading toward the mac-and-cheese bar. In my hasty pursuit, I bumped into someone, nearly toppling her over. "Sorry."

Her head whipped up so fast, she nearly knocked it right into my chin if I hadn't deftly moved out of the way. Wide eyes stared up at me. "I'd know that 'sorry' anywhere."

There she stood, clad in a sensible dark red pantsuit that

did nothing to hide the curves I'd been privileged enough to enjoy a few months ago. It was as if I'd conjured her. "You."

"Yes, me." She blinked a couple of times, as if really bringing me into focus after thinking she was mistaken. "What are you—"

"Why are you—" It was clear we had the same thought, speaking over each other.

"Who's your friend?" The man I thought was Dominick, the man I'd been searching for, stood next to Mary, a small plate of mac and cheese with shrimp and bacon sprinkled on top in hand.

I quickly scanned the file I had stored away in my memories to connect the name *Mary* with Dominick. He had three sisters, but none named Mary. His wife had died over a year ago. Could Mary be his girlfriend? If so, this recruitment would likely be over before it even started.

Mary's mouth worked for a moment with no sound forthcoming, so I spoke up. "Hullo."

He frowned and threw Mary a furtive glance but reached out his free hand. "Hi. I'm Andrew."

I shook the hand, disappointed. I swore this was Dominick. Should I give him my name or the name I used with Mary in London since she stood right there, listening intensely? "Leon. Nice to meet you." I looked to Mary by way of explanation. Was this her man?

Andrew seemed to pick up on my confusion and smiled. "I'm her cousin."

A woman called from across the room, waving and pointing at an empty table, a plate piled high in the other hand. "Andrew."

"That's my girlfriend. Nice to meet you, Leon." He kissed Mary on the cheek. "I'll catch up with you later."

She only nodded, then rotated back to me. Several emotions played across her face. First contemplation with her eyes squinting at me, as if to make sense of my very existence, then confusion related through her pursed lips. Finally, her eyes narrowed. "What are you doing here, Leon?"

"Well, I've only just moved here. About three months ago actually. The day after I met you."

"Moved here?" The skepticism written all over her face made my stomach drop. "You're kidding, right?"

I realized this was quite the coincidence, but there was no need to be snippy about it. I was as surprised to see her as she was me. "Yes, Mary. I moved here. When I met you with my brother, that was a going away outing for the two of us."

Her shoulders relaxed slightly. "This seems like a huge coincidence."

I agreed with her, and my stomach tightened with the thought. Was this serendipity? Or a distraction?

I didn't need a distraction right now. What I needed was to find this Dominick Hawthorne fellow and begin laying the groundwork to recruit him. As much as I'd love to take up with Mary again, a one-night stand was called that for a reason.

"That's all it is. A huge coincidence." I grabbed up her hand and immediately regretted it as the memories of her soft skin flooded my senses. "Listen, let's catch up later." I squeezed the hand and let it go, then retreated to my side of the ballroom.

CHAPTER SIX

Margaret—Coincidence, happenstance, or enemy action?

WHAT DID IAN Fleming say about coincidence? *Once is happenstance. Twice is coincidence. Three times is enemy action.* Looked like we were in enemy action territory. But why? What reason would Mr. Posh have for hooking up with me, then following me? And halfway around the world, no less? Did he know who I was when he tried to rob me of my chair? That didn't make any sense though. What would his end game be?

I watched as Andrew loaded up a bowl for two with ice cream, bananas, hot fudge, caramel, and chopped nuts. My stomach grumbled just watching him down all that richness. My cousin wasn't a Hawthorne; he was Aunt Deborah's son who'd moved in with us during his junior year of high school after his father died. He usually didn't come out to industry events either, but he'd been dating a flight attendant for a couple of months, so he tagged along.

"You don't want one?" he asked.

"Nah. I think I'll get one of those pecan-pie tarts I spotted on the way over here." I didn't move to get one though. "What do you make of Leon?"

Andrew eyed me. "What do you mean? Is he a friend of

yours?"

I shrugged noncommittally. "Not really. I met him recently." No sense weighing down Andrew with the details that didn't matter anyway.

He sort of dipped his head back and forth as if in contemplation. "I mean, I only met him for, like, a second. He seemed nice. British, right?"

"Yeah." I wasn't sure what I expected from Andrew. Of course he hadn't had time to form an opinion. What did it matter anyway? Leon couldn't seem to get away from me fast enough.

My stomach clutched at the thought. I hadn't expected to see him either, but I was...not glad. But maybe pleasantly surprised.

Andrew waved his overflowing banana split in front of me. "Do you want to join us?"

"You go ahead. Jaymes should be here any minute."

He gave me a quick hug, and he was off.

I watched as he joined his girlfriend back at their table. They were cute together but Andrew lived in Austin, and long distance, even three hours away, was a chore on any relationship. They'd met in the airport there and hit it off. Then again, maybe they'd make a go of it. He came to town often enough already to visit his mother, so the possibility was there.

I quickly scanned the room and noted Mr. Posh speaking with a group of men I was acquainted with. Well, at least one of them. Brian. He flew with my airline, and we went back at least ten years. We were friendly but not close. I had to fight hard to become a captain at my airline—met with prejudice, racism, sexism, and discrimination at every turn. Most believed I got by on my family name. People like Brian were rumored to have said as much. But if I isolated myself from everyone who said something similar about me behind my back—and honestly, sometimes to my face with a microaggression—my work life would've been quite lonely.

Leon spotted me watching him and winked.

Who cared if he saw? We'd seen each other naked, so playing coy at this point seemed futile. I strolled over to another table, this one surrounded by women, all women who belonged to the association who hosted this little soirée; as did I. It was the only reason I came out tonight. "Hello, ladies. How's everyone?"

We exchanged pleasantries.

Then one of them, a flight attendant I'd flown with too many times to count, sidled up to me.

Michelle leaned in close, then pointed at Mr. Posh. "Is that you?"

No, Mr. Posh did not belong to me. We had one heated night that curled my toes even now, but that was all. "No. I hardly know him."

Michelle bit her lip, the lust clear on her face. "Can you hook me up?"

If I recalled correctly, she asked my brother out a couple of months ago. Even though it had been over a year, Dominick still wasn't ready for a new woman in his life. His excuses ranged from his business at work to needing to be there for his sons. Both were true, but if he really wanted to date, he could find the time. We all stepped in with the boys even when not needed. His family support system was solid.

I tried to smile at Michelle, to provide some sort of sisterly solidarity, but I didn't have it in me. "You'll have to track him down on your own."

"What did I miss?" I turned to my approaching best friend and restrained myself from jumping into her arms. If I had to converse with Michelle one more minute, I wasn't sure I wouldn't have blurted out just why I was hesitant to "hook her up" with Posh.

I'd probably need to examine that reaction later. "Nothing much. Have you seen the quesadilla station?" I turned her toward the food setup across the room and walked, throwing a wave over my shoulder to the frowning women standing around the high table.

Jaymes giggled. "What in the world was that all about?"

"I'll tell you later."

She eyed me suspiciously. "Later when? And what if I don't want quesadillas?"

I walked faster and loud whispered at her. "Just come on." The quesadilla station stood farthest from Posh, and I needed to clue in my best friend in case we ran into him again.

"Seriously, Mags. Did you see the shrimp-and-grits bar?"

The only person I'd ever given permission to call me by a nickname was my bestie from way back. Even my family knew better. "Wow, your Creole roots jump out at the wrong time more often than not."

"I don't know what that means, but let's head that way."

We looked like fools running from one side of the reception to the other. Either that or two people who couldn't make up their minds on what to eat. Hopefully anyone who might've been watching would think the latter. "Fine, but I'm getting tacos." Why would the taco bar be next to the shrimp-and-grits bar? That didn't even make sense. It should've been next to the quesadilla station.

While Jaymes piled her plate with shrimp, brisket, and who knew what else, I helped myself to one of each of the street tacos. My stomach rumbled, and I searched my memory for the last time I put something in it. Must have been the grapes I had around lunchtime, intending to grab a sandwich or something, but then I got busy and forgot.

I took a bite of each one as I checked out Posh from the corner of my eye. Still talking, now a little more animated, as if he was having the best time. I wish I knew his game and why he'd be at an industry event. I just couldn't get over this being a coincidence.

All the tacos were great, but the barbacoa was to die for, so I finished it off while waiting for Jaymes to finish fixing her plate.

She grabbed a second dish and placed some sliced tomatoes on it. "Let's find somewhere to settle in."

I chuckled. "Looks like we better."

"Oh, hush." Of course she walked toward Posh and his crew but thankfully hooked a left, finding a table a few over from his. Close enough I could watch him in profile all I wanted, but far enough I could speak freely to Jaymes as long as I kept my voice down. The tasteful music that filled the room helped with that too.

I waited for Jaymes to get through a good amount of her food before cluing her in. That gave me time to polish off my own snacks. I enjoyed my tacos, but the smoky brisket from her plate filled my nose and had me second-guessing myself.

She wiped at the corner of her mouth with a napkin. "Okay, what gives?"

"Remember that hookup in London I told you about?"

She snorted. "How could I forget. *I* wanted a cigarette after you told me about it. Did you call him or something?"

"I didn't even give him my real name, so we definitely didn't exchange phone numbers."

After frowning at me, she took a spoonful of her grits mixed with a good amount of cheese. "What was his name? Lance or something like that."

"His name is Leon. I don't even know his last name." I glanced around before saying anything else out loud. It was one thing to talk about someone with them in the room. Quite another to blatantly toss around their name.

"Okay, so what about Leon?"

I tilted my head to the right and slow blinked.

Jaymes didn't make a sudden move. Instead she picked up her fork and slid her gaze toward the table where Posh stood with his new buddies. My friend knew how to be discrete. She looked back at me with raised brows. "Oh, he is *fine* fine."

"Yeah."

"But what's he doing here?"

"That's the question of the hour. He said he moved here but didn't offer any other information."

Jaymes narrowed her eyes but didn't stop stuffing her mouth. When she swallowed, she said, "You don't normally let anything pass. You don't know his last name or why he moved here?"

I shrugged. "I was a little flummoxed."

"I'll say. Well, how will you find out what your London lover is doing here?"

"I have no idea, but this industry is really small, especially here in Houston. I'll get to the bottom of it."

A sly smile spread across my best friend's face.

"What?"

"Nothing."

It wasn't like I didn't know what she thought. She knew me about as well as anyone, siblings included. I wanted to know what Posh was all about.

In more ways than one.

CHAPTER SEVEN

Margaret—Sexism is built into the charter

THE GOLF CART I'd driven over was still outside the rental office. That wasn't a given. I couldn't count the number of times I'd parked one, gone inside a building or even out to the forest trail to take a long walk, and come back out to nothing. Thankfully they were haphazardly left everywhere, so nobody had to walk too far before stumbling on another one.

While driving back to the main office, I replayed the evening before. Mr. Posh had been attentive and charming, endearing people in the room, a position I'd shared a few months before. I got what I wanted from the exchange, and I assumed Leon did too, but I couldn't figure out how he could possibly be here. And why he attended an aviation event. He was both personable and secretive, two qualities that most found difficult to employ at the same time. Leon did it effortlessly, never revealing anything important about his move or the company he worked for.

I couldn't waste too much brain power thinking about Leon and his suddenly showing up here.

I had bigger fish to fry. Priority number one was reading through the company charter before I made my outward play for CEO. If it were solely up to Daddy to name a replacement, I believed in my gut he'd choose me. Even with Granddaddy's old-fashioned sexism at play. But there was a board to satisfy, even if my siblings made up the bulk of the governing body. The rest were extended family members from Granddaddy's brother's family. Uncle Joseph had since passed but had descendants, five in all, spread around the country with board votes. We weren't a public company, so the original charter dictated how we ran the business. There had been some amendments over the years but very few since more than a simple majority was needed. In order to amend the Hawthorne Family Flying Eagles charter, there needed to be a qualified majority of three-quarters. In today's terms, that meant out of the twelve members of the board, nine had to vote to pass it. No easy task in my family.

It reminded me of something Chana often said: *Two Jews, three opinions.* My family could definitely appropriate that saying.

I stuck my head in the door of Daddy's office and waved. "Hey."

"Hey there yourself." He narrowed his eyes. "Where are you coming from all dressed up?"

"I'm not dressed up." I had a penchant for sundresses when off from my day job, especially given the heat. "I was at the flight school, now I'm here."

Jaden walked in with a multicompartment food container, and I stood aside so he could enter Daddy's office. "Hey, Margaret." In addition to the wide smile he gave, his green eyes sparkled instantly reminding me of Leon.

I cleared my throat. "Oh, hey. What do you have there?"

"Don't you worry about that," Daddy couldn't help but

answer, most likely not wanting to share his lunch.

Whatever. I had a protein bar in my purse to hold me over until I made my way back to my house. "Nobody cares."

"Then why'd you ask him?"

After placing the container on Daddy's desk, Jaden turned to me. "Do you want me to go back up to the house and get you something? Mom asked me to bring this down for your dad since I was heading back to the rental counter."

The main house was only a short walk away, but my schedule fluxed so much, I tried not to burden Chana. The house manager already had plenty on her plate. And I definitely didn't like to take advantage of Jaden. This wasn't his job after all.

"Nah, I was just teasing Daddy."

He nodded and headed back out the door.

Daddy called behind him. "Thank you, Jaden."

"Of course." The words trailed behind Jaden as he exited the building.

After finishing his degree in aviation sciences from Texas Southern University, Jaden had returned here at his mother's insistence to get his commercial pilot's license. In all honesty, the degree more than likely was her idea too. And I was certain my mother had input, both women thinking they knew what was best for him. Maybe he loved it all, but Jaden never gave me the impression he was truly happy. Personable, courteous, and friendly, yes, a ready smile bestowed on everyone he came across. But there was a sadness lurking just beneath.

Since he was closer in age to Miranda and Donovan, they

knew him more as a friend and peer, the younger set growing up together and sharing everything, including all their secrets. Miranda never flinched when Donovan announced his business degree while the rest of us nearly fainted.

"What are you up to?"

I blinked away my distraction and glanced at Daddy. "Nothing much. I'll let you enjoy your lunch. See ya." Then I went down the hallway to the other office and settled in.

The charter could be accessed by board members from a private server, so I logged in to have a look. Times like these, I wish I had my baby brother's business degree to make sense of it all. As I read through the nearly fifty pages (obviously my ancestors hadn't believed in brevity), one theme leapt from the pages: The charter was written by men for men. No wonder Granddaddy felt so entitled to his misogynistic options. If I wanted to be CEO, it would take an amendment.

Sexism was codified in the family business charter from the beginning.

THERE WEREN'T MANY places in the western world where I hadn't flown. And I'd vacationed in many others. I still said hands down, pound for pound, Houston had the best food scene. Mostly because of the diversity of the population. A true melting pot, folks brought their recipes from their homeland all around the world.

Really good Mexican food was practically on every corner, so I met Jaymes at one of our favorite spots in North

Houston bordering Autumn. I'd been smarting after reading the charter the day before and needed some best-friend time. Margaritas were an added bonus.

Jaymes waved me over when I entered the medium-sized restaurant with shadowy lighting. I couldn't figure out if they were going for romantic or not considering there were plenty of families dining every time I came. Since the tables were smaller and adorned with tea lights, maybe they were going for a romantic feel after all.

Of course, Jaymes had secured us a booth where we could spread out and lounge until our heart's content. It could seat four but the place wasn't full, so my conscious remained guilt free. She'd been leaning against the wall of the red-leathered booths, clad in a blue sundress identical to my red one, perusing the menu. We'd purchased those dresses and a couple more on our last shopping spree at the Cypress outlets. "Hey."

I fell into the booth and shoved my purse down the seat as far as it would go. "Whew, hey."

"*Whew* indeed. I already ordered us smoky margs. No salt for you." She lifted a brow and grinned, knowing that would be the first question out of my mouth.

"Thank you. This heat is not playing. When will fall be here?" Considering it was mid-September, autumn might've been on the calendar, but the milder temps wouldn't hit us until late October. I'd worn short sleeves on New Year's Eve before, so honestly, who knew what we'd get and when.

The waitress sat our drinks in front of us along with tall glasses of ice water, condensation already running down the outside.

I eyed my drink while the waitress took a pad out from her apron, then I took a sip. No margarita mixes here. Another reason I enjoyed this place. The food was all from scratch too. "Yum."

The waitress smiled. "Are you ready to order, or do you need more time?"

Jaymes still scanned the menu.

I hadn't even looked at mine because I pretty much had it memorized. "Looks like my friend needs a little more time." I smirked at her. "Do you want to start with some guac and queso?"

Jaymes nodded. "Yeah, that sounds good."

"Okay, I'll go put those in." The waitress walked off, placing her pad back in her apron as she went.

I took another sip of my drink, then picked up a chip and dipped it into salsa. "You already know you'll get the enchiladas." She probably needed to decide which ones.

My bestie looked over the menu at me with narrowed eyes. "You don't know my life. What are you getting?" She bit her lip and searched the menu again.

"Grilled shrimp poblano."

Jaymes closed the menu and dropped it on the table. "Fine, I'll get the shrimp enchiladas." She finally noticed the drink in front of her, and her eyes lit up. "So what were you saying about the charter?"

There was no sense rehashing the basics. I'd already load-ed her up on the phone with my incensed babbling. Now it was time for a plan. "Basically we need an amendment to include women in the management of the company."

"I'm thinking that's a lawsuit."

I tilted my head and stared her down. "Exactly who do you think I should sue? My family?"

She shrugged. "Okay, that probably isn't the way to go. But I think about everything you've been through at work, and it doesn't seem fair you have to fight the same fight."

I snorted. "Listen, if they had their shitty old boys'-club policies actually written out, I would have gone the lawsuit path. As it was, fighting against invisible policies turned out to be much harder."

She only shook her head and took another drink.

I followed suit, the cold tangy liquid coating my throat on the way down. "These really are good."

"Mmmm, yes." She smacked her lips, then smiled at the waitress as she sat down our appetizers. "Thanks."

"Sure. Are you ready to order?"

This time we were. After we placed our orders, I spooned some guac onto my small plate and dipped a chip in. We both ate several chips dipped in guac or queso before speaking again.

I swallowed and took a big gulp of water to wash everything down. "Here's what I'm thinking. I've already made a list of the board members and which way their vote would go if it were held today. Obviously my sisters would be a yes. And because my brothers aren't cavemen, I'm guessing theirs would be yeses as well."

"Yeah, but you'd need to pin Donovan down to even attend a vote." Her voice raised the slightest on my brother's name. She seemed to have a soft spot for him. Maybe because he was the baby and we were nearly ten when he was born, really able to relish in that new baby smell. Jaymes didn't have any younger siblings of her own, just an older brother.

"True, but I would hope he'd make the time knowing how important this is." That was more wishful thinking on my part. I couldn't remember the last time Donovan attended a board meeting. They were only quarterly, but it had been some years. I frowned at my next thought. "Just as obvious, Isaac is a no."

"Oh, you're big mad if you're calling your grandfather by his first name."

My stomach clenched. "I stay big mad at him."

"Understandable."

Another snort worked its way out of my nose, unbidden. "Yeah. I would love to automatically put a yes in Daddy's column, but I'm leaving it blank for now. It's not that I didn't trust the man, but too much seemed to be in flux. The remaining members are cousins—three of Daddy's first cousins and two of their children who are of age. If I count the two younger, I would assume they'll vote yes. Daddy's first cousins are two men and a woman. Let's say a yes for her."

"So where does that leave you?"

I sighed. "Eight votes. And that's if all my siblings cooperate. I need nine. With three outstanding, I like my chances. Men from Daddy's generation can be a little…" I searched my thoughts for a good descriptor and came up short.

"Just go with *traditional*. That's the nicest word I can think of."

"Yeah, *traditional* fits. But if I can just sway one of them, it'll pass. The odds are on my side." For the first time in the past week, my shoulders relaxed.

"Yeah, I just have one question."

I stopped mid chip dip and studied her face. "And that is?"

"Do you really want to be CEO?"

An elephant sat on my chest and slowed my breathing. So much for relaxed shoulders. "Why would you even ask that?"

"You love flying, Mags. I can't imagine you cooped up in the office every day."

I opened my mouth to protest, but she raised a hand. "I'm not saying you couldn't do the job—probably do it better than anyone who has ever done it. I only question if you really want this for what it is. Rather than showing everyone what's what."

Of course I wanted to prove Granddaddy wrong. And even show Daddy how much of an asset I would be. But I also felt pulled to continue the Hawthorne family legacy. "I want it for me."

"Okay." She shrugged and picked up her glass. "That's all I wanted to know." Her gaze turned toward the door. "Hey, isn't that the guy from the other night?"

I rotated and stared right into the face of Mr. Posh.

"Goodness, what's he doing here?" I'd turned my head so fast, there was a good chance I had whiplash.

"If you don't know, I really don't know." Jaymes raised her hand, waving it toward the table. And us.

I lowered my voice and hissed. "What are you doing?" My stomach turned flips at the very sight of him. But then I remembered how weird it was he kept turning up.

She shrugged and spoke, keeping her mouth in a smile, ventriloquist style. "I'm inviting him over. Duh."

"But why are you—" It was too late to finish that question because the man himself stood at the end of our table, a tight smile in place that didn't quite reach his eyes. What was that about? "Um, hi."

"Sorry—did we have a meeting I forgot about?"

That explained the puzzled look. Although he knew full good and well we didn't have a meeting. Why would we? What would be on the agenda of a meeting between the two of us? I still didn't know exactly what he did and what it had to do with aviation.

"I might ask you the same thing. I was sitting here enjoying a nice dinner with my best friend, and here you come."

His eyebrows shot up. "Sorry—I thought…"

Lordt, I was beginning to hate the word *sorry*. "Another coincidence, I'm afraid."

Jaymes popped her head back into the mix then. "I remember you from the other night. At the mixer at the JW, right?" She didn't give him time to reply. "If you're here for dinner, you're welcome to join us."

I shot my former bestie the scowliest glare I could manage.

He wiped his palms on his pants, which appeared to be linen. Smart choice in this Texas heat. "I couldn't intrude." He looked around, probably searching for an out.

"Oh, are you meeting someone?" Jaymes could be relentless, especially when she dealt with someone else's business. Mostly mine.

"Uh, no. Actually."

"Please, sit." For some reason, she gestured across the table at my side. Seemed like if you were going to invite someone to sit, you'd at least pat the seat next to you.

Because of his close proximity, I couldn't convey my feelings of dismay to my bestie. As I was sure she planned.

"Do you mind, Mary?" His smile turned weary.

Jaymes's shoulders shook with the chore of holding her laughter in. I felt bad allowing him to think my name was Mary, but I didn't really know him like that. I decided to see where this all went before I revealed anything too personal.

"Not at all." I scooted over, pressing my body against my purse which was flat against the wall of the booth. Maybe this was a good thing. I could drill him on what he really was doing here. "Help yourself to some guac or queso. We already ordered dinner."

"We just ordered though. Do you know what you want? I'm sure the waitress can hurry back."

Although Jaymes posed the question, he leaned into my personal space. "What's good here?"

Goose bumps rose on my arms despite the tepid temperature. Almost everywhere you went in Houston, the AC was cranked way too high, so you went from one extreme to another. Keeping the temperature normal was another check in the plus column for this spot.

I turned toward Leon, my face inches from his, and inhaled his sweet, herbal scent. If I had to guess, I'd say he wore something with bergamot. The lime undertone was unmistakable. "I've had nearly everything on the menu and can safely say you can't go wrong with anything you choose." I glanced at his lap, then up again. "It depends on what you want."

He released a quick breath and looked back at the menu.

I glanced at Jaymes and winked. Yes, I flirted with him. I didn't mean it. Not really.

Her shoulders shook again, ever so slightly.

As long as he was here, sitting right next to me, someone I'd left in London for what I thought forever, I couldn't resist messing with him. I wasn't 100 percent sold on these accidental meetings. Running into him after our one-night stand might've been serendipitous...or maybe there was something more nefarious afoot.

The waitress walked over. "Oh, one more for dinner?"

He closed the menu. "Looks like it. Could I get the shredded-beef tacos please?"

"Okay. Beans and rice okay?"

He looked around the table for answers, and Jaymes gave him a thumbs-up. "Yes, that's fine. Thank you."

"Sure." She reached for his menu. "Anything to drink?"

"I'll have what they're having."

"I'll put that order in." She walked off toward the back. Hopefully she was picking up our food. Just because Mr. Posh was here now, I hoped she didn't deliver our meal together. My stomach rumbled to register its protest.

He clasped his hands in front of him on the table. "Sounds like you come here often."

I supposed that comment was directed toward me since I had just told him I'd had everything on the menu, so I responded. "It's nearby to home, and they have really great food."

"I've heard. That's why I thought I'd check it out. You

live near here?"

I tilted my head and studied him. His question seemed sincere enough. "I live in Autumn."

"Oh. That is nearby. Do you live alone?" He said it congenially, no malice detected. Just curious.

So I responded in kind. "I have my own house on a family compound. My siblings all have one as well. Except for my youngest brother, who owns a condo in downtown Houston."

"Brilliant. That sounds like a lovely family setup."

"Yup. We all have houses off a circular driveway behind the main house where my parents live along with my grandfather and an aunt."

He nodded, then looked at Jaymes. "Do you live there too?"

She snorted. "No, but I do live close by in Autumn. We grew up together."

"I hadn't realized. You've been best friends a long time, then."

I gave Jaymes a fond smile. "She's more like another sister. I've literally known her longer than my youngest sibling. Do you have any friends like that, Leon?"

He stared at me, not saying anything, a small smile turning up the corners of his mouth. His lush mouth that suddenly gave me memories on what it could do to my own mouth, my neck, my body.

I shivered.

He chuckled, knowing full good and well what he'd done. "Not really."

"That's vague."

Twin pairs of green eyes gawked at me.

"What? I'm just saying. It was a nonanswer."

"Don't be rude, Mags." Jaymes grimaced at the slip.

"Mags, is it?" He gave me a sultry look, bit his thick lower lip, clearly not upset by my previous words.

"It is to my bestie."

He licked those pretty lips and smiled ever so slightly. "Noted."

The waitress came with a tray loaded with plates of food, enough to feed three people. Hopefully mine wasn't cold, or that would be something else to hold against Mr. Posh.

Because the universe knew I was looking for anything and everything I could to keep thoughts of lips, eyes, and hands out of my head.

CHAPTER EIGHT

Lewis—The target, finally!

WHEN I WOKE up this morning, running into Mary at dinner was not on my list of to-dos. The way she studied me, she obviously believed quite the opposite about my intentions. I'd long given up on the conspiracy that she'd somehow orchestrated our meeting in London. To what end? That night together didn't benefit her in any way other than the obvious. And if I remembered correctly, it had benefited her a couple times that night. I smiled at the recollection, then took a sip of my margarita.

"What's that grin for? Looks like you had a good memory." Mary's friend was not shy about asking me whatever came to her mind. Neither of them, really. Which was the opposite of what I preferred.

"It was. I thought about the last time I had a meal with Mary in the same restaurant." I slid my gaze to Mary momentarily, then back to her friend. "The night ended very pleasantly."

"So I've heard."

My brows rose unbidden. "Have you now?"

Mary cleared her throat. "I don't have secrets from Jaymes."

I nodded. "Good to know."

We tucked into our food, everyone giving appreciative groans as we ate, including me. I hadn't had a lot of good Mexican food in my lifetime given where I grew up, but this place had to be top tier. Even the rice was spiced up and delicious.

After using my margarita to wash down a particularly large mouthful, I spoke to the table. "This will be a favorite spot for me, so when we inevitably run into each other again, know that we're playing with the law of averages."

"Mm-hmm." Mary apparently didn't believe in maths. Pity that, her being a pilot and all. Something I learned when running into her at the mixer at the JW Marriott.

Her friend chuckled. "You know, y'all could run into each other on purpose."

I raised a brow.

Jaymes yelped. "Ouch." Apparently Mary had kicked her under the table. "What? You're both grown, and it's not like you're strangers—at least your bodies aren't."

I had better reel her in. I had one job to do before I could relax into my new life; it would be better to keep our distance. Although if I could taste her once more…

I cleared my throat. "As enamored as I am by your friend, I've just moved here and am still settling in. A relationship wouldn't be fair to anyone right now."

"Who said anything about a relationship?" She moved over in her seat, then gave Mary a pointed look. "Don't kick me again."

Mary threw up her hands and rubbed her face. Then she looked at me with narrowed eyes. "Ignore her. Pretend you don't hear anything out of her mouth that pertains to the two of us. It's easier that way."

I nodded. "Noted."

Jaymes went back to her food, and Mary looked at me longer than what would be considered polite. "Why did you move from London to Texas of all places?"

"Was there a better place to move than Texas?" I'd had a lot of practice deflecting since Sheila: Answer a question with a question. Always steer them clear.

"Respond please."

Steered the usual person away. Mary apparently wasn't usual.

Her bluntness caught me off guard, and I sputtered and reached for my water. When I had myself reasonably pulled together, I faced her head-on. "For work."

"What does that mean exactly? Did someone here offer you a job you couldn't refuse? Or did you know you wanted to move to the US and looked for suitable employment?"

I picked up my water glass again and took a long pull. Mary's level of concision far exceeded anyone I'd met before. She wouldn't be easily assuaged.

She waited patiently for what must have been the longest drink of water in history.

Resigned, I put down my glass. "I was offered employment, and it was a good opportunity." No need for her to know I ran as fast as I could from Sheila, from my parents.

"Do you miss Charlie?"

"Who's Charlie?" Jaymes, of course, had followed the conversation while she pretended to eat and give us privacy.

"Charlie is his brother. I mentioned him to you. I met them both at the theater." She rotated my way. "A going-away party for you, I believe."

I only nodded.

"So do you miss your brother?"

"I'm not certain what sort of question that is. Wouldn't anyone miss their sibling?"

She raised one brow and tilted her head. "Depends on which sibling."

She and Jaymes cackled at that little dig at one of her brothers or sisters.

"We don't have to date, but would you like me to show you around Houston?" The laugh ended quickly, all manner of mirth dissipated. Her mouth said *friends*, but her eyes said *I want you now*.

"I...um, yes, that would be lovely." My mouth spoke the words without input from my brain. If I had to guess, the suggestion probably came from a completely different part of my body.

She reached her hand out. "Give me your phone and I'll put my number in."

I glanced around in a panic, but there was no getting out of this. I slipped the phone from my pocket and unlocked it.

Mary tapped in her contact details and called her own phone.

Sweat popped out on my brow, and it had nothing to do with the spice in the food. I felt trapped and elated in equal measure.

Somehow I needed to figure out how to get out of any more contact with Mary. Women, even the luscious woman next to me, were not in my plans. I had to prove myself before I even thought about one-night dates. Definitely not anything more.

I studied her while she drank her margarita. She sucked a piece of ice into her mouth and worked it with her tongue, closing her eyes.

Mary would be trouble. I just knew it.

I'D BEEN THINKING of Mary ever since we ran into each other two days ago at the Mexican restaurant. Having her on my mind was the opposite of what I needed. Or even wanted. Yet as I sat here waiting for Dominick Hawthorne to meet me at a lunch spot near his flight school, only one person filled my thoughts.

My intention was to block her number. I never got around to it, and when a text message popped up from her, it still caught me completely unawares. She'd planned a museum day for Saturday. I should have told her I couldn't make it, that I had another engagement already. I couldn't force my fingers to type the message. Instead I agreed quickly. Too quickly.

While I waited, I reread the first email from Shawn Sperry: *"Make sure to be at the JW Marriott by the Galleria at 7. If you go much later you'll miss him. He has kids to get home to and doesn't stay out late. Your name's on the list."*

Of course I knew about his kids already. He wasn't a big social media poster, but the few pictures he did post were of his sons. For my purposes, his personal life wasn't much use, but it was nice to know some of the basics. My main focus was his unique skill set. He'd managed his family's flight school for years, and while that usually would be a red flag for recruitment—it was hard to lure anyone away from a family business—my intel discovered he wasn't happy with how behind the school was, needing many improvements.

The corporation I worked for had a newly built state-of-the-art flight school. This should be an easy sell.

According to Shawn, it was because of his kids that he didn't make it to the JW Marriott. This time, Shawn took a more direct approach and set up the lunch with an introduction. As far as Dominick knew, I was new to the area and wanted to meet with some of the area flight-school directors, maybe even tour a couple.

Dominick was accommodating enough.

When the man walked through the glass door, familiarity hit me. There was a reason I'd mistaken him for Mary's cousin, Andrew. The two men could definitely be related, cousins if not brothers. I shivered at the thought because that would make Mary related to Dominick too. What a cluster-fuck that would be if the man I needed to recruit to fulfill my new employer's desire was somehow related to the woman I'd had a—could we even call it a one-night stand anymore now that I ran into her whenever I left my home?

He stopped at the hostess stand, and I raised my hand to get his attention, waving him over to our table in the center of the room. Surprisingly, there were a few high-end restaurants to invite him to near his suburb. I'd chosen a steakhouse, feeding into the Texas stereotype. How stupid would I look if the man turned out to be vegan.

I stood and held out my hand. "You must be Dominick."

He gave me a wide smile, but sadness tinged the edges and shone through his eyes. This man clearly had a lot on his mind. Hopefully one of those things was being open to changing his surroundings. "Nice to meet you. Lewis, right?"

"Right. Lewis Watson-Grosvenor." I winced at the sound of my own pretentiousness. "We have a mutual in Shawn Sperry."

"Shawn's a great person. I've known them for..." He scrunched his face up in thought. "Going on five or six years, I think. Maybe more." He sat, and I followed suit.

The waiter came over and inquired about our drink order.

I stuck with water whilst Dominick ordered a cup of coffee.

Another clue to his disposition. Perhaps he was overworked. Or maybe just overwhelmed with his new single-father situation. Either way, I had an answer for anything that troubled him at Hawthorne's flight school.

"I'm really grateful to Shawn for making the introduction. And to you, of course, for agreeing to meet me."

He shrugged. "It's no problem at all. They said you were newly here from London." He raised a brow.

"That's right. I've been here about three months now. Still getting settled and learning the lay of the land."

He nodded. "Quite a difference between there and here. I can imagine you're having a bit of culture shock."

He'd hit the nail on the head. So much difference between here and back home. I'd had to actually buy an automobile. Never in my lifetime did I believe I'd own one of those monstrosities, but the mass transit here was nearly nonexistent, so I purchased the car, under protest. The list grew every week of things I said I'd never do. The auto was only one of the first of them.

Recruiting a man away from his family was next on my list.

The waiter deposited our drinks and asked for our order. Of course, we'd been talking and hadn't even picked up the menus, so he left us for the time being.

I took a sip of my cold water and shivered. Everywhere I went in this town, the air-conditioning only knew one setting: full blast. "It is a bit of a difference, but I'm taking it all in." I picked up my menu. "We'd probably better peruse the offerings before the man returns. And please, order whatever you want. It's on my company." Another recruitment perk—the hefty expense account.

He gave me a knowing smile and picked up his own menu. "Thank you."

I'd just decided on my lunch order when the waiter returned. I ordered their scallop pasta, and Dominick ordered the salmon. I laughed to myself because neither of us had actually ordered a steak. "Do you eat meat?"

"I definitely do, but I usually do something a little lighter at lunch." He sipped from his coffee cup.

"I'm much the same." I wasn't much for a big breakfast either. Usually, once I'd finished up at the gym, I stopped by a local tea shop for some masala chai. Luck didn't begin to describe the feeling when I finally found a decent cuppa here. Had to kiss a lot of frogs for that one, didn't I? Then I'd have a smoothie or maybe scramble a couple of eggs. I'd never been much of a cook. Mostly because I hadn't the opportunity. "Tell me something about yourself. And the area. Your school."

"Well, let's see." He leaned back in his chair as if readying himself for the long haul. "I grew up here, in Autumn. Got my degree from University of Houston, then pilot's license from the very flight school I now run. I have a big family—three sisters and a brother—and we're all mostly in the family business one way or another."

"That's quite interesting. I met someone who lives here in Autumn, and she has several siblings as well. Do families have more children than the norm here?" I was genuinely curious because I couldn't think of a single former friend who had more than two siblings.

A pain shot through my gut at the thought of people I'd grown close to only to abandon me at the first sight of scandal. I could blame Sheila, but she only exposed these people weren't my true friends after all.

He rubbed his chin in thought. "I don't believe so. Then again, I'm not sure. I haven't paid much attention. What's the person's name? Maybe I know them."

I hesitated a moment. If I gave him Mary's name, would he know her? I wasn't sure why, but I didn't want his path to cross with hers. Especially since I hadn't had the lay of the land yet. Then again, I didn't even know her last name and her first name was quite common. "Her name is Mary, but I don't know her well. That's really all I know about her." That and how her body felt and tasted.

My dick twitched, and I reminded myself I was in the middle of a business meeting.

Dominick scrunched his face in thought. "I don't believe

I know a Mary. Is she in the business?"

I supposed that was a natural question considering our circumstances. "A pilot, I believe. We met in London briefly earlier this year before I moved. Then I ran into her here." A few times actually, but Dominick didn't need to know that. I'd already given him more information than I intended. Something about him made the man easy to talk to.

I put that away because it was time to get down to business. I wanted a tour of his flight school and to ease myself into his good graces, laying the groundwork to make an offer I hoped he wouldn't refuse.

CHAPTER NINE

Margaret—Tranquility is nice. Don't get used to it.

I WAITED IN my car for any sight of Leon. I had no idea what sort of car he drove, but I arrived fifteen minutes early and the lot wasn't especially full this early on a Saturday morning, so hopefully he'd find me. I'd instructed him to park in the lot between the Japanese Gardens and the Museum of Natural History and Sciences since my plan included both.

I'd thought about picking up some Shipley's doughnuts and coffee, but I knew nothing about the man, other than how the dips between his ab muscles felt. He was English, so maybe he only drank tepid tea. And with crumpets only, not doughnuts.

I rubbed my head in frustration. Turning a one-night stand into a friendship probably wasn't the best idea in any situation. Especially not when he turned up halfway across the world under suspicious circumstances. Well, suspicious to me anyhow, however unearned.

Right on time, Mr. Posh drove up in a large dark green SUV and parked about four spaces down from me.

I hopped out of my much more conservative nondescript sedan and dug my backpack out of the back seat. I met him right as he exited his vehicle and turned as if searching for something in one of the compartments. I had to catch my breath when I saw the white pants tastefully clinging to his slim hips and tight ass. The red polo hugged his biceps perfectly, and I had to turn my head. I wondered why he wore my signature color. It matched my coloring perfectly, which was why I wore it along with the occasional deep greens and neutral browns.

No complaint from me on how he pulled it off though. When he spun around to face me, I had to consciously close my mouth. "You made it." Should I lean in for a hug? A handshake? Damn, he had me frazzled. I settled for a small wave and a smile.

"I made it. Have you been waiting long?" He walked up to me and bent.

I offered my cheek in response.

He kissed it but lingered a moment past casual greeting.

I stepped back and cleared my throat. After all he was the one who said he didn't even have time for a friend and definitely not a relationship. "What type of car is that?" I knew airplanes, but automobiles somehow eluded me.

He gave me a sheepish grin. "A Range Rover."

"Like the queen?" She was gone now, but I always associated that type of car and those little corgi dogs with her.

"You'd be surprised how many people in the UK drive them."

"Interesting." He wasn't in the UK anymore, but I supposed a car could give you the comfort of home. For some people at least. I angled to the right and tipped my head. "This way."

As we walked, I peppered him with softball questions. If

all went to plan, we'd have hours to spend together and learn more about each other naturally. From the little I knew of Leon, he liked to keep his cards close to his vest.

"So this is the Japanese Gardens." I swept my hand toward the entrance. My heart swelled with pride to show off this beautiful place nestled in the middle of Houston. I couldn't count how many times during college I would drive over here between classes to study in a peaceful surrounding or even just decompress.

"Brilliant." He glanced around the outside. "Where do we purchase tickets?"

I grinned. "It's completely free." Then I winked and headed past the small structure separating the outside from the inside and the stone lantern just beyond.

Posh kept in step beside me. "This is really nice. It's so tranquil."

A couple people meandered through the paths around us, but at this time of day, we were mostly isolated.

I nodded. "It is. Do you have anything like this at home?"

"This is home now." His shoulders stiffened ever so slightly.

I almost said *You know what I mean* but decided against it. I tried to put myself in his shoes. Not only leaving his family and home but his entire country. I still lived a hundred feet from my kinfolk, and I wouldn't have it any other way. "That's true, which is why I wanted to show you around today. May as well know what your new home has to offer."

He relaxed and kept the pace with me. "I hope you know

how appreciative I am. You didn't have to do this."

"I wanted to. It would be weird for me to pretend like I don't know you and just keep running into you." I directed him to the small Japanese Friendship Pavilion, and we settled on one of the benches. "Am I mistaken, or are we in the same industry?" Hopefully with the soothing surroundings, Posh would let his guard down and open up a little. I held my breath waiting on his reply and stared up at the hewed ceiling, painted in reds, greens, and golds. Breathtaking.

"Tangentially." He stared off into the calm water; a turtle perched on a rock.

When I realized he wasn't about to say anything else, I prodded on. "How so?"

His throat worked until he finally huffed a small breath. "I'm a recruiter in the industry."

My ears perked up. "How does that work? Like if you were looking for a pilot, you might call me?"

Posh rocked his head back and forth. "Sure, there are recruiters for that. I work for a company and recruit exclusively for them."

"That's really interesting. Who are you recruit—"

"Did you see that?" He jumped up and pointed at the water.

I followed his pointing finger but didn't see anything unusual. "See what?"

"The fish jumped up out of the water and hung there for a moment. I wonder what it was after."

I stared at his profile and frowned. A fish jumping out of the water didn't seem that interesting. We had a whole lake at home where this was a daily occurrence. Maybe that was why spotting marine life where they were supposed to be didn't seem like a big deal to me. I shrugged it off and took my seat.

He came back with raised brows. "You don't fancy fish?"

"I guess I don't get quite as excited at their spotting." I chuckled, and he patted his warm hand on my thigh. I'd worn walking shorts today, so there was skin-on-skin contact. I intentionally slowed my breaths before they got out of hand at his touch. It amazed me how much my body remembered his feel.

He stared at me with hooded eyes.

I wanted him to lean in. I would meet him halfway, if only to taste those sultry lips again just once.

A nearby duck quacked loudly—too loud—jerking Leon's attention back to the water.

The spell was broken. I knew I'd been about to ask him something important, but for the life of me, I couldn't remember what it was.

We still had the entire day before us.

Maybe it would come to me later.

CHAPTER TEN

Lewis—You can't be serious

I WASN'T SURE what I expected, but the research I'd done hadn't prepared me for the Hawthorne Family Flying Eagles. In order to get to the flight school, I passed along a paved road that ran miles along a chain-link fence. On the other side of the fence at some point was a big house with a huge statue out front and other buildings, maybe houses, behind. From my research, I learned the Hawthornes' legacy began with a Tuskegee Airman, so the statue was probably of the man. I itched to get on the other side of that fence and really check out the family-only portion of the vast property.

Security waved me through the gate after showing my ID and checking the list against it. Seemed like that should've been computerized. I started making mental notes of short-comings to use as leverage in the future.

Dominick stood outside the first hangar I approached and waved me his way, guiding me toward a small parking lot behind the large building. Another note that the parking lot could use some pothole fill-ins, maybe even get complete-ly repaved. Three more hangars littered this side of the field, but only the one nearest us was open. From the outside, all the buildings could use a coat of paint. Not that hangars needed to be perfect, but appearance could seep into the psyche of potential flight students.

Once I parked, I got out and strode over to Dominick, hand extended. "Thanks so much for taking the time to show me around. I hope I'm not keeping you from lunch." I probably should have offered to bring him something to eat.

"No problem at all. Someone from the house usually drops something off for me, and I eat at my desk while poring over ledgers. It's good to get out and stretch my legs." He took the lead, walking toward a smaller building.

"Doesn't sound like you're the one giving lessons." Maybe I'd misunderstood, but I could have sworn he had his pilot's license.

"I did before, but there's so much to do in the office nowadays. My sister helps out, which takes some of the burden off, but she splits her time between here and the plane rental." He pointed off in the near distance. Looked like the rental business was interconnected with the flight school.

The two buildings weren't very close, but she could easily walk between them. "Right, your sister. What was her name?"

He chuckled and opened the door to the office, waving me through, the AC a welcome relief from the heat. "I have three sisters, man. The one I'm talking about is my sister Miranda. She's the youngest sister, while Margaret's the oldest. I have another one in the middle named Meredith. And a younger brother, Donovan."

"I don't know how I forgot how large your family is." It wasn't so much that I forgot, but most people liked to talk about themselves and I wanted him to talk so I could tell where his priorities lay.

"Did you say you have siblings, Lewis?"

I nodded. Usually I wouldn't reveal anything about myself, but I'd mentioned it to him at lunch the other day offhandedly. Honestly, Dominick had me talking just as much as, if not more than, the other way around. "One brother, I'm afraid. Nothing like your brood. Do you enjoy having such a large family?" Better to learn this up front. If he couldn't do without his relatives even the smallest amount, I shouldn't waste my time.

"I do. And I don't." He shrugged. "Listen, I wouldn't trade any of them for the world, but privacy is a luxury around here. Plus I have a lot of bosses. Everyone has an opinion."

"I can only imagine."

He sat behind his desk and gestured for me to take the plush chair across from him. There was a smaller desk in the room, presumably for Miranda. The small window behind Donovan showed the other part of the building. From what I could see where I sat, there appeared to be a counter and waiting room with chairs.

He drummed his fingers on the desk. "Don't get me wrong. It's a trade-off because they give so much of themselves too. I never want for anything, and neither do my sons. Someone is always around to lend a helping hand."

I nodded because that made sense. A family business would have its pros and cons, especially the way the Hawthornes seemed to do it. "Sounds lovely."

He smiled. "So before I show you around, can you tell me why you're here? I don't want to give you a blanket tour if you have certain objectives."

Here was where I really needed to employ some finesse. Lying was out of the question considering when it was time to offer him a job, he wouldn't likely forget. "I've just arrived in the States at the beginning of the summer. I work for an aviation company that has built a state-of-the-art flight school not too far from here actually."

He nodded. "That must be Gibson. They're a huge outfit. We're not even on the same scale."

"Yes, Gibson Aviation. The school is lovely, certainly, but I also wanted to get a feel for..."

A plane landed, and I turned and watched it through the big picture window behind me. Soon, two people hopped out, both in flight gear, although one had more of a swagger while the other trailed behind.

"That's Andre back from a lesson."

"Related to you?" The man was average height like Dominick and had the same bulky build like he lifted a lot of weights.

He grinned. "No, we employ people outside the family too."

"Yes, of course." I wasn't sure what happened, but my insides melted a little. There really was something about witnessing all the Black excellence that surrounded me. Aviation was not somewhere the average person looked for that. Perhaps it was different in America, I reckoned.

"You were saying?"

I watched until the men disappeared into the office next door. "Uh, yes. Where was I? Oh, right. I was saying I wanted to familiarize myself with other outfits in the area.

Although this is a much smaller school than Gibson, it's still sizable and has a great reputation. Coming from England, I image we do things a little differently."

"I imagine so." He stood. "Let's go have a look around."

And just like that, we were out the door. No more questions asked. If Dominick was this laid-back, my chances with him would be a piece of cake.

NO SOONER HAD I stepped outside back into the heat than Mary showed up with hair whipping around her head and a brick-red sundress flowing behind her like she had large fans set up, Beyoncé style. In reality, another plane took off, sans Andre, who still talked with the student in the building behind us.

She shielded her eyes against the sun and focused on Dominick. "I thought Jennifer was sick."

"Probably just a twenty-four hour something or other." Dominick turned my way. "Jennifer actually is a relative. Our cousin." He grinned and shrugged.

That snagged Mary's attention, and she glanced at me, then really looked at me with wide eyes, her mouth agape. "What are you doing here?"

Dominick looked between me and Mary. "Have you met my sister Margaret?"

I narrowed my eyes at her. "I don't believe I've met a Margaret." I stuck out my hand, amused by her lie. The same one I'd told and held on to.

She reluctantly put her hand in mine.

I gave it a squeeze instead of a shake.

Dominick didn't notice.

She narrowed her eyes. "And your name?"

So much for my high horse. My lie to Mary—er, Margaret—was about to be exposed too. "It's Lewis. Lewis Watson-Grosvenor."

I expected her to be cross, but Margaret cracked a smile. "Quite a mouthful, Lewis." She put more than enough emphasis on my name. I couldn't blame her, but we'd both lied to protect our identities. And neither of us revealed our true identities to each other until forced. I knew my motives, but I wondered about hers.

Not that I could blame her. If I hadn't needed to work her brother, I definitely would have given her shit. This was quite the coincidence. Then again, was it? Could that one-night stand been some sort of setup? But to what end? Her body language didn't give conspiracy, and in addition to having a good memory for details, names, and faces, I prided myself on reading people, their expressions, both facial and body. Maybe just a coincidence, but I'd tuck all his away in the back of my mind and proceed accordingly.

If she wasn't inclined to let on that we'd met before tonight, I would happily go along. If this meeting was all happenstance, then I should ensure I didn't tip my hand. "Do you think that's a mouthful?" I raised brows in challenge, my mind flashing back to that wondrous night.

"I've heard bigger." She released a bright smile.

Dominick's head swiveled between us. "What's going on here?"

Mary—er, Margaret (would I ever get used to this new

name?)—schooled her expression. "Nothing. Just getting to know your new friend. Are y'all just…" She shrugged and twisted her mouth. "Hanging out? How did you even meet?"

Dominick eyed his sister warily. "We met through a mutual. And I'm giving him a tour of the school." He tilted his head and narrowed his eyes quizzically.

Margaret couldn't just let that go on face value. Of course she couldn't. "Why exactly do you want to tour the school?"

That was none of her business, and I sorely wished I could respond in kind. Doing so probably wouldn't endear me to her brother though. As it was, I had no intention of either of them knowing my reason until I had lured him in completely. Instead I did my usual deflection. "Is that an issue? Is there some sort of objection?"

She blinked. "That's not an answ—"

"Give the man a break, Margaret. He asked me, and I'm perfectly fine with it." Then Dominick turned his attention my way. "Are you ready to have a look?"

I was more than ready. "Yes."

"Great. Let's go." He rotated back to his sister, who stood there like a statue, staring daggers. "Did you want to come, Margaret?"

I would bet all of my parents' money she wanted to go with us. That didn't stop me from trying to discourage her. "Nice seeing you." I rotated to Dominick, refusing to show her anything I felt. Which was nothing. Why would I feel anything? "I'm ready when you are."

He frowned between me and Margaret. "Am I missing something?"

"Not at all, little brother. I think I will tag along."

Dominick scrunched his face but apparently decided to let it ago. He turned and walked to the open hangar nearest us.

I hung back just enough to remain out of earshot from him. "Is there anything on your mind...*Margaret?*"

She hissed at me. "Stop saying my name like that. I don't just hand out my name to perfect strangers. Besides, you lied too, *Leon.*"

"You don't hand out your name to strangers, but you don't mind handing out—"

Dominick looked back then. "Everything okay?"

We both nodded, and I plastered a reassuring smile on my face.

Neither of us spoke again, at least not to each other, while Dominick walked me through the operation. One small plane sat inside the otherwise empty hangar with space for two more. I assumed those were the ones being used for lessons currently.

Dominick motioned all around. "This and the hangar right next door is where we keep the Cessna Skyhawk single engines. For beginners or people who only want to learn enough for reasons like crop dusting."

Nodding, I asked, "Do you rent space out to private planes?"

"No, we never have. Any airplane you see today is owned by Hawthorne Flying Eagles."

"Did you leave *Family* out of the name, or am I mistaken?"

"Family is never left out." Margaret obviously had been

biding her time to check me.

"Hmm indeed."

Dominick only chuckled. "Normally I just say *Hawthorne*. Most folks around here know what I'm talking about. Especially if they're in the business."

The Hawthorne Family Flying Eagles were well respected in Autumn, Texas, and in the Houston aviation circles as well. I'd learned that much this past summer. "Noted. How many airplanes does Hawthorne own?"

"What a curious question. Why do you want to know exactly?" Margaret released a saccharine smile.

"We've already talked about all that. Leave the man alone please."

Fire lit up her eyes, but when she looked at her brother's calm face, she nodded.

Thank goodness for Dominick. He let me off the hook, but I had a feeling Margaret wouldn't be so easy to dance around.

"As for how many, we have planes both for the school and a separate fleet to rent out. For the school, we currently have six planes."

"What type of programs do you offer?" I had to keep my eyes strictly trained on Dominick's face because the heat radiating off Margaret behind me was a bit maddening.

"We have a transport pilot program as well as a career pilot program, like what my sister here went through."

That explained London. My own internalized misogyny blocked the possibility of her being a commercial pilot. I'd guessed flying for FedEx or the like. I turned toward her, genuinely impressed, and bowed slightly. "That's quite an accomplishment."

Those big brown eyes narrowed, and I realized she hadn't taken the compliment as I intended.

"That is quite an accomplishment in general. That's what I meant."

"Thank you." She didn't smile, but her face relaxed considerably.

"Our baby sister tried her hand at it too, but the politics of it wasn't for her. She quit after two years."

"Well, Dominick, you have quite an impressive family. Truly. I'd love to meet them some day." I glanced at Margaret, my gaze snagging on her lips in somewhat of a pout. For a moment I lost myself, remembering the taste of that beautiful mouth. "I mean, aside from your sister here, of course."

"We'll have to have you out soon for Sunday dinner."

"Before you invite people for dinner, you should probably check with Chana, don't you think?" She didn't appear angry, but something else flashed across her face, almost like she was hopeful despite the words she threw at her brother.

Dominick gave his sister a tight smile. "I said soon, not this Sunday."

Yes, there it was. Quick, but there nonetheless. Disappointment.

I shook the thought right out of my head. Now that I knew they were siblings, I reminded myself I was here for Dominick, not Margaret.

I'd do well to keep remembering that.

CHAPTER ELEVEN

Lewis—Breakfast of champions?

THE DAY I'D spent with Margaret almost changed my mind about getting back into the relationship game. She displayed warmth and attention—maybe too much attention considering I had to bob and weave, deflect left and right. Her sarcastic humor kept me chuckling even in the Museum of Fine Arts when everyone around us seeped themselves in such seriousness. The paintings were beautiful, and Picasso's black-and-white exhibition tour was truly magnificent, but there was no need for such somberness.

Feelings were almost caught, but then she showed up at Hawthorne—my target's sister, no less—and that broke the temporary spell she'd put me under. I looked down at my tattoo and nodded. Lesson relearned.

One thing about my day spent with Margaret that stood out in her consistent questioning: I did miss Charlie. I wanted a new start far away from anyone who knew my last name, from anyone who might expect something from me because of it.

But taking a job at a new company in a new country might have been a bit more than I was cut out for. My days were filled, yet loneliness clung to me. Despite being peppered with questions I had no intention answering, being with Margaret was the highlight of my week.

I couldn't think along those lines though. My attention was better directed at recruiting Dominick and finding a place in my new company. There were plenty of coworkers, and working from home wasn't conducive to forging new relationships.

My mobile chirped, and I had to smile when Charlie's face filled my screen. "I was just thinking about you, bro."

He tapped the side of his head. "I know. Must be telepathy or some shite."

My silly little brother. The only member of our immediate family whose calls I never dodged. Even when he talked nonsense, his conversation outperformed anyone else's.

I checked the time on my open laptop. "Ending the day a little early, are you?"

"What makes you think my day is done? I'm leaving the office, but Dad set up dinner with a client."

I only nodded. I didn't want to talk about our father or the business. "Well, you have fun." I hesitated, but it couldn't hurt to ask. "How's Mum?"

He grimaced, then shrugged. "Be a lot better if you'd return her calls. She said she's barely heard from you since you moved."

Although Dad worked quite a bit, he and Mum were essentially tied at the hip. The company was a family affair, even reeling her in. I always took a chance she'd be with him when I contacted her. "I've talked with her."

"Once, maybe twice? At least that's what she related."

That had been the gist of it. "I'll ring her tomorrow. The time difference is really messing me up."

His expression broadcast his displeasure and disbelief. No need for words. "How's the job going? Did you land that big fish yet?"

"This one will take quite a bit of finesse, I'm afraid."

"Color me intrigued."

"Do you remember the woman from the theater? The night before I left?"

He chuckled. "Certainly. You were enamored."

"I was not enam—" I huffed. "She's the sister of the man I'm recruiting."

"Really? How did that happen?"

I shrugged. "Coincidence, looks like."

"Some coincidence." He glanced behind him. "I've got to run. The table's ready, and I see the client at the valet."

"Good luck."

He nodded and saluted. "Be good."

When the call disconnected, I looked up at the ceiling and studied the smooth, white surface. Maybe I would paint it black. Then I opened the box I'd just received and admired its contents.

After setting my newest atlas on the shelf, I sat on the mattress of the guest bed and admired my find. There were no linens or anything else to make this room homey—I wasn't expecting house guests in my new Texas digs. Charlie would visit at some point; I wouldn't be able to keep him away for long. But until then, I'd relish this room as a safe space to unload my thoughts. Now all I needed was a comfy sofa.

Although I'd been here for more than three months, there were still many missing items for my town house. If all worked out with my new job, there would be plenty of time to finish furnishing the place.

I'd make sure it worked out.

My mobile chimed again. I frowned before looking at it. My device rarely rang with an actual call, and this morning I'd had two. I had to admit I was a little surprised, something that had been happening a lot since I moved to Texas, when I realized who called.

I answered on speaker. "Dominick, hello."

"Hey, man, how you doing?"

"I'm good." I waited for him to state his business. Maybe this was about Sunday dinner.

"Listen, I wondered if you wanted to meet up. You mentioned a couple of improvements we could make. I've been thinking about those a lot and have even taken some to my father before, but nothing ever came of it. I'd like to put together a comprehensive plan to present to him again, this time with related time and costs. And I'd love to pick your brain on what you saw. You know, get a fresh perspective from someone in the industry."

This couldn't have gone better if I planned it. I thought it would take at least a month or so of calling, dropping in for chats, and other ways to keep myself in front of Dominick.

I rubbed my hands together in anticipation, glad this wasn't a video chat. "I'd be happy to meet with you and discuss improvements. Gibson built a state-of-the-art school, so I can compare and contrast for you. Then you can use whatever makes sense for your smaller operation." Subtle reminders we have something much better without pushing him that way. At least not yet. "When and where?"

"Are you free this morning? I just dropped the boys off at school. We could have breakfast at the main house."

I hesitated just the slightest. What if Margaret breakfasted at the main house too? I wanted to see her. And therein laid the problem. Keeping my distance was a must, yet I thought of her until I went to bed last night, and she remained on my mind when I woke up this morning. I couldn't let my preoccupation with her cause problems. There was too much at stake. "Will that be okay with your house manager? I remember your sister scolding you."

"I've already cleared it with Chana. She's pretty flexible because you never know who'll show up for breakfast. Plus everyone else has probably cleared out by now. Or close to it."

My stomach sank. This sounded like a gamble, but one I couldn't afford to ignore. "Count me in."

"Excellent! See you soon."

"Looking forward to it."

That was the problem. I looked forward to entering the Hawthorne family realm a little too much—not for the right reasons.

SINCE I'D BEEN in Texas, I hadn't actually gone inside anybody's house. I'd met colleagues for drinks, been out to the new build site, and attended a couple meetings in the offices of headquarters but never inside an actual Texas residence. I wasn't sure what to expect, especially after matching Margaret's story with the Hawthornes and realizing almost all them lived on the property.

Dominick greeted me at the large wooden door before I could ring the doorbell. "Good morning. And welcome." He stuck out a hand.

I completed the gesture and walked across the threshold. "Delighted to be here." As I followed Dominick through the entryway and down a hall, I noted a large living room through a glass door to my right and an even larger room to my left, with a long wooden table appearing to seat at least fourteen or fifteen people for dinner. It was empty, and since Dominick continued walking, I concluded we must be dining elsewhere.

The house might have been brick on the outside, but in here, it was all glass and wood, tastefully decorated in an almost minimalist style with obviously expensive furnishings. We spilled out into another space, a great room with a large television mounted on the wall and comfortable, plush chairs, recliners, and sofas spread throughout.

We finally arrived at a smaller dining area just off the kitchen, which was partially visible from this room. There were two tables here, one large and round and another rectangular, which was where Dominick ended our walk, lowering himself into a chair. "Have a seat." He pointed to a chair just to his right as he was seated at the end.

The house appeared empty otherwise, the quiet pulsing in my ears. I half expected Margaret to round any one of the turns we made or seated at the table when we arrived. With so many family members, the lack of noise or movement seemed odd. "Are we the only ones here?"

He chuckled. "When you're here, you're never alone. Trust me. Although my parents and at least one sister ate earlier with the boys before they headed off to their various responsibilities. Mama made us some breakfast, and Chana kept it warm for us. I'll go get it as soon as she lets me know it's ready."

"Chana? Oh, the house manager, right?" I thought I remembered Margaret mention her but wanted to double-check.

Dominick nodded. "She keeps the Hawthorne family together. I don't know how we'd manage without her. She first started here as a housekeeper when her son was still a toddler. Now he's done with college and back for flight school."

"That's quite a long time. Do they live here?"

He nodded. "Well, not here in the house. They have their own house on the property."

Interesting. This was a much larger operation than I realized. I had so much intel on the flight school, but little else. "Convenient, that."

"Definitely a perk. I know from personal experience—there's nothing like living five minutes from your job."

That was a strike but not wholly unexpected. Gibson's flight school wasn't terribly far from here, so the commute would still be minimal. "I work from home mostly or out in the field, so I understand what you mean. I'm still gob-smacked by the lack of public transportation here."

"A common complaint. But there's a lot of land to cover, so it's difficult. Plus the politics of it all. It's a shame."

"Dominick," a woman called from the kitchen, although

I couldn't see anyone attached to the voice.

"Be right there." He rose, and I followed suit but he stayed me. "I can manage. If you need to wash up, there's a small bathroom through there."

I glanced where he signaled. A different hallway leading farther into the house. "Thanks."

This hallway was complete glass and gave me a glimpse of a swimming pool and large backyard. It was barely visible, but I believed there was some sort of court. I hoped for tennis, although if all went to plan, I probably wouldn't receive any invitations.

When I returned from washing my hands, several plates covered the space near the end of the table where Dominick and I had set up. The buttery smell of croissants hit my nose first, followed by a steaming platter of sausage and another with scrambled eggs. My stomach grumbled in anticipation. "Your mother made this?"

"She loves to cook, but we all pitch in for big meals, like Sunday dinner." He passed the basket of croissants to me after taking one for himself.

"Well, it smells delicious."

"You'll have to try some of these preserves. Mama and Margaret put them up…" He looked at the label of the two jars before him. "Looks like summer before last. There's muscadine and apricot."

"Muscadine?"

"It's some sort of grape. I think. Margaret can tell you about them."

What made him think I would talk with Margaret again? Odd thing to pronounce. I grunted noncommittally.

"Would you like some coffee? Oh, or do you drink tea? I'm sure we can muster some up."

"I had some earlier—thank you." The first bite of croissant melted in my mouth. "This is amazing."

He smiled, despite his full mouth.

"Does everyone eat breakfast here?"

He shook his head, then swallowed. "Mostly Miranda, and sometimes Meredith and Margaret. They have their own houses. I mean, Miranda does too, but you know, she's the baby girl so…" He took another mouthful of eggs and shrugged.

"And you and your sons?"

"Most days, that's true. Dinner too usually." He seemed suddenly solemn, and I didn't want to push the issue. His wife died less than two years ago, so I imagined it was a difficult adjustment.

"You ready to talk about those improvements?"

"Yes, thank you so much again, by the way." He pulled his mobile from a pants pocket and laid it on the table between us. "Do you mind?"

"Of course not." It wasn't my favorite, but if it was easier for him to record, so be it. I wasn't giving away state secrets after all. "When I drove up, the first things I noticed were a need for new pavement on the roads and parking lot, and the hangars needed painting. Obviously these are only cosmetic issues, but they give potential students the first impression of not being in good condition. Maybe they'll wonder if the planes aren't very sturdy."

He nodded along in agreement.

"The classroom is far from the parking lot, but that's just

an inconvenience and shouldn't be at the top of the list. It would probably be costly to move an entire building over closer to where your offices and front desk are."

"That would be a pipe dream. It's within walking distance. Plus I like the idea of keeping the school separated from the administration."

That was a good point. Dominick Hawthorne was extremely good at his job. The flight school had a steady rotation of students through their commercial-pilot program, most who went on to actually fly for the big airlines. The training program was unmatched, and while Dominick didn't originally create it, he overhauled and honed it to what the program was today. Clearly that had been more of his focus than the aesthetics, although that appeared to be higher on his radar now. "I know it's expensive, but the flight simulators could use an upgrade."

"Agreed. That one is on the top of my list."

Not a surprise considering it was a part of the actual training. "No notes on your planes or inside of the hangars. From what I hear, your curriculum is top notch and you've graduated some fine pilots."

He grinned then, pride spreading across his face. "Thank you." He looked beyond me. "Good morning."

Although rude, I didn't rotate my head. Somehow deep in my bones, I already knew who it was.

"Good morning indeed. I didn't realize you had company."

Now I did turn as her voice sounded right behind me. "Hullo there, Margaret."

Her hair was piled on top of her head, and she waved

away an errant strand from her face. Beautiful as always.

"Well, hello to you, Lewis."

Serendipity. Coincidence. Happenstance. I began to think whatever this was between us was inevitable.

CHAPTER TWELVE

Margaret—Meet my sisters

T HIS MORNING I'D gotten off to a slow start, having been up most of the night constructing my plan to approach various board members for their affirmative vote and determining in what order to make those advances. Plus stressing over my assignment for Thanksgiving that I'd received via email from Chana late in the evening. I was in charge of transportation. No easy task juggling all of our extended relatives' schedules. Seemed like a task better suited to my baby sister, and first chance I got, I'd trade with Miranda. Depending on the task she was assigned, of course.

I continued musing as I walked through my parents' house. Lewis Watson-Grosvenor seated at one of the kitchen tables for breakfast was not on my bingo card.

For his part, Lewis's expression was as surprised as I felt. He recovered quickly though. "It's nice to see you, Margaret."

"It's nice to be seen, Lewis." I tilted my head and smiled sweetly. "Can I have some?"

He sputtered, nearly choking on his own spit because from what I could see, he and my brother demolished breakfast. "Can you...sorry?"

"Just wondering if there was any breakfast left." I widened my eyes innocently. "What did you think I meant?"

Dominick stood then. "Thanks for letting me pick your brain, Lewis." He walked toward the closest exit. "I'm sure Margaret can handle it from here. I'll be in touch."

I sat and picked up the last remaining sausage. No longer warm, but edible. I stuck part of the sausage link into my mouth and twirled my tongue around the end, then bit into it, unable to help myself, feeling so flirty this morning. "Not much left."

Lewis groaned and looked away. Once he'd gathered himself, he rotated my way and lowered his voice. "What are you playing at, Margaret?"

Sometime between our day together the Saturday before, flying to Boston and back, poring over plans, losing sleep, and missing breakfast, I'd thought a lot about Lewis. Too much. The truth was I had a lot going on right now and no time for romance. Sex wasn't romance though, and we were two consenting adults who'd enjoyed each other's bodies before. Surely we could continue in that vein without complications. "Do you have anywhere to be?"

His brows shot up. "Why?"

"Since breakfast is good and done, my next stop is a hike. Care to join me?"

He looked down at his spotless shoes, not made for hiking for sure. "I don't think I'm dressed for hiking. I have trainers in the car if you'd rather go for a walk."

My skin tingled with anticipation. I was happy to no longer fight against this attraction. Hopefully we could get on the same page and have a little fun. "Sounds like a plan. You go out to your car, and I'll meet you there."

When I pulled around to the front of the house in a golf cart, Lewis hopped in, no questions asked. Maybe this was how they got around at Gibson too, but I doubted it.

He looked up at my great-grandfather's replica. "Can I get the history on that rather large statue?"

I ran it down to him. How he and his father and brother founded this land. How he started the Hawthorne Family Flying Eagles business. How he was part of the elite Red Tails.

"If the brothers started the family business, why's there only a statue of your great-grandfather and not his sibling as well?"

That was the hundred-thousand-dollar question I'd yet to discover. "I'm not sure. Family mystery, I guess."

His expression twisted, ready to ask another question, but he quelled the desire. He held on to the roof on his side. "Where are we off to?"

"Not too far." Most of our hiking trails were mild, but he probably wouldn't appreciate going through our little dense forest like I'd originally intended. Overall, the entire Houston area was relatively flat, but we had a hill or two here and there. A walk around the lake would better suit for today.

"This is quite a property." His gaze traveled over the vast open land. Most of the aviation happenings were in the opposite direction we rode. This way laid untouched acres where we entertained ourselves with all manner of outdoor activity.

"Did you ever go to the country back home?"

"Not really." We hit a bump, and he grabbed the seat

between us, brushing his hand against my thigh.

That small brush of his hand was enough to bring back memories of his soft but sure caresses a few months before. I shivered in response.

He turned to me, eyes alight.

Clearly we were on the same page when it came to recollections.

Lewis turned away just as fast.

We might've been in concert when it came to the past, but the here and now might be a different story.

We pulled up to the lake and got out.

Lewis shielded his eyes from the beaming sun and looked around. "This is so peaceful."

Ducks glided through the water in small groups while water rushed over rocks placed to create a small waterfall. It would take too much time to walk around the entire lake, as big as it was, but we could go quite a distance, then turn back.

"I come here to sort through my thoughts. There's no other serene place that I like better than here." I led him to the packed-dirt path one of my ancestors had created. "We fish here too sometimes. Miranda likes to take a kayak out." I chuckled.

"Tell me."

As we walked, I thought about simpler times. "Once, Meredith got it in her head to take a canoe out and roped me into getting in with her. So I was in front, and we were rowing." I huffed a laugh. "Only we weren't making any traction, just going in a circle. I kept telling her to row opposite me, but when I glanced over my shoulder, she rowed on the same side as me." I never understood why she wouldn't listen. She wasn't stubborn by nature, but sometimes listening to her older sister was a bridge too far for her.

"She kept rowing with you?" He stopped and picked up a rock, then skipped it across the surface of the water.

Something I've never mastered. "Yes." I threw out my hands in frustration at the memory. "I'd yell back at her to row opposite and she'd yell back that she would, then we'd go in another circle."

"Maddening."

"Right? I was at my wit's end by the time we stumbled to shore."

"Did she say why?"

I shrugged. "It was basically some version of 'you're not the boss of me.' We were only thirteen and eleven."

He laughed then. "Okay, that makes a lot more sense. I thought you were grown women out there being foolish."

What if we were? We weren't made to be serious and proper all the time. Or maybe that was the American in me. We couldn't all be posh like Lewis. "Do you never do anything silly?"

He turned his head toward me as we kept the pace. "Not that I can remember."

"You're very vague, you know."

"Am I?"

Every indication was he knew just how much he withheld. My guess was it was intentional, which only made me wonder again what he was hiding. Maybe even casual sex would need to go on the back burner until I got more measure of the man.

Too bad because I'd been looking forward to an afternoon romp.

ONCE I'D DEPOSITED Mr. Posh back at the front of my parents' house, I headed over to the repair shop. The memory I'd relayed to Lewis by the lake had my sisters top of mind. Time to roll out my strategy.

When I stepped inside the shop, music blared from somewhere deep within and the AC blew as hard as possible, causing me to shiver and rub my bare arms. The smell was consistent with the odors of any type of repair shop: thick grease, faint burnt rubber, and electrical shortages. Plus this one had the added olfactory assault of jet fuel.

I spotted Meredith high on top of a ladder, hunched over an engine, and stepped that way. At least until Grumpy Grand, as we liked to call him (behind his back because no one dared say that to his face), stepped into my path.

He crossed his arms and stared down at me. "Where do you think you're going?"

"Um, to holler at my sister real quick."

He shook his head and narrowed his dark brown eyes at me. "This isn't a social club. It's bad enough she"—he stuck out a finger Meredith's way and stab-pointed in her direction—"is in here under foot whenever I turn around, but here you come to gab." Despite Grand's dark brown skin, red undertones made themselves known.

Everyone knew Meredith was the bane of the shop manager's existence, but Grand couldn't do anything about her, considering her last name inked his paychecks. And as much as they'd like to, neither could Mama and Daddy. My sister was determined to spend her days covered in grease instead of up in the sky.

Offended, I placed a hand over my heart. "Listen, Grand. I'm not here to gossip like some teenager. I need to speak with my sister about business."

"Then take it to an office somewhere, not my shop."

His shop? His shop! This man had more nerve than I could ever muster. But everyone put up with him because the repair shop boasted strong profits. He ran a tight ship, keeping accidents low and billable hours high.

I ground my teeth, then unhinged my jaw. "Okay, fine. Can you at least let her know to come down and meet me in the waiting room?" I'd walked through there on the way in, and it was completely empty.

He inhaled a large amount of air and quickly let it go, exhaling the sigh of the long suffering. "Fine."

"Don't break your teeth, grinding them so hard." I circled back to the outer office, hoping Grand would follow through. If not, I'd have to catch her later once she left the shop. Truth was I didn't want to go another round with the shop manager. I didn't want that smoke.

The water dispenser in the corner of the waiting room was too much to resist, so I slipped a cup out from the sleeve and filled it with the cold H_2O, then deposited myself in one of the metal chairs lining the wall. There wasn't much to look at in the small room; two airplane engine posters dotted the white walls and the white tile floor gave off an unnervingly harsh reflection. My mind raced a mile a minute through everything I needed to get done today. Tomorrow I'd fly out to Miami and wouldn't be back until the day after, which was by design—my cousin, and her vote, lived there. Thoughts of my morning with Mr. Posh were close at hand as well. I shook the thought out of my head.

Luckily I didn't have to ponder my attraction long because my sister finally opened the door. She wore unflattering overalls, hiding what we all called body yoddy. And by we, I meant me and our baby sister, Miranda, who had the perfect tits, while I boasted the big ass and shapely legs, but Meredith had it all. Too bad nobody ever saw it.

As usual, grease streaked her pretty brown skin and even worked its way up into her close-clipped sandy-brown hair. She released her bright smile, which lit up the room, helped by the reflective tiled floor. "Hey, sister." She leaned down as if to give me a hug.

I scooted my chair away, the legs scraping along the tile, and just dodged the greasy embrace. Instead I reached out and patted her upper arm, the only patch of clean I could find. "Ew—I have too much to do today, and going back home to get cleaned up isn't on the list."

She rolled her pretty brown eyes, good natured as always, and plopped into the chair a couple seats down. "To what do I owe the pleasure? Must be important if you braved Grand."

I shook my head. "That man. I don't know how you do it."

She shrugged. "He's really not that bad." She looked toward the door, and I imagined the man beyond.

When she turned back, I quirked an eyebrow.

"What?"

"Is there something going on I should know about?"

"Like what, Margaret?"

I tilted my head and stared her down.

Her innocent gaze stared back.

"Okay, never mind. Listen, I don't want to take up much of your time, but I need your support." I went on to explain my plan of getting the votes to update the charter.

"Of course you know you have my *yes* vote. You'll make an amazing replacement for Daddy." She stood.

Mist filled my eyes, but I blinked it away. "Thanks. I knew I could count on you." I stood then too. "I'll let you get back to work."

She left the room, and I watched after her. She passed Grand without a glance, but once she'd walked a couple steps, she looked over her shoulder at him, a very sly move.

I knew it. My intuition about these things never failed. She had a little something going on with the shop manager. Or at least, Meredith thought about it.

MY NEXT STOP was either the school or the rental office. Miranda could be close to either. I fired off a text message, hoping she was free to respond.

While I waited for a response, I drove that way. The two were connected, so I'd catch her at one of the other.

By the time I arrived at the customer parking lot, my phone was quiet, no messages of any kind. I left the golf cart at the edge of the lot, nearest the flight school office, and headed that way. A quick peek into Dominick's window didn't yield my sister, but my brother sat at his desk, nose buried in his computer. I knocked and waved, and he started, then held up a tentative hand.

Moving on to the rental office, I thought about my brother and his new relationship with Lewis. They seemed awfully chummy fast, which didn't necessarily sit right in my spirit, but I couldn't begrudge my brother someone outside the family to talk with. It seemed ever since Lisa passed, he hadn't been out there much. Old friends probably didn't know how to navigate a relationship with him still grieving, and he hadn't shown much interest in reconnecting with any of them. More than that, job satisfaction wasn't at the highest it could be with him either. He wanted some improvements made to the school and had been shot down. Hopefully that wouldn't cause him to give up.

Janine stood behind the rental counter, checking in a plane someone had returned. Miranda must've been outside looking over the plane, which explained why she didn't return my text. I gave Janine a wave, then entered the back office.

Miranda sat behind the desk, a fat salad before her, and Jaden across the table, heads bent together whispering.

"What's the big secret?"

They popped apart as if I'd lit a firecracker under the desk.

"What?"

"Why are you sneaking up on people?" Miranda sat back in her chair and stared up at me.

Jaden glanced my way, then stood. "I'd better get back to the school. Hey, Margaret." He rushed out the back door before I could finish my response.

"Um, hey." Something ticked in the back of my brain, but I couldn't capture it. I took the recently vacated chair and studied my sister.

Apparently the salad was intriguing because she stared into its leafy depths.

"What's going on?"

"Nothing. Jaden stopped through on his way to class to check on things."

Not much information there, so I let it go. Miranda would tell me in good time. Plus now wasn't the time to antagonize her. "Looks good." My stomach took that moment to rumble loud enough for the customer in the other room to hear.

We busted out laughing, breaking the slight tension that had filled the room.

"I forgot I haven't really had anything today."

She pushed the salad across the desk. "Have some."

I pushed it back. "Nah. I've got some spaghetti in the fridge back at my place that's calling my name."

My baby sister took a bite of her greens and closed her eyes.

"That good, huh?" Aunt Deborah must have made it. She was the salad queen. Her concoctions held more calories than a Sunday roast with mashed potatoes.

Miranda nodded and chewed.

While she ate, I launched into my plan and outlined the support I would need.

She waved a fork in my direction. "Obviously I'm a *yes* vote."

"I'm not taking anyone for granted."

"What time does your flight leave tomorrow?" Her expression was grim, the corners of her mouth turned down. Any mention of flying for a commercial airline left a sour appearance on her pretty face.

"It's a ten-a.m. flight, so I'll be up at zero dark thirty per usual."

"You love it."

The only response was to smile. I did love it.

"And you'll have enough time to see cousin Barbara?"

"That's the plan."

She placed her fork in the empty container and sat back. "Tell me about this Lewis guy."

My eyes bugged and my breath caught. "Who told you? Jaymes?" I couldn't believe my bestie would rat me out. Plus she hadn't been out here that I knew of. Jaymes looked at Miranda as a little sister too, but they didn't chat on the phone. Unless something had changed.

Miranda narrowed her eyes and leaned toward me. "Well, well, well. Do tell."

"What?"

"Clearly I've missed something. I was asking about Dominick's new friend, but maybe he's a little more than that." She waggled her eyebrows.

"I'll tell you as soon as you tell me what's going on with Jaden."

She snorted and sat back. "Well played, sister. Well played."

We stared each other down for a long moment, then I stood. "Good talk. Thanks for your support."

"Anytime." She winked.

With two votes in the bag, I decided to wait until I returned from Miami, hopefully with a third, to approach my brothers at Sunday dinner.

CHAPTER THIRTEEN

Lewis—Fond memories? Or lusty desires?

B ECAUSE MY CURIOSITY and search for knowledge was always at one hundred, I latched on to the tidbit of the Hawthorne ancestor and why he didn't have a statue. My nose said conspiracy, and I made it a habit to listen to my nose. Something shady happened with this bloke, and I intended to uncover what. It wouldn't help in my quest to recruit Dominick, but I needed to know.

A perk of my job was I had access to certain databases for cursory background checks. We used an outside company for something more thorough to clear a recruit before setting the wheels in motion, but in the beginning, it was me and the computer.

Once I'd established his name, nothing untoward immediately came up on Harrison Hawthorne. He'd had a deed to one of the houses on the Hawthorne land but naught else titled to him. There was his service notice but no mention of the Airmen he supposedly flew with.

I ran a rough hand over my face and looked at my calloused palm. When had I picked up those nubs? Then I remembered my outing with Shawn the day before. We'd played some tennis, and my borrowed racket had done a number on my hands. They'd beaten me solidly, which hadn't exactly sat well with me. I loathed losing.

Maybe setting aside my task for now would help, give me a bit of distance to think on it. My thoughts were quickly replaced with Margaret's smooth brown skin, glistening as we walked around the lake, enchanting me with her many childhood stories. Talking with her made me almost want to share little ditties of my own sibling relationship. Almost. Then I remembered the last time I'd opened up to someone so completely. She took me for a ride, that one. Never again.

But the pull Margaret had on me couldn't be denied. I had to physically restrain myself from reaching out so many times, casual touches so instinctive, they had to be contained. Remembering that one night when she opened her body to me, allowed me to worship that soft skin. Tease the tips of her breasts until they peaked. Run my tongue through her salty-sweet folds until she came.

I shook myself and released my cock I'd inadvertently clutched through my pants.

After checking the time, I chanced a text to her. *"Do you have plans this evening? Would like a chat."*

Dots danced on the screen and her reply came quickly. *"Early flight tomorrow, but I can spare an hour or so. Where?"*

Since it was early evening, I took a chance. *"Have you had dinner yet? We could meet there."*

That was a bit of a dick move. I wasn't ready to share my space here with her. And for obvious reasons, I couldn't visit her house. I clutched my head in admonishment. What was I doing? My relationship with Dominick was just beginning to gel. Being half in with his sister was not a bright business move.

My mobile pinged. *"Meet me at Prey in 30 minutes. Reservation under my name."*

What I should have done was sent a message back, making up an excuse, something I'd forgotten about. What I did was just the opposite: *"See you in 30."*

Most of the time, I made solid choices. There were times, few and far between, where I didn't. Sheila being at the top of that list. I couldn't let Margaret be another bad decision.

When I got to the restaurant, I'd tell her we shouldn't be involved.

CHAPTER FOURTEEN

Margaret — I just can't resist

J AYMES SAT HER bag back down on my coffee table. "Who are you texting and smiling with?"

I fixed my face. "There you go."

"Yeah, there I go. I already know who it is." She placed a hand on a well-proportioned hip.

"Well, if you already know, why are you asking?"

She rolled her eyes and plopped herself onto my couch.

"Nuh-uh, don't get comfortable. I have somewhere to be."

Jaymes raised her brows.

"Fine. I'm meeting your boy for dinner at Prey."

She rolled over onto her side laughing. "Oh, he's my boy now, huh?" Jaymes patted her stomach. "I love me some Prey."

"Who you telling? We'll see what Mr. Posh is talking about. If it's nothing, I can at least relish in the fact that I'll have an amazing dinner." I couldn't imagine it being nothing though. At the lake today, we conversed so easily. He listened to my silly stories and laughed like I was the most interesting person in the world. For about an hour, I forgot about my familial duties and fights. I felt closer to him than when we'd merged our bodies back in London. Not that I learned anything new about him, but there was an easiness to our interaction.

"What do you want him to be talking about?" Her expression turned serious, and she leaned in toward me, her green eyes sparkling.

"I don't know. It's a bad idea to fall back into anything with Lewis, but I'm having trouble resisting his charms." The timing was way off. There was too much on my plate, and anything resembling love wasn't in play for me. Not yet. There was a little thought, buried deep in the recesses of my mind that said, *If not now, then when?* Everything had come between me and love since I finished flight school.

"Why resist, sis?" She grinned at her little rhyme.

"Besides the timing being off, I always have in the back of my mind that he's up to something, but I can't figure it out, so maybe it's nothing." I shrugged.

"It's probably nothing, but I wondered about him and Dominick. Seems like they're more than business associates. Like Lewis is Dominick's new buddy." She frowned briefly. "It's probably nothing, like I said."

"No, I've had the same thoughts." I held up a finger. "First, he finagled his way into taking a tour of the flight school. And just this morning, he was perched at the kitchen table like he was part of the family. All of this in the span of less than a week." When I put the interactions together, maybe there was something more there. My intuition hadn't steered me wrong yet. Well, actually it had, but my confidence was on point this time.

"Wait, what? At your kitchen table?" She waved her hand in that direction.

"No, I mean at my parents' house. He and Dominick had their heads together when I walked in. I'm not sure what it was about, and I guess it's none of my business what they have going on. I don't want to interfere."

Jaymes cocked her head. "What are you saying? That if he and your brother are friends, then you and Lewis can't be...*friends*?" She lowered her voice seductively.

I thought about that a moment, a sour feeling filling my stomach. "It's been really hard for Dominick. You know that."

She nodded.

Tears flooded my eyes, and I quickly blinked them away. "He was so in love with Lisa. And they were perfect together. Then came two perfect boys, and their family was the envy of all the rest of us. But we were so happy for them too." My voice quivered, and I had to take a breath. "To have that snatched away with no warning...it was too much for all of us. But devastating for my brother."

My best friend wrapped an arm around my shoulders. "I know, babe. I was there, and even from the outside looking in, I've seen how much Lisa's death affected everyone. But you rallied around him, all of you, and ensured the boys want for nothing, most of all love."

"They're great kids." I sniffed. "But you also know that Dominick hasn't been the same. He's been more withdrawn, rarely talking to me, at least about anything important. I asked Meredith—you know those two were thick as thieves—and she says the same. So if he has someone in his life, someone who might be a good friend, who am I to swoop in and take that person away from him?"

Jaymes dropped her arms and sat back and looked at me. "Why is this a zero-sum game? You know that's how my parents met, right? My mom's best friend was my dad's sister. And they're still best friends after all these years. Literally the same."

I snorted. "Not exactly. I've seen Lewis naked. And that was before he met my brother."

"What does that matter. Talk to your brother and see what's going on with Lewis." She tapped a finger on her chin. "Or better yet, mention it to Lewis and let him know your concerns."

"Well, you're jumping ahead a little bit. I'm assuming Lewis wants to rekindle, but he could very well be asking me to dinner to talk about something aviation related. Or Dominick, even."

"I guess you'll have to see." Jaymes checked her watch and stood. "You should probably get going."

I stood and hugged my friend. "Thanks for your words. Your advice means everything, and I'm listening."

She squeezed me back. "Let me know how it goes."

I picked up my purse and keys and headed toward the garage. Time to see what Mr. Posh was really about.

THE VALET TOOK control of my car, and I looked up at the second floor to the Prey balcony. The last vestiges of daylight remained but were slipping rapidly. I'd made the reservation for inside because the heat was still doing its thing and the bugs hadn't gone back to the underworld or wherever they went when it turned cold.

Maybe I'd beat Lewis here even with Jaymes's attempt to waylay me because the man was nowhere to be seen. Then again, perhaps he was already seated, so I walked over to the escalators and rode up to the landing that led to Prey.

He stood next to the wall, looking down at his phone.

I took the opportunity of his preoccupation and really checked him out. From the looks of it, he'd received a fresh cut since I saw him earlier. He'd changed clothes too.

He looked up and smiled, slipping his phone into his periwinkle pants. The muscles in his forearm flexed with the motion, and I momentarily thanked my good fortune to witness the pushed-up sleeves of his Henley. Inside, the AC would likely blow too cold and he'd return those sleeves to their intended place.

I gave him a small smile and wave before walking up to him. "Hi."

"Hullo there. You look lovely as usual."

A small rush of heat flew up the back of my neck. "Thanks. You too. I love that color on you." I turned and moved toward the restaurant door.

He placed a hand on the small of my back and guided me through the outdoor patrons.

Looked like we might've been on the same page because my back heated where he touched me through my linen pantsuit and his fingers pulsed ever so slightly. A small tingle lit up my clit, my body clearly remembering his touch and responding as it did the first time.

Once the hostess seated us, I opened my menu and hid, suddenly aware of every nerve ending in my body, practically panting. Thankfully the lights were low, creating a romantic atmosphere but also hiding my nervousness.

"What's good here?"

I peeked over my menu. "You always ask that, and if I'm eating there, I'll probably always say anything on the menu."

He studied his menu again, not hiding at all. "Surely you have your favorites."

"Well, tonight I'm getting the oxtails, but if you like seafood, the catfish and shrimp in Acadian sauce is stellar." I did a chef's kiss for emphasis. It really was that good.

"You've sold me. Some nibbles?"

I scrunched my face in confusion.

"Uh, something to get us started."

"No, I don't have enough time."

"Cocktail? Or no because you have an early flight?"

I pointed at him. "Bingo. My flight isn't until ten, but it's still an early morning for me."

He nodded. "Another time, then."

We placed our order and relayed we were time constrained.

Without my menu to disguise my facial expressions, I practiced some deep, steady breathing instead and kept eye contact. "So?" There was so much I wanted to say. To ask him. But he asked me here so my questions would wait.

"So." He scratched his head, then pulled out a bottle of sanitizer. "Have some?"

"Sure." My purse contained a full-size bottle, but since he had his out anyway, why not?

He handed me the little plastic container and held on a beat too long, his skin caressing mine as he looked into my eyes. Initially, his expression was almost pained, then it lightened and finally heated. Decisions were going on behind those orbs that I wasn't privy to.

"What's on your mind, Posh?"

"Posh?" He chuckled. "Is that me?"

"A little nickname I conjured before we exchanged names. I guess I could switch to Leon if you like." I released a winsome smile.

He chuckled again and shook his head. "What am I going to do with you?"

"The question of the hour, I think."

"Yes, I suppose so. Do you feel the draw too, Margaret?"

Of course I did, but there was so much else to discuss. I only nodded.

Encouraged, Lewis continued. "It's strong. At least for me. How do you feel about picking up where we left off in London?"

"I think we should talk about Dominick first. What are your intentions?"

"I have nothing but respect for Dominick."

A nonanswer per usual. "He's been through a lot over the past couple of years. He lost his spouse and has two kids to raise on his own."

Lewis frowned and gave a sad nod. I couldn't tell if he already knew about Lisa or not. "Not quite on his own though. Your family seems to be a tremendous support system for him and his sons."

"Yes, that's true, but my brother hasn't really put himself out there much. He's been understandably withdrawn, but he seems to have taken a liking to you."

"I like him too. And as you know, I've only just moved here and don't know many people yet."

"So, you want to be his friend?"

"I'd be honored to have a friend such as Dominick."

This man never gave a straight answer. Before I could protest the waitress placed our food before us and I momentarily lost my mind, the strong seasoning from the oxtails hitting my nose. My mouth literally watered.

I looked up to an amused Lewis studying me. "Mine smells wonderful too."

All I could do was laugh, then say a quick blessing over my meal and lift a forkful to my mouth. "This is so good."

He cut off a piece of catfish and loaded his fork with rice, then dragged the whole thing through the sauce. When the food hit his palate, he groaned. "This is too good."

"There ought to be a law against food tasting this good."

We ate and exchanged the occasional glance, but no words passed between us.

With a full belly, I wiped my mouth with my napkin. "So what will it be, Posh? If we continue what we started, will it hurt my brother?"

"I have no intent on hurting Dominick. That I can promise." His face broadcasted seriousness.

I could only hope that was the case. I guess we'd put it to the test when I returned from Miami.

CHAPTER FIFTEEN

Lewis — The force is strong in this one

EITHER MY LUCK changed or I'd sunk into delusion because I had two events to look forward to this weekend, and I hadn't felt that way in a very long time. Margaret's plane landed an hour ago, and I'd dropped my defenses enough for her to come round and have a look at my place. Obviously I was hoping there'd be more to her visit than that, but this was a huge first step for me.

Tomorrow I'd been invited to the Hawthorne family's famous Sunday dinner. Turned out Dominick and I shared a love of golf, so whilst spending time with the sport yesterday, he asked me if I wanted to join their weekly family get-together. Although this was a business move, I'd come to enjoy Dominick's company and found we had a lot in common, not just golf. There was the aviation aspect, of course, and our shared goal of having him be in charge of a state-of-the-art flight school. Although our paths to get there were quite different for now. We also shared a lot of the same attitudes about relationships. Again, we diverged on our routes but had both ended up deciding that they weren't worth the effort.

So when I saw Margaret this evening, I needed to make it clear this was not a relationship in the making. I wanted to continue what we started in London, on a physical level. Hopefully that was what she meant as well, but best to clear up any misunderstandings now. Because true love was not in the cards for me. That had been proven time and time again, Sheila being the latest, if not most consequential, installment. I doubted Margaret knew anything about my family—it was the whole reason I'd escaped to the States—but one couldn't be too sure. And once she found out, then what? She had plenty going for her, but once those familial connections and wealth were dangled in front of a person's eyes, it was difficult to pass up what the Watson-Grosvenor name could do. What doors it could open, even secret ones.

I'd been gullible before. Never again.

While I waited for Margaret, and since I really didn't have anything else worth doing in the short time before her arrival, I opened my laptop and revisited the background-check databases to further investigate her ancestor. I dove into whatever military records were available and occupied my time reading through firsthand accounts of the Red Tails, as they were called.

Many accounts of James Hawthorne's heroics were well documented, however there was little to account for Harrison, only passing mentions as events related to his brother. Curious, that.

A knock on the front door sounded from below, and I momentarily startled. I saw that my mobile yielded a missed text from Margaret letting me know she was en route. My attention to the history of the Tuskegee Airmen had enthralled me so much I missed the ring notification both on the mobile and from the front door. Quickly, I packed up my research and ran down the steps of my town house to let in Margaret.

She was a vision in her signature brick red, this time a tank top and shorts hugging her luscious ass and thick thighs. My dick twitched at the memory of sliding between those beautiful legs.

"You look flushed. Did you forget about me?" She screwed her face into a suspicious expression, narrowed eyes and tightened lips.

"Sorry? How could I?" In truth, I had for a moment, so wrapped up in her family history. I could've contributed the flush of my skin to my errant thoughts though. Not something I needed to highlight at the moment. "Please, come in."

Her face relaxed a bit before stepping through the doorway. She looked around into the living area and the dining room connected beyond. The blinds opened to the small backyard I hadn't done a thing to. "This is nice."

Gardening wasn't really in my wheelhouse, and I suddenly heated with embarrassment thinking back to the land Margaret lived on. There were patches of gardens spread throughout. A large one behind the family houses as we passed by on our way to the lake, but other smaller ones boasted fat tomatoes practically bursting to be picked, peppers in varying colors, vines of plump watermelons sweetening in the sun, and other gourds. Not to mention all the herbs.

"Thank you. As you can see, I haven't much of a green thumb. Who tends to all your gardens?" I waved her to the sofa, and we sat side by side.

"You noticed those, huh? Chana is in charge of the gardens, but she has a staff that live on the property. My aunt Deborah is heavily involved too. Most of us have rotated through their care at one time or another. My parents don't believe in us being waited on. We've been assigned every job there is on the running the compound at one time or another."

My eyebrows flew up in appreciation, and I blew out a breath. "Big job." The Hawthorne philosophy ran completely antithetical to my family's. They believed in servants aplenty, and neither myself nor my brother learned any domesticated skills, which hurt us in the long run. Well, hurt me mostly because I'd turned my back on that life. Now I barely knew how to boil an egg or launder my own clothes. The back of my neck heated. These were ideas I couldn't share with Margaret without revealing too much. Instead I kept the conversation superficial. "I didn't notice too many flower beds."

"We're a practical family, so the land is used to sustain us and our...caretakers. That's what Mama calls them, but the name sounds so..." She shrugged and pinched her nose. "Bougie." She laughed uncomfortably.

"Not at all. It's better than *servants*." I inwardly winced, having given away too much.

"Is that what you would call them in England?"

I shrugged noncommittally. "Can I get you something to drink? Or some snacks?" I stood, ready to change the subject.

"I could go for some really cold water." She stood too and followed me into the kitchen.

I opened the sparsely stocked refrigerator to remove the

pitcher of filtered water.

"Wow, where's your food?"

From her perspective, it was clear that the fridge lacked basic nutrients. However, I had several bottles of green juice and eggs in view and frozen fruit in the freezer for protein smoothies I made after my workouts. "I suppose I eat a lot of takeaway. I mostly make scrambled eggs and smoothies. I never learned to cook." I poured her a glass of water and set the pitcher back in the refrigerator, happy to close it away from her prying eyes.

She placed a hand on my upper arm. "I get it. Even though I do know how to cook, I rarely get the chance, except for Sunday dinners. And that's when I'm home." She picked up her glass of water and walked back to the sofa.

That declaration was very generous. I stumbled behind her, trying to get myself back on track. "Speaking of Sunday dinners, guess who's invited tomorrow?"

She turned to me, surprise clearly on her face. "Really? So you talked to Dominick?"

"Yeah, we golfed. It was a great afternoon although scorching hot. He wasn't available earlier though."

She bit her lip, then squinted at me. "We should probably talk."

Never a good sign.

CHAPTER SIXTEEN

Margaret—Granddaddy is still sexist

MANY THINGS SURPRISED me about Lewis, and I hadn't really gotten my bearings where he was concerned. I'd connected with him several times over the past couple weeks since we'd been reunited, and I still couldn't tell anyone anything new about him other than where he lived. And even that was so completely generic—the town house told me nothing about the man. Downstairs was...nice but plain and void of personal touches. Maybe it was different upstairs, but until I learned more about Lewis Watson-Grosvenor, I'd have to be more reserved with him.

I could've googled him, but that always seemed like such an invasion of privacy and the wrong way to begin any sort of relationship.

Yes, I was undeniably attracted to Mr. Posh, but all physical and surface level. How could I take the measure of the man when he wouldn't reveal anything about himself? I'd yet to figure out if his lack of candidness was intentional or part of his nature.

And if intentional, what was going on? My bones told me it was something to do with Dominick and the flight school. Lewis was too interested, too eager to see the operation and make suggestions. Even though he technically worked for the competition. Maybe not in the same capacity, but then again, maybe it was. I really didn't know what he did for Gibson because of his vague responses.

I placed my water on the glass table, no coasters in sight. "Listen, Lewis. I enjoyed what we did in London. And I'd like to do it again, but I think we need some ground rules."

Surprise registered on his face, and he leaned in closer. "Go on."

"Until you and Dominick are on solid ground and I get to know you a little better, let's keep anything we're doing under wraps."

What was surprise before has turned into shock. His face creased into a giant question mark.

"I'm just saying. Dominick invited you to dinner tomorrow. I'm not asking you to pretend like you don't know me, but don't go out of your way either. Sit next to my brother, which is usually on the opposite end of the table from me. Get to know others or whatever he has in store for you." I shrug. "Are you okay with that?"

He blinked. "Sorry? Are you saying you want to have an intimate situation but nothing in the way of a romantic relationship?"

"I suppose that's one way of putting it. Is that a problem?" If anything, I'd say he was in full agreement but surprised I brought the idea to him packaged this way.

Lewis's expression was usually schooled, but not this time. Every thought ran across his face. "No, not a problem." Now the mask was back in place. He sat back and crossed his legs, placing an ankle on top of his other knee, then grinned ever so slightly allowing his eyes to close, then open again at half-mast.

Now that we'd settled on the stipulations, Lewis pulsated with sex appeal.

I took a long drink of my water and rested my back against the couch, my leg brushing his.

He knocked his leg against mine, then reached for my hand. "I guess we'll have to always meet here." His tone sounded resigned, and he glanced around the town house.

"There are no secrets at the compound, so yes."

"You don't mind?"

"Why would I?"

"That means you driving every time, sometimes at odd hours."

A clear signal that overnights had been snatched off the table. Looked like Lewis and I were absolutely on the same page about this non-relationship.

I unlinked our hands and dragged his across my stomach, essentially lifting the hem of my tank top and uncovering a sliver of skin. "I'm used to driving to the airport at all hours of the day or night. Your place is closer."

He might have heard me, or maybe not, because his gaze was locked on his hand placed on my stomach. The hand twitched, and he slid it back and forth, heightening the gap between where my top ended and my shorts began.

I'd intentionally worn casual attire to keep down the fuss. There was never a doubt in my mind Lewis would agree to my terms and we'd fall into bed together tonight. At least, I hoped we ended up in bed and not just on this couch. This was his house, so I'd follow his lead, but I wouldn't be happy about it. We weren't teens.

I placed a hand on his firm chest and felt up the muscles underneath his shirt, relishing in the thought that I'd have my hands back in a place they'd been craving for more than three months, since we first slept together.

My touch seemed to awaken Lewis completely. He growled and placed his lips on mine. I eagerly welcomed the kiss and ran my tongue across the seam of his mouth, encouraging him to open. He complied, and we deepened the kiss, our hands getting reacquainted with each other's bodies.

"I've been thinking about this for weeks." He trailed a line of kisses down my neck and back up, nibbling my ear.

The admission surprised me, buttoned up as he seemed. "Me too. Yes, right there." He clearly remembered what my body responded to and resumed his sensory assault on the shell of my ear.

"Want to take this upstairs to my bedroom?"

Thank goodness, yes. "Uh-huh" was all I managed to reply as I followed him up the stairs and down a short hall to the first door, which stood open. The made-up queen-sized bed welcomed me, and I pulled my top over my head and dropped my shorts before plopping down in the middle of it. Lewis's scent rose up from the duvet, herbal and citrusy. My core squeezed.

I reached for him and unbuttoned his shirt while he stood perfectly still, eyes absorbing my nearly unclothed body. All thoughts of brothers, family commitments, and obligations faded away as Lewis's golden-brown skin came into sharp focus. All I could think about is how much I missed his caress and touching his body in return and how happy I was we'd come to an arrangement.

After pushing the shirt off his shoulders, I went for his chinos next, but he grasped my hands and made quick work of the button and let the trousers fall to the floor. "Lie back, please, and let me look at you."

As requested, I relaxed in his bed, making sure to give him a side view to highlight my best feature—my ass.

He grinned, completely onto what I tried to accomplish, then slid a hand up my leg as he settled himself next to me, his erection pressed into my hip. "I love the view, but it's difficult to keep my hands off you."

The feeling was mutual, and I flipped to turn toward him and ran my hands up his arms and around his neck. He grabbed one arm and kissed the inside of my wrist, sending tingles to every single nerve ending I possessed. I closed my eyes to savor the tenderness, to drink in the softness that Lewis employed, to relish the connection.

When he moved his lips to my breast, I gasped and opened my eyes, locking gazes with him. "All good?" he asked.

"More than good." I pulled him closer to me and rubbed my body against him, yearning for the closeness and more, as he pulled a nipple into his mouth with a groan. My whole body responded, every cell reaching for him, wanting the connection now. "Condom. Now please." I could barely huff the words, my breathing completely uneven.

When he entered me, twin sounds of excitement rose up both of our throats, and we moved together in the harmony we'd composed back in London. It wasn't a first time together, and the way our bodies reacted and joined proved that all nervousness dissipated now that we knew each other a little more, even if not completely. It was enough. Enough to run my blood hot, to ignite the bundle of nerves between my legs, and to find my glorious release.

Lewis held me tightly against him through my orgasm, allowing me to ride it through completely, before he moved again, finding his own completion.

This was the part Lewis wanted to share with me, and at the moment, it was enough.

THE SMELLS COMING from the main house dragged me by the nose all the way there. I had potato salad in hand along with some yeast rolls. Miranda and Daddy had tag-teamed on the barbecue and clearly had smoked up some deliciousness for Sunday dinner. From the menu assignments Chana sent out earlier in the week, looked like Donovan was tasked with banana pudding. My stomach rumbled just thinking about it. Baby brother could make the hell out of some banana pudding.

My rumblings soon turned to butterflies as I wedged my way through the door with my full hands. Was Lewis here already? How would he react when he saw me? Would my family know what was up after one look at us? I quelled all the internal noise and headed for the kitchen.

Meredith came around the corner, a grease spot smudging her khaki-colored romper.

"Careful."

"Ooof, let me help you with those." She took the bowl of

potato salad and walked with me to the kitchen.

"I forgot. What did you make?"

"Mac and cheese."

I looked at her romper again and decided the stain probably came from butter instead of engine oil. Thank goodness. "I didn't get a chance to eat breakfast, so I'm looking forward to all those melty carbs." I had to get up at the crack of dawn to get the rolls started so they'd be ready in time. Luckily I thrived during the early-morning hours. The definition of a morning person.

She laughed and placed the bowl on the counter.

"Hi, Mama." I kissed her on the cheek while she stirred beans in a big pot.

"Hey, baby. Woo, I smell those buttery rolls from here." Her eyes shown bright as she smiled. "I haven't seen you in a few days. What's been keeping you so busy?"

Mama kept better track of all our schedules than we did—with Chana's expertise of course. But I humored her. "I had an overnight in Miami." No need to mention the extracurricular activities I'd been involved in.

"Is Jaymes coming?"

"Yes, ma'am."

"Your brother is bringing a guest by the way. He's from England but moved here recently. Have you met him?"

Ah, my mother. Not the queen of subtlety. Her spidey senses clearly tingled.

"I have. Those beans sure do smell good."

"Thanks. What's he like?" No way would she let me bring that weak-sauce deflection without lobbing it back at me.

I shrugged. "British?"

She gave me a sidelong glance and went back to stirring her beans. "Mm-hmm." Dorothea Hawthorne beat everyone by a mile in this family in the intellect department. She'd bide her time on this though, get the lay of the land before she pounced, so it was doubly important Lewis and I held each other at arm's length this afternoon.

"Where's everyone?"

Mama tapped the wooden spoon against the rim of the pot and put the lid back on. "Well, let's see. Your aunt Deborah is out back icing some drinks. I haven't seen your brothers yet, but Miranda and Daddy are out by the barbecue pit on the side of the house." She looked around at me and Meredith, who had busied herself with ladling the potato salad into a serving dish. "Did I miss anyone?"

Not that I cared much, but she hadn't mentioned her father-in-law. "Granddaddy, I guess."

She withered me with a stern look. "Your grandfather is in his room watching that show he loves. He'll be out when the table is set. What time is Jaymes getting here?"

My bestie has never been late for a Hawthorne-family Sunday dinner. I pulled my phone from the pocket of my capris. Sure enough, a text from Jaymes waited. "She says she's on her way. That was about five minutes ago."

Mama nodded. "She ought to be here any minute."

The front doorbell rang, and I looked around in a panic. Jaymes wouldn't ring the doorbell, so it could only be one person.

Mama eyed me suspiciously. "Can you get the door?" The implied *since you're looking around all anxiously and clearly something's going on* was silent.

I cleared my throat and swallowed hard, my mouth suddenly dry. "Sure."

Meredith threw me a furtive glance, her eyebrows raised.

The start to this afternoon opposed everything I intended. I shuffled to the front door, but by the time I got there, Dominick and the boys were walking in with Lewis in tow. Thank goodness my brother arrived before I could get to the door.

I took a deep breath and relaxed. "Hey, guys." I spoke to my nephews more than anyone else.

They ran over to me and hugged my legs, then took off toward the backyard.

I glanced at Lewis briefly, then took my brother in.

Dominick's perma-scowl had abandoned his face, and he looked more mellow than I'd seen him in quite some time. He actually looked his age instead of a grumpy old man, Granddaddy's twin. "Hey, brother."

"Hey. Where's everyone?" He grabbed at Lewis's arm and led him past me, presumably to find *everyone* without waiting for my reply.

Lewis threw a wink over his shoulder, and I nearly melted from the covert contact.

Somebody help me get through this dinner.

I trailed them back toward the kitchen but stopped at the powder room to wash my hands in case any last-minute help was needed. The powder-room vent connected to the laundry room next door. The voices of Dominick and Lewis were clear but reduced.

"I'll make a last bid for improvements, but watch them

shoot me down." My brother, who'd been so cheerful just a minute ago, sounded resigned.

"They may surprise you," Lewis, the voice of reason, countered.

I smiled to myself and dried my hands. It wasn't my objective to eavesdrop.

"They won't. And when they refuse, I'll be looking real hard at Gibson."

My hand was on the doorknob, but I snatched it back. Looking at Gibson to do what?

"The decision is yours."

My mouth dropped open, and I hurried out of the bathroom, my mind on confrontation.

"Whoa, where's the fire?" Daddy's hands were full, and he handed me a rather heavy roasting pan. "Get that for me, honey."

Like I had a choice. Maybe interrupting me from challenging my brother and his new bestie was for the best because my mind wasn't right for that conversation.

Instead I'd bide my time to figure out what's what. When Dominick aired his objections during dinner, others would grill him on his intentions. But from where I stood, it sounded a whole lot like my brother was considering leaving our family business. And maybe my lover had something to do with it.

I knew something wasn't right.

DADDY BURPED AND rushed a hand over his mouth. "Excuse

me." He laughed and picked up another spoonful of beans.

Aunt Deborah leaned her head to the side. "Dorothea put her foot in those beans, didn't she?"

He chuckled. "She sure did."

The atmosphere mostly swelled with frivolity, but Dominick remained quiet throughout.

After everyone grilled Lewis about his background and he dodged like a pro, the family settled in to the business of devouring all the food at the table.

Jaymes leaned into me and spoke low, but not low enough to whisper and be rude. "What's going on? I feel some tension."

I wiped my mouth of barbecue sauce. "I have an idea, but we'll have to see how this plays out."

Donovan leaned over Jaymes. "What are y'all whispering about?"

Jaymes swatted him away with a pat and a giggle. "We're not whispering."

I narrowed my eyes. "Since when do you giggle like a schoolgirl?"

She shot Donovan a hurried look, then rotated back to me with pursed lips. "Hush."

What was this about?

Before I could ponder further, Dominick cleared his throat.

Here we go. Dinner was winding down, so this was expected. I only hoped this wouldn't ruin dessert because that banana pudding was calling my name.

He pushed his chair back from the table but didn't stand. He looked to Lewis for a moment before speaking. "I need to bring up something."

Mama cocked her head. "Go ahead, son."

I tensed.

"It's about the flight school. I've put together a comprehensive project plan for the various improvements that are needed for us to be competitive."

"Competitive with who?" Heaven help me, but I couldn't keep my mouth shut. I'd been primed for this conversation since I overheard them in the bathroom earlier.

Dominick swung his gaze to me and cocked his head. "The other flight schools, obviously." The look on his face was giving *are you new?* vibes.

The truth, as I understood it, was that we'd put together competitive research on Gibson and concluded they weren't in the same landscape. We were a much smaller operation and targeted. Sure, they would take some business away from us when they finally opened, but we really serviced different demographics.

Daddy spoke up. "We've already talked about this. The board has already approved some upgrades."

"Superficial ones. Throwing a coat of paint on the buildings and repaving the parking lot won't cut it."

No doubt Dominick had a point, but the thought of Lewis having something to do with my brother's push didn't settle right in my spirit. I kept my mouth closed though.

"We do a good business, son. We have what we need for the market we serve."

Frustration laced my brother's face, and my heart went out to him. Work motivated him more than anything the past couple of years, and he'd put his whole self in growing the clientele. He was already a great director, but recently he'd really upped his game.

I said, "Daddy, let's look at Dominick's proposal at least. Maybe there's more we can incorporate."

Granddaddy just had to add his two cents. "That's not your place, girl. Running the business is up to your daddy and the board."

I fumed at the old man. "You know that I'm on the board, right, Granddaddy? And Daddy is retiring soon, so others need to step up." I threw my hands up in frustration. "I'm a commercial airline pilot, a captain, and it wasn't an easy route getting there. I'm not some little girl." That man could get under my skin like nobody else, and I hated that I always went to stating my bona fides as my response to him.

"No woman has ever run the Hawthorne Family Flying Eagles, and I'll be damned if one will on my watch." Spittle dribbled down his chin, and his eyes bulged, burning fiery red.

"Our CEO is a woman and quite a capable leader, and I see a lot of kindred qualities with Margaret."

Everyone's eyes snapped to Lewis, whose hardened expression took me by surprise. Apparently the rest of the family too, judging by the looks on their faces. He hadn't said a word while Dominick, his friend, laid out his plea for upgrades, but as soon as Granddaddy hopped on me, someone he supposedly had no connection to, fury ran across his face and reflected in the tone of his voice.

This was not good.

Yet I couldn't help softening at his defense.

Mama looked between me and Lewis and covered her

smile with a hand. She lived for being proven right.

Granddaddy approached stroke territory, his eyes bulging to an unhealthy degree. "You need to stay out of family business. You're the reason my grandson is all riled up?"

"I'm not riled up, Granddaddy. This is about business, and as the director of the flight school, I have a right to bring this up."

For the life of me, I couldn't remember why we allowed business talk at dinner. Growing up, there was a rule against it, but somewhere along the way, that principle went out the window. Maybe we needed to reinstitute it.

Granddaddy grumbled, and Aunt Deborah placed a glass of water in his hand.

That exchange pulled something into sharp focus for me: I'd never gain my grandfather's approval, but maybe I could do something to keep my brother happy and firmly in the family business. I'd look at Dominick's plans, and we'd bring them to the board for approval. So while I shored up the vote count for my ascension to CEO, I'd hustle votes for the flight school too. Hopefully that would be on the plus side for winning my brother's vote.

I chanced a look at Lewis.

His face remained stern.

CHAPTER SEVENTEEN

Lewis—But I don't know how to fly

HAVING NEVER BEEN up in a small plane, I wasn't sure what to wear or expect. I ended up in jeans, my only pair, and layers of T-shirt, then long-sleeved shirt, then sweatshirt, then jacket. Although I hadn't been up before, I understood the air in the sky cooled considerably, and I had no desire to be caught unawares. With everything that had transpired the past few days, I wouldn't put it past Margaret to freeze me out, in more ways than one.

I looked at the text exchange again to ensure I hadn't missed anything.

Margaret sent me a message after the disastrous family dinner where I spoke completely out of turn to her vile grandfather. *"How about a quick flight before we head back to your place?"*

"Flight? Like we go to the airport? Or you pilot us?"

The dots jumped on her end, then disappeared. A few seconds later, they jumped again, then stopped just as quickly. Finally a message came through. *"The latter. Just for a few minutes."*

I wasn't sure how to feel about going up in a smaller plane. But any chance to spend time with Margaret was time well spent.

"What time?"

I waited for a reply. No dancing dots, just my message hanging out there on read.

Finally, she sent, *"How about 4:30? Meet me at the rental shop."*

"Okay."

Considering I didn't have any instructions other than meet her at the rental place, I parked in the only parking lot I knew of and made my way across the grass toward the destination she gave me.

I hadn't made it a dozen steps before Margaret came out of nowhere and redirected me. "Hello, Posh. We're this way." She walked just ahead of me. Her intentions escaped me, but whatever went on in that pretty head of hers, she intended to lead me like a dog with that fine ass covered in tight-fitted red trousers.

It didn't take much for me to be led.

I guess I misjudged after all because her whole outfit was made for the summer, not sub temperatures in the air.

"Am I overdressed?"

She glanced over her shoulder and rotated back, her shoulders shaking. "Goodness, what in the world are you wearing?"

I lengthened my stride to walk next to her. "Will it not be cold up there?"

"We have a heater in the cockpit, Posh."

At this point, I hadn't processed my feelings about her little nickname for me. It dredged up memories of being put on a higher level. Then taken advantage of for being there. Margaret didn't mean it that way, I was sure of it, but context clues told me it wasn't a compliment either. "I hadn't realized."

She grinned at me then, a genuine smile, her shoulders dropping in relaxation. "I would never set you up to fail like that, Lewis."

As we walked toward a white plane with blue stripes, I stripped off my many layers until I got to the T-shirt. Hopefully the plane contained storage space, at least enough for my clothes. "I'm happy to hear that. Where are you taking me?"

"Just a short trip, as I mentioned, then we can head to your place."

"And the purpose of this short trip?"

We'd arrived, and she opened the door for me. "Does it need a purpose? You can stick your stuff back there."

Nice deflection. On par with my own diversions. I placed my clothes where Margaret instructed and folded myself into the small airplane. Joy sticks and instruments arranged on both sides, and it suddenly dawned on me that she might try to give me a lesson. My blood pounded in my ears. I had nothing against flying, but all of my experience so far in my life had been on large commercial airplanes or the occasional private jet with my family. Riding was fine, driving quite another.

Once Margaret settled herself, she turned to me. "Ready?"

"You don't plan on my flying this thing, do you?"

She tilted her head and drew her eyebrows together. "What would give you that idea?"

"I'm serious, Margaret. I don't want to fly."

"I, too, am serious, Lewis. I have no intention of placing my life in your novice hands today."

I relaxed just a bit. At least I could hear better against the slight pounding in my ears. "*Novice* implies some level of training. I have none."

She continued through her preflight checks while I stewed in my seat.

There was no reason for me to act so unreasonably, but my body had taken over. "Are you familiar with this plane?" I took a shuddering breath, trying to calm myself.

"Yes. If you don't want to go up, just tell me. I thought it would be fun to see the operation from a higher level, but you look really nervous."

The truth was I was actually excited about going up although apprehensive. Looked like the equation between apprehension and excitement was rather unbalanced. "I want to."

She patted me on the thigh. "Okay, let's go, then." She gave me a list of instructions on what I could do or touch and a longer list of what I shouldn't do or touch. She needn't have bothered because I planned to keep my hands entirely to myself until my feet touched the ground again.

The last thing she did was place a headset on me. She sat back and looked at her handiwork, then gave me a thumbs-up.

I returned the gesture.

We graced down the runway and into the air with ease. Five minutes in, after we leveled off, I relaxed and took in my surroundings.

"What do you think?"

"It's amazing." We weren't so far up that the landscape blended together like I was accustomed to. We flew low enough that I could see everyone's backyards and swimming pools, of which there were many. Soon housing subdivisions gave way to open land. "I thought maybe I would be sitting separately from you in the back."

She grinned. "Although Hawthorne Family Flying Eagles was founded by a couple of Tuskegee Airmen and their father, we don't actually still fly their airplanes."

"Noted."

She winked and looked out over the landscape.

"I'd love to learn more about your Airmen." The mystery I'd been tracking down about her great-uncle still hadn't yielded much information. My time had been limited the past few days with work, so I hadn't much time to research either. What little I had learned gave me great appreciation for Margaret's ancestors.

"Did you know I'm the current family historian?"

"I did not."

"Yup, so you've come to the right place. And I love talking about them. Honestly, you can corner any member of my family and get an earful. We all love to talk about the men who faced so many roadblocks but still excelled and came out heroes." Margaret's enthusiasm shone through.

I stared at her profile and took in the incredibly accomplished woman who zoomed us through the air high above my new home. "Your great-uncle. You mentioned a mystery surrounding him." Even though she indicated previously she didn't have much information about him, I reckoned any small tidbit might be something I could latch a hold to in my research.

She frowned and looked out over the expanse of sky ahead of us. "There's something there, but I've yet to find it. Anytime my granddaddy gets tight-lipped or vague about something or someone, there has to be a story there. I've talked with my father's cousins about it before, but nobody knows why there isn't a statue of him out front too." She shrugged and clicked a switch over on the gauges in front of her.

That part about the statue was what really hooked me into the mystery. It did seem strange to attach the founding to both brothers but only give one a physical representation. "That's quite unusual. Assuming your father doesn't know anything either?"

"Nothing. It really is a family mystery." She shrugged. "Most families have them. What about you? Does your family have any interesting tidbits?"

Since the moment I met her, Margaret had always turned the conversation back to me. This should have been expected, but I enjoyed her company and view too much to keep my head straight. "Quite boring, I'm afraid. Nothing like your interesting family. You're quite proud of them, rightly so."

She nodded and glanced my way, relaying her thoughts of my bullshit completely in her eyes. Then she smiled and shook her head, mostly to herself. "Yes, I'm proud. We have a long, storied history, and there's almost nothing more important to me than preserving that."

For the first time since working to recruit Dominick, guilt grabbed me by the neck. It caught me off guard actually. I'd been looking at this as a job only, but the more I got to know the Hawthorne family, the more I realized they were nothing like my own family. The Hawthornes embraced family legacy and community. My family raided companies and tore them apart. We were not the same.

An urgent need to come clean worked its way up from my stomach and up my throat, but I caught the words before any slipped through my lips. Margaret was onto me, that much I was sure. But she would have to continue her supposition on her own. I wouldn't feed her information. The decision ultimately would be up to Dominick, an adult man old enough to make it.

I was only a facilitator. Surely anyone could understand that.

CHAPTER EIGHTEEN
Margaret—Oh no

AFTER SPENDING ANOTHER exuberant evening with Lewis, I'd finally accepted that pulling information from him would be impossible. There was a moment there, flying high above the ground below, where he struggled with something he wanted to say. I could see it in his eyes, but he just as quickly closed off.

No one was born this way, so controlled and protected. Life had done something to Lewis Watson-Grosvenor to make him closed off even to a romantic interest. Then again, we agreed romance hadn't defined our situationship. But I had to believe that if my brother wasn't involved, he'd be at least a little more forthcoming.

My phone buzzed. *"Where are you?"*

I rolled my eyes and got out of the car, walking the few steps from the parking lot to Jaymes's condo. The front door was cracked open, so I pushed it the rest of the way. "Hey, I'm here."

We'd long ago exchanged keys but also assured each other we'd never use them without the others' permission. It was easier to leave the door ajar slightly when we were expected.

Jaymes called from the kitchen, "I'm in here. Wash your hands and come help me."

"Okay." After a long flight to Rome, I was ready to relax with my bestie with some good food and maybe a movie, depending on how long I could keep my eyes open.

I washed up in the guest bathroom and strolled to the kitchen, following the scent of jambalaya. Having a best friend who could cook recipes handed down through her Creole family was a big plus. Jaymes's food was better than anything you could find in a Houston restaurant, and that included Prey, which had some pretty fantastic Creole food.

Plump shrimp fused a bed of rice with tomatoes, bell pepper, and celery. Not to mention the spices that set Creole cuisine apart from anything else. My stomach rumbled too loud to hide.

Jaymes turned to me. "Wow, hungry much?"

"No lies detected." I gave her a side hug and pulled down some wineglasses. I'd only have one drink with dinner considering I was already tired. Then again, maybe I'd just make myself at home in the guest bedroom. It certainly wouldn't be the first time.

"Grab the salad from the fridge, and we can eat."

Nobody needed to tell me twice. I removed the greens as instructed and picked up a couple bowls, then went out to the small dining room and settled everything on the black lacquer table. I teased her about her late-eighties style, but the table belonged to a dear aunt and Jaymes refused to part with it.

When we sat down to eat, my stomach growled again. "I guess it's reminding me I can't even remember when I've had a decent meal. This looks delicious. Thanks for thinking of me."

"Always, bestie. We both know when your schedule gets hectic, eating is the first thing to fall by the wayside." She poured wine into both our glasses and sat the bottle back on the table.

"Maybe not the first thing." I thought of Lewis and the last time I'd had sex before London. Even now my schedule didn't allow for nightly nookie. Not that either of us expressed a need for that.

"Oh, do tell. How has it been with Lewis? You're still getting on okay?"

I shrugged and took a swig of wine. "It's all very surface level. He refuses to open up to me."

"You're okay with that?"

I thought I was, but where did all this come from? "We set ground rules. They were my ground rules. I didn't want to interfere with his relationship with my brother, but now I think I made a grave mistake."

Jaymes raised her brows. "That sounds ominous. How so?"

I finished chewing the too-big spoonful of jambalaya I'd wedged into my mouth before responding. "I finally googled him." I sighed, then took another sip of wine. This wasn't something I made a habit of doing. My preference was to learn about a potential partner organically. Lewis hadn't really left me a choice with his tightly closed lips. "He's a recruiter for Gibson and from an extremely wealthy and connected London family. There's a story there because he obviously could work for his family. Instead he's breaking up mine."

"Oh, Marg, you don't think that's his goal, right?"

"I don't know. Maybe not his goal, but he has to know it would be a biproduct if he recruits Dominick away."

"What are you going to do?"

"I—" My phone shrilled from the other side of the room where I'd left it on top of my purse. I ignored it. "I'll check it later." It rang again, then proceeded to ding one after the other. "What in the world?"

"You better see what's going on."

I took another bite of my food and got up to check my phone. A couple of missed calls and several text messages from my siblings and parents clouded my device. My stomach dropped. "I've gotta go. Looks like Dominick called a family meeting." I dreaded leaving the comfort of my best friend's warm condo. Especially knowing with confidence what this meeting would be about.

"You don't think…"

I nodded.

No matter the concessions we'd made in giving Dominick nearly everything he wanted, he would still leave.

CHAPTER NINETEEN
Lewis—I'm guilty, your honor

RESTLESSNESS TORE AT my body, had me pacing, doing push-ups, and pacing again. My spirit would not settle as I kept replaying the last conversation with Dominick that should have left me elated. I'd successfully recruited this target that I'd been hired to bring over to Gibson. It was my first test at this new company, thousands of miles from home, where nobody knew my family. I might've even been able to put Sheila in my rearview finally. The higher-ups trusted me. I'd aced the first power serve quite spectacularly.

Why did I feel like such shite?

I sat on the edge of the guest bed because my bed smelled like Margaret and I didn't want to think about Margaret right now. Looking around at my prized atlases should have made me feel on top of the world. All I could do was think about Dominick and what I'd said to finally seal the deal.

We'd met for golf, this time early in the morning. *It was clear his mind was preoccupied as he played mindlessly, so I finally asked him what was going on. "Hey, bro. Everything all good with you?"*

He nodded and set up his tee.

I waited for him to swing. "I'm not complaining, but how did you get away from work so early?"

Dominick balanced on his golf club and took in our surroundings. A bit of dew still hung to the nearby oak and magnolia trees as well as the grass. The overcast sky slowly allowed through streams of sunrays, but they were few and far in between.

Not that I complained. The clouds kept the heat at bay, but my new friend seemed affected by the gloom.

"Here's the thing. I did that proposal for the upgrades to the flight school. Put all the improvements in we discussed, and my father felt the need to revise it to clarify the return on investment. It's like they don't trust or believe in me even though I've been running the school exclusively for nearly a decade."

Technically it had been almost six years, with the two years prior co-directing with his grandfather. In those six years, he'd improved the bottom line exponentially with programs put in place to focus on four licenses and certifications whereas they'd had nearly twice as many before and standardized the training programs. Dominick had also instituted a community-outreach program that went beyond flight training but opened up the possibilities to a whole new group of people. There were scholarship programs he'd set up and lobbied to fund. So many intangibles he brought to the management of the school as well, like higher-qualified teachers instead of the family members used before that his grandfather had insisted on because that was how they'd always done it.

That was Dominick in a nutshell: Despite his family legacy, he incorporated contemporary ideas while still preserving traditions. The man was a huge win, and I understood completely why Gibson wanted him to be my first target.

I walked closer to him and stared down the fairway. "Sometimes with family, they never quite see you as a full adult." This sentiment was firmly in my wheelhouse. Family controlled and punished.

"That's why I need to get out, man. I'm tired of someone looking over my shoulder at every turn. I've been fighting for improvements for years, but they can't even see how I've taken the flight school to the next level and want to continue to do so." He spit on the grass and sighed.

I'd made Dominick aware of the open flight-school-director position with Gibson. I hadn't pushed or even asked but laid out the benefits and salary for someone with his expertise and experience. It was folly for him to think he wouldn't have an overseer. This was a corporation, and multilevel oversight was built in. I remained silent on that point though. "The position at Gibson is yours for the taking. All you have to do is submit your application, and I can fast-track it." I cleared my throat and relaxed my face, trying to keep the elation at bay.

"Yeah, let's do that. It's time for a change."

"Okay." I took out my mobile and forwarded him the application. I'd ping HR and my boss as soon as I returned home.

"Okay." His shoulders were somewhere around his ears, and anxiety rolled off him.

"Are you sure? You seem…tense."

He chuckled and shook his arms out, letting his club fall to the ground. "I'm sure. What I'm not sure about is how I'll tell my family. There are Hawthornes who live across the country and have nothing to do with aviation, but this will be the first time someone from my direct line has left the family business. It will not be well received."

I searched my memories and landed on Donovan. "I thought your brother left."

He shook his head and released a half grin. "Donovan was

never in. From day one, everyone knew what was what. Mama and Daddy forced him to go through the school and get his pilot's license, but nobody thought it would take."

"Wow. Forced him how?"

He shrugged and picked up his club. "They threatened to withhold money for college. Rice University is not cheap, believe me. And my brother is nothing if not sensible. He took the deal and never looked back."

I suddenly felt a kindred spirit with Donovan. I understood that path too well, but where he was still able to spend time with his family every Sunday without every comment erupting into an argument, I'd never been able to achieve that.

I followed Dominick to the golf cart and settled in for the ride to the next hole.

It wasn't until I returned home after contacting work about the big win that my mood turned sour. The Hawthornes had treated me well—except the grandfather, maybe, but I'd also stuck my nose in where it didn't belong in defense of Margaret.

That was the real reason for my acerbic disposition. Margaret loved her family, loved their legacy, and loved to fly. It was apparent when she took me up for our quick escape and her nonstop talk about it when she arrived at my house before we finally fell into bed.

I'd missed her the past couple of days she'd flown to Rome, and now I'd stepped all the way in it.

She would never forgive me for what she would see as a betrayal.

CHAPTER TWENTY

Margaret—Endings can be beginnings, right?

B Y THE TIME I arrived at Mama and Daddy's, the dinner dishes had been removed and most of my siblings were waiting in the family room.

I looked around at my kinfolk, most faces broadcasting confusion. Except Dominick. Dominick fidgeted with his belt, the cuffs of his shirt, any part of himself where he could grab a hold and rub or pick. "Where are the boys?"

My brother looked up then, obviously relieved for something easy to answer. "They're upstairs in the game room with Aunt Deborah."

Granddaddy ambled in, assisted by a cane, staring Dominick down. "What's all this about?"

Mama took the question. "We're waiting for Donovan, Daddy."

"Well, where is he? I'm ready for bed."

Daddy sighed and looked at his phone. "He'll be here in about five minutes. You know he had to come from downtown Houston."

None of this felt good. Or right. Why drag Donovan out here in the middle of the week? A lump formed in my throat, and I swallowed hard. He was a member of the board—that was why. His presence only confirmed my suspicions of what this meeting was about.

As far as Granddaddy was concerned, I didn't remember him retiring at eight in the evening but maybe I'd missed something. He was aging, no doubt about that. I occupied my thoughts with musings of him stepping back from the board and allowing our generation to finally take over unencumbered. Fat chance of that happening—he'd vote against us from his death bed.

"Anyone want some coffee?" Chana came into the room balancing a tray with a pot and cups, her long light brown curly hair pinned up out of her way. Thankfully this was happening today instead of tomorrow, the beginning of Shabbat, or we'd have to fend for ourselves.

"Yes, please." I raced over to help her with her burden and sat it on the wide coffee table. Sweeteners and cream already lined the opposite end of the wooden structure, and I filled a cup with coffee and a little cream. The wine hadn't affected me, I only had half a glass, but I needed something of a pick-me-up. I wasn't sure if anyone else had a clue what was to come tonight, but if they guessed, Chana would've probably brought out the whisky instead.

Donovan glided in then, defiance and resentment creasing his face.

I didn't blame him. Being summoned out here from Houston last minute couldn't have been fun. My baby brother had a whole separate life with big oil that was just as important to him as any business out here. Not to mention his string of love interests we couldn't start to keep up with.

Dominick cleared his throat but remained sitting. "Thanks for coming out, brother."

Donovan checked his watch. "You're welcome, but what's all this about?" He sat next to Miranda on the sectional. Meredith perched on her other side near Mama and Daddy. Granddaddy had settled into his recliner.

I remained standing near the door. I didn't want any part of this.

"What's this about? Yeah, the question of the hour. I've asked you all here because I have some news. And it'll affect everyone in this room." He still didn't stand. Kind of a coward move, but honestly, if I were in his position, I probably wouldn't be any bolder. Our family could be tough and judgmental at times—all of us, not just Granddaddy.

I held my breath and braced for impact.

"I've been offered a job at Gibson, and I'm going to take it."

Silence all around as the air sucked out of the room.

Sweet Meredith creased her face in a question. "How can you take on another job? You have the boys and the flight school. I don't understand."

Mama's face crumpled in realization. Although she wasn't a Hawthorne by birth and couldn't serve on the board, she'd given her life to growing our family and our business. Sometimes it had been a thankless job.

Miranda turned to Meredith next to her. "He means he's leaving the flight school."

Meredith gasped.

Donovan sat forward. "Good for you, brother. Follow your heart."

Daddy's booming voice broke through the muted reactions. "Follow your heart? Since when is your heart not with this family, son?" He stood and placed his hands on his hips. If anyone besides me knew this was a possibility, it was Daddy. Maybe he thought we'd done enough to placate Dominick by accepting his revision plan and putting it into review.

"Of course my heart will always be with my family. I'm suffocating here though. You've made me the director but don't allow me to direct. My hands are tied at every juncture, with someone always looking over my shoulder."

Miranda snorted. "Good luck with all this autonomy you think you'll have at Gibson. Corporations are full of red tape." She left commercial flight for much the same reason.

"At least I won't have my sisters improving every idea I come up with." The quotes around *improving* were evident, loud and clear.

Miranda's head whipped around. "What's that supposed to mean?" The implied *The hell is that supposed to mean?* was clear, but none of us dared curse around our parents. I don't despite how grown we were. Especially not under their roof.

Dominick held up his hands. "I'm not saying you haven't been a great help to me. That's not what I mean."

She deflated some. My tough baby sister hid her sensitive side well, but her facade began to crumble. Her chin quivered and she sucked her lips inside her mouth, evidently to keep from tearing up. "What do you mean?"

"For instance, with this improvement plan I've been pushing for years. Nobody took it seriously until Daddy came along and fluffed up the numbers. Now you've got it in review to take it before the board to give the flight school the money to make necessary upgrades. Not on my word, but

Daddy's. And Margaret's."

Donovan covered his mouth and whooped. "Big sis catching strays."

I gave him a hard look and turned my attention to my other brother. I'd done nothing but try to help him and keep him here. "I think that's a misrepresentation of what happened."

Daddy looked at me, then at Dominick, then shook his head. "We work together as a family. That's why we have grown a small crop-duster operation into the multi-operations conglomerate it is today. Nobody has autonomy, even me. I answer to the board. Of which you're a member."

"I'm sorry, Daddy. I know this isn't the news you wanted to hear, but I've made up my mind. I wanted to tell everyone to their face, so consider this my two weeks' notice."

Granddaddy seethed in his recliner. "You're in line for CEO, and you're parachuting five minutes before the landing? What's wrong with you, boy?"

Daddy placed a calming hand on his father's shoulder. "Don't let this upset you. We'll work it out."

Of course the only thing of interest to Granddaddy was ensuring Dominick leapfrogged me to head the company because I was a woman.

Dominick finally stood. "Daddy, we can meet in your office another time to work out logistics. I'm going up to get the boys."

Mama wiped at a tear. "I'll go with you." Knowing our mother, she had other logistics on her mind concerning how he'd manage with the kids and how we still fit in their lives.

Lots of head shaking and grumbling followed, but I'd had enough. There was only one thing on my mind.

Seeing what Mr. Posh, aka Lewis Watson-Grosvenor, had to say for himself, the dirty conniving bastard.

As soon as I extricated myself from my family, I ran back to my house and got into my car. Before I drove off, I sent a text message: *"I'm on my way to your place."*

There was no reply. One wasn't needed. Surely he had to expect this visit.

He waited for me in the open doorway of his town house and stepped aside when I pushed through. The lights were low, a single candle flickering on the counter leading to the kitchen.

I rotated to him, my eyebrows drawn together. "I hope you don't think this is a booty call."

He huffed a laugh, deadpan in his demeanor. "Nah, love. That's not what I expected at all."

"Good. Just so we're clear." I moved toward the sofa, then thought better of it and circled around to one of the single chairs on either side of the couch.

His shoulders rose and fell, accompanied by a sigh.

"I guess you know we're over, right?"

"I had a notion." He was stone faced, no tells to give away his actual feelings.

"You really have nothing to say for yourself?" I crossed my arms over my chest and stared at him. This man who had pleasured my body so many times but never nourished my emotions. How could I think he would care about any of this?

He threw out his hands in frustration, finally some sort of spirit from him. "What can I say, Margaret? What you and I have had has been absolutely lovely. Our"—he waved between the two of us—"whatever it is you'd call it eased me into my new life here, made me so much less lonely than I could have been after leaving everything behind. But we both realized our relationship was only temporary. You didn't even want your family to know."

There was a lot to unpack in those few sentences. I hardly knew where to start. "I—" After a couple of deep breaths, I tried again. "It's good to know I kept you less lonely while you sabotaged my family."

"Whoa, whoa. *Sabotage* is a strong word. I'm helping your brother. At his request, I might add."

I shook my head in rapid succession, nearly braining myself. It didn't matter because my head hurt ever since I quelled the tears leaving my parents' house. Anger drove me now, and thank goodness for that because I wasn't prepared to deal with any other emotions. "At his request? Well, that's a lie, and I'm not a fool. You're a recruiter for Gibson."

He narrowed his gaze.

"Yeah, I looked you up. After I began putting two and two together. You're always so cagey. The only real thing I know about you organically is that you have a brother. I doubt I would have known that if I hadn't been acquainted with the man the same time I met you." I felt no shame in this admission. Most people looked up their dates before going out. These days it was almost stupid not to. I haven't dated enough lately to care about such things, but Lewis left me no choice.

"And what did you find when you 'looked me up,' Margaret?"

"Don't try to deflect, Lewis. The point is I found out you're a recruiter for Gibson. That's what's at the center of this discussion. Don't forget when Dominick first met you, you sought him out, said you'd been referred to him by a mutual friend. Shawn, right?"

"Yes, that's right. So what?"

"So, your mission in even meeting him was to lay the groundwork to recruit my brother. So saying it was at his request is a bold-faced lie. Admit it."

"What is it you want from me, Margaret?" He leaned forward, true curiosity lining his face.

It was a good question, albeit his deflection was evident in the asking. The truth was I wasn't sure what I wanted from Lewis. There was no point in coming over here other than to vent. Nothing would be changed. I pursed my lips in thought. "I want to know how you could be so underhanded."

There—that was the crux of the issue. I felt used by Lewis and wondered if I could be so wrong about someone.

He scrubbed his hands across his face then searched mine. "Do you think what's happened between us wasn't real? Is that what you're implying?"

I didn't say anything, only stared.

"Margaret, we met before I knew Dominick was your brother. Yes, he was my target, but I didn't know your connection to him until I saw you at the flight school. At first I wondered if you somehow orchestrated our meeting in London."

I gasped. "What the fuck?"

He waved a hand. "No, I realized pretty quickly that didn't make sense. It's all happenstance, but there have been people in the past who've tried to get close to me for less."

Now I was genuinely confused. "What? Why?"

"You said you looked me up. Surely you've gained knowledge of my family."

Other than his family being richer than the queen, I hadn't dug too deep. "I don't know what you mean."

"Hmm, okay." Lewis deflected with the best of them.

"This isn't really about your family. It's about mine. Maybe you only found out about my connection to Dominick when you met him. Okay. Why would you start any sort of relationship with me knowing your whole goal was to poach my brother away from our family?"

"Margaret. That was never my intention. Your family and your business are two separate entities. You know that, right?"

"How do you not know by now that they aren't?" I stood because really, what was the point of all this? "I'm going because I know nothing more now than before I arrived. Really, no more about you than when we first met. You never had any intention of letting me. At least now I know why."

I walked through the door before he had a chance to reply.

What else was left to say?

CHAPTER TWENTY-ONE
Lewis—Google is the devil

I GUESSED THERE were worst things in life than being proven right. My weary body didn't know what they were though.

Almost everything Margaret said was true. I should have never entered into a relationship with her, no matter that it was only physical, knowing I headhunted her brother. Something I would have loved to talk with her about was that they didn't appreciate what they had, and that was how they lost him. I only facilitated the process.

I was happy to do it and I reached my goals of this move and new job in the process, but there was more going on out at that compound than the mean old British guy rolling in to rob them of their family.

And maybe justification remained in my corner though. She admitted to researching me. Surely she realized immediately my background, my family's background. She hadn't used that information against me or asked me for anything though.

None of that was a comfort now.

An unexpected knock sounded on the door, and I frowned. Surely Margaret wasn't returning. Then again, maybe she thought about it and realized we had a good thing going. No need to let something like this, something that didn't affect our physical relationship, interfere.

I yanked open the door. "I'm so glad you..." Not who I expected.

Dominick stood on my porch, arms crossed, looking a bit worse for wear. "Hey, man. Sorry for just dropping by like this."

"Uh, yeah, okay. No problem. Come in." He'd picked me up for golf once but never actually came inside. I supposed I shouldn't have been as shocked as I felt. "Can I help with something?"

"No. I wish you could, but we both knew the conversation I needed to have with my family wouldn't be easy." He sat on the sofa and stretched his legs before him, scratching his close-cropped hair.

"That bad, huh?" I'd already been beaten up by his sister. Listening to him wax poetic about family matters wasn't something I wanted to spend my night doing. It was his decision to leave, and I only did my job. My gut clenched.

"Nobody got it. Well, except my brother, but I expected him to understand. In all honesty, I'm not sure he did, but he sided with me at least."

"Why would you say that? About Donovan."

"Aviation wasn't really his interest. Or maybe family-legacy stuff wasn't his jam. I'm not sure why he refused to join the business, but it was never in the cards for him and everyone knew it. I'm leaving because..." He scratched at his scalp again.

"Because you weren't appreciated for the talent you are." It was simple and an easy way to lure him away. I understood that about five minutes after arriving to the flight school. I built my strategy from there.

"Hmm, I suppose. What happened with you and my sister? She couldn't have been too happy."

I froze and my airway closed. "Your...your... Sorry?"

He dipped his head and looked at me from under his eyes. "Man, be serious. You can't possibly think you and Margaret were flying under the radar."

Margaret assured me we were indeed flying quite that low. "Does everyone know?"

"Definitely. Maybe not Granddaddy, but I'm pretty sure the rest of the brood is caught up. Nobody's business is safe at the compound."

Somehow that made me feel worse. I slumped back in my chair. "I can imagine what they think of me these days."

He chuckled. "Persona non grata for sure. I wouldn't visit for any more airplane joy rides if I were you. And maybe wait a few weeks before you return for a Sunday dinner."

"I can't imagine ever being invited round for one of those again." I would miss the Hawthorne food almost as much as Margaret.

"Are we friends? Or did you just get close to me for one reason only?"

I thought about it a moment. He was a target, plain and simple. At least that was how it started. "We're friends, bro."

"And Margaret?"

I cast my eyes down. "That's more complicated." My stomach was seriously doing some flips. I hadn't explored my feelings like this in quite a while—two years, to be exact. Not since Sheila snatched my heart out of my chest and stomped on it.

"Yeah, I can see how it would be. Let me ask you something." He leaned forward. "That day you initially visited the flight school wasn't the first time you and Margaret met, was it?"

"I'm not entirely certain that's my story to tell."

"Yeah, I figured it wasn't." He chuckled again. "The way you two kept stealing glances when the other wasn't looking... Then the way you spoke to each other. Like there was an inside joke."

I stretched my collar, suddenly too tight.

"You don't have to say anything. All this really is between the two of you. From now on my name is Wes."

I raised a brow.

"You know—I'm staying out of this mess."

"Ah, one of those American idioms I'm not quite acquainted with."

"I suppose so." He chuckled and stood, then headed to the door. "I guess I'll get out of your hair."

I followed him and opened the door for him. "Dominick."

"Yeah?"

"Why did you really come over?" Maybe he wanted to back out of the verbal agreement now that it had become so real. This deal was of great importance to me, but I would never convince him of something he didn't want. That would not a happy employee make.

He shrugged and stepped down to the walkway.

Mosquito hawks zoomed by, hopefully doing their job so I wouldn't wake up itchy in the morning.

When Dominick turned back toward me, his expression appeared a lot more relaxed. "I just wanted to talk to someone without the last name *Hawthorne*. You know, a friend."

I smiled and nodded, happy for his friendship.

At least one thing went Margaret's way. She wanted her brother to reenter the world and form associations.

Now we'd need to maneuver through all these tangles those associations meted out.

CHAPTER TWENTY-TWO

Margaret—You get an assessment. You get an assessment. Everyone gets an assessment.

TURNED OUT, I figured out a way to get Dominick what he wanted without having to take it to the board for approval. Something all of us secretly knew wouldn't be an easy vote. A fund was already set up, and as CEO, Daddy could make it happen. Now my top mission, even more than securing my votes, was to get what Dominick wanted and make him happy. My brother leaving our family business completely was not an option.

Gah, the thought of him working somewhere else turned my stomach. We were a family, and sure, there were strong personalities and opinions, but we were still a family. We loved each other and held each other together. We shared in an incredible legacy, and I thought we were all committed to that legacy continuing. I understood why my brother might waver, considering how impacted his life had been since Lisa died. But I also didn't think he'd thought this through all the way. Decisions were made on emotions, which again, I understood, but these were life-changing decisions.

He hadn't said, but I felt it deep inside he would move away if he left for Gibson. Their flight school wasn't close to us—actually on the other side of the kids' school by some distance. It wouldn't make sense for him to live here in the compound and drive back and forth around their schedule. Here, when he picked them up from school, there was always someone around to care for them. To help them with homework or supervise their chores. To play with them and make sure they were fed. To love on them as much as humanly possible, understanding that love could never replace their mother's but could at least provide some sort of salve.

I couldn't imagine him losing the support all of us provided him and the boys. My nephews certainly didn't need to be separated from their family and with a new work schedule. How would Dominick manage their care alone? At least here he had flexibility.

So that was it. My number one priority shifted to ensure my brother was happy.

Daddy's office door stood open, so I waltzed right in. He bent over his desk, his sports coat relegated to a nearby chair, reviewing a pile of spreadsheets, then looked up at my entrance.

"You're single-handedly killing all the trees in North America."

His quizzical expression made me smile.

"I meant all this paperwork, Daddy. You have a computer."

"I can't see it on the computer well enough."

I shook my head but couldn't help but smile. I guess everyone had their method. "Well, unfortunately for you, I have a bunch of items to share with you and they're all on my laptop." I held it up for him to see.

He rubbed his eyes. "Can we at least project in the con-ference room?"

"We absolutely can."

We walked down the hall to the larger room, and I set up my laptop to project against the pull-down screen. "Okay, Daddy. I've been doing a ton of research and reviewed Dominick's proposal again with the added ROI changes we came up with."

"Oh, that's what this is about." His disinterested tone surprised me.

"Daddy, do you want to lose Dominick? Because he has one foot out the door. He was serious when he gave his notice."

He frowned. "And you think this will change his mind?"

"I'm not sure, but Dominick deserves our attention to these issues even if we can't change his mind."

"Did you see the bottom line of what he's asking for? That's a big number, Margaret."

I fired up my laptop and opened the documents Dominick emailed us. "He's made some excellent points here, Daddy." I walked him through the list of improve-ments and the estimated ROI Daddy and I put together.

"I agree he has, but I'm not sure it's needed. I think it'll be a hard sell to the board."

"Ah, that's the thing." I switched over to the budget and related documents, pulling up the text I'd identified the night before. "See this?" I pointed at the line item in the budget for an infrastructure fund. Judging from the amount, we'd never tapped into it and it must have rolled over year after year.

An oversight by the CEO.

His frown deepened. "Hmph."

"Okay, I get it. But this is good news, Daddy."

He heaved a heavy sigh and sat back in his chair. "Do you really believe Dominick would leave?"

I slowly nodded.

"It's that new friend of his. Before that Brit came around, he was perfectly happy."

I agreed that Lewis was deep into this decision, but Daddy's characterizations were unfair. "I don't think Dominick has been happy since Lisa passed away. If anything, his disposition has been a bit brighter since Lewis showed up."

He huffed. "He wasn't thinking about leaving though."

I couldn't believe I took up for Lewis. This was about getting Dominick to stay though. "What he's asked for isn't unreasonable."

He nodded. "Before I agree, I want an assessment of the repair shop and the airplane rental."

I blinked. "Do you mean for me to do that?"

"You want to be CEO, right? This is a step in that direction. You've inelegantly pointed out my shortcomings, so show the board what you've got instead of running around the country trying to talk our relatives into a *yes* vote."

My mouth dropped open. "You know about that?" Nausea hit my stomach.

He dipped his head and looked at me over his glasses. "Do you really think you could rally support from individual board members without it getting back to me?"

I shrugged, hiding my annoyance, trying to maintain an air of professionalism. "I wasn't hiding it from you."

He chuckled. "Sure. So are you up to the task?"

I thought about having to interact with Grumpy Grand and almost threw in the towel. "Yes, of course I'm up to the task."

The rental assessment would be easy. Not so much for the repair shop. If I could work with Grand and get his cooperation without one of us mangling the other one, it would be a minor miracle.

This was clearly a test, but Daddy should've known by now—broadcast to me I can't do something, and I'd prove you wrong every time.

STANDING OUTSIDE THE aircraft repair shop, I rubbed my hand over my face. I had two assessments to complete, and considering the shop manager, this one would be the most difficult. It also had more moving parts than the rental, so doubly difficult. I had to fly to New York yesterday but it was a turnaround, so last night, I put together a checklist for both operations. Hopefully this process would make the assessment less painful, but knowing Grand, he would do everything in his power to make me uncomfortable.

Once I pulled out my tablet from my messenger bag, I strolled around the massive building, taking my time and checking off needed repairs. Unlike the hangars at the flight school, this building was constructed of sturdy white brick. It didn't need a paint job. Even if it did, the repair shop's outwardly appearance did not hold the same importance as the flight school. Dominick had a great point there.

Honestly, most of his points were more than valid, and although he hadn't qualified the ROI as well as he could, we put a shine on that part of his proposal. Made me wonder how much Lewis was involved in putting it together. I didn't believe I played in conspiracy territory when my thoughts ran toward Lewis giving Dominick advice on improvements but not on the return-on-investment aspect of the plan. If I was right, and I truly believed I was, Mr. Posh set my brother up to make demands so that when they weren't met, Dominick would leave us for Gibson.

Having spent as much time as I reasonably could on the outside, I ventured inside. Three aircraft were actively being worked on, and another two stood without any activity around. I spotted my sister on top of the largest airplane where scaffolding had been set up. She wore bright blue overalls, and I had to bite back a smile because I was quite sure Grand required black. The clothes could be regular pants and a shirt, even shorts, but the shop manager wanted black. Meredith didn't believe in wearing black, even to funerals. Clearly Grand had lost that battle, and I would have paid good money to have seen it.

Others sat on stools for smaller planes, stooping over to get into the compartments they needed, while many workers reassembled parts on long tables. The space buzzed with energy and testosterone, Meredith being the only woman visible. I wrote a note on the assessment because Grand's hiring practices should be evaluated.

When I spotted Grand, it was clear he'd been watching me. I headed his way, and he focused his attention on the computer in front of him, a line of batteries lining the table nearby.

I took a couple of deep, cleansing breaths on my way over and stopped across from him. "Hi, Grand. Did you get my email about the assessment today?"

He grunted.

"Grand. I need your cooperation. Or do you not think any upgrades are needed here?"

He frowned and closed his eyes for a moment, then opened them, turning that sharp gaze on me. "I've already made a report of what's needed."

"That's great. Where's this report?"

"I sent it to your father," he said, emphasizing *father* with a smirk, which said all anyone needed to say about Grand. He didn't think much of nepotism. Which…fair. But also, this had always been a family company, had been for over a hundred years, and he knew that when he signed on nearly ten years ago. None of this was news.

"Okay, well, since I don't have it and my *father* tasked me with assessing this operation, I guess I'll do it from scratch." Sometimes a gentle reminder went a long way.

Not with Grand apparently. "Suit yourself."

I huffed. "Well, I'll need your undivided attention to assist me. Obviously you know the ins and outs of the shop better than I do."

He snorted. "I don't have time." He waved in the general direction of all the batteries.

I'd had enough of this misogynistic bullshit. I doubted this would be the attitude if this were Donovan over here carrying out Daddy's wishes. "Listen here, Grand—"

"Hey, what's going on? I could see the steam coming out

of both your ears from across the building." Meredith appeared, her kind face diffusing the situation already.

"And here you are." Grand snickered.

"Yes, here I am. You think you'd be used to it by now."

They stared each other down for an uncomfortably long time. My sister actually surprised me with her temerity. She was the calm sister, laid-back in every way, and not prone to gossip. Not usually this bold either.

I broke the stalemate. "Hi, Meredith. I'm doing an assessment, and Grand doesn't want to cooperate."

Meredith gave the man one last stink eye, then turned my way. "Is this something I could help with?"

Grand actually smiled. "See, there you go. A win-win." He turned back to his laptop, essentially shutting down further conversation.

One of these days, once I was CEO, we would have a reckoning about professionalism and respect. Today I only wanted to get through this task and get to the next.

I turned my attention back to my sister. "Are you sure, Meredith? Looked like you were busy."

Clearly Grand was still engaged in this conversation because he released a rather loud exhale.

Meredith shook her head and placed her arm in mine, leading me away from the grumpy man. "It's no problem at all. Where do we start?"

I showed her my tablet and the checklist. "It would have been great if we had the report Grand sent to Daddy. He already outlined the shop's needs."

"Can't you ask Daddy for it?"

I could, but asking for a report from him instead of the

person standing in front of me wouldn't exactly instill confidence in my managerial prowess. "I don't want to bother him."

Meredith shook her head and pulled out her phone, scrolling through email. "Yeah, as I thought. It's probably the same report Grand sent out to the team a few weeks ago, asking everyone to provide feedback. I'll forward you the end result." She made a few more clicks, and my phone buzzed.

I opened the attachment in her email to guide us through our walk-through. "Thank you. This is perfect."

My phone buzzed again, this time with a text. *"Can I see you today?"*

I buried the phone in my pocket and tried, unsuccessfully, not to think about the message.

"Was that from Lewis?" Meredith peered over my arm and must have seen the text.

"Why would you think that?"

"Well, Mama said…"

I released a deep sigh. "I was just thinking how you weren't a gossip."

She laughed. "Listen, everything I know about Lewis, and possibly you, has been against my will. Sunday dinner was…interesting."

"Ugh, to say the least. What does Mama think she knows?"

"Now you want me to gossip?"

"Is it gossip if it's about me? I'm the literal subject of this conversation."

She tapped a greasy finger on her chin, leaving behind a wide smudge. "Okay, she thinks you met Lewis at an industry event and that Lewis has been courting both you and Dominick, but separately."

So Mama really didn't know anything at all other than what Dominick had probably told her about meeting Lewis. Of course, Mr. Posh and I had intimate knowledge of each other before that industry meeting.

"Margaret?"

I blinked. And turned my gaze back on my sister. "She's wrong."

Meredith shrugged. "Okay. Let's get to this assessment because I really should get back to my task before Grand gets someone else to do it while I'm not looking." She shook her head and sighed.

It was unfortunate that at least two of the Hawthorne sisters had to fight the patriarchy on a daily basis. Miranda waded into those waters and quickly paddled back to shore. Two years flying commercial was two years too long, according to my baby sister.

I followed Meredith through the stations, checking possible issues against the opened report on my phone and logging them on the checklist on my tablet when necessary. The problem with that was that I couldn't forget about Lewis's text because I kept having to view my phone.

Did I want to see him? My body hummed with the thought, but he'd betrayed me and my family.

I didn't text back.

MY NEXT STOP was Jaden and Miranda, who I sent texts to

before leaving the repair shop. Although officially Jaden managed the plane rental, Miranda had a lot of input just the same as she did at the flight school under Dominick. She spent more time at the rental for some reason, even though it had a lot less moving parts. Like Jaden, she seemed to still be working out where she really fit in. I supposed that was fair for someone still in their twenties.

My sandals clacked on the bright flooring as I made my way down the hall, passing an empty office where Miranda usually sat, ending up at the office Jaden claimed. He spent a lot of time away from the office though, between working on his commercial pilot's license and running errands for his mother, but Miranda stepped in to pick up any slack he might have left behind.

They made a good team.

As expected, they sat next to each other behind Jaden's desk, huddled over his laptop.

"Hey, y'all."

Both sets of eyes looked up at me, registering slight surprise.

"I literally just texted you ten minutes ago letting you know I was driving over."

Miranda recovered first. "Sorry—we were checking the bookings. Looks like we've double-booked a rental, so we'll have to borrow one from the flight school." She shook her head. "This system sucks."

I sat and pulled out my tablet. "Looks like that's a great place to start with the assessment."

Jaden, reserved and quiet, nodded his agreement.

I opened the assessment for the plane rental and checked

the appropriate box, making notes in the comments section about the double bookings.

Miranda looked at the computer in front of her and back up at me. "Did you book a plane last week?"

I responded cautiously, hoping this wouldn't be another semi-interrogation. "Yes."

"Okay, good. Just making sure it wasn't another glitch in the system."

Crisis averted.

I relaxed and put a series of questions to Jaden from the assessment, which he answered with ease. That was the thing with Jaden: Even though he didn't seem fully in, he was smart as a whip and picked up easily. It was a no brainer for Daddy to pair him with Miranda on running the rental operation.

"Okay, let's take a walk and check everything out." I checked the time, and luckily this part wouldn't take long because I had a long list of items to check off my to-do list.

The outer office was of main concern because, like the flight school, appearance mattered for confidence. Nobody wanted to rent from a dilapidated building or a rickety plane, even those who crop dusted and didn't want to maintain their own equipment.

"Do you know why we have this reflective flooring?" I squinted at the tile bouncing sunrays all over the room.

"I've always wondered that myself." Miranda scrunched her nose. "It's really bright in the summer."

Jaden shrugged. "I haven't got a clue, but it doesn't really bother me much."

Jimmy, working the front desk, glanced up like he wanted to add to the conversation but must have changed his mind because he went back to whatever he was doing on the computer.

"I'll check with Daddy and see what he says."

Other than the tile, countertops were pristine and the folding chairs were in good repair. The seats were padded to provide a little comfort, but if all went to plan, a customer wouldn't spend much time in here. Which could be different for the repair shop, which was why I recommended better seating in the waiting room there.

The planes were at the flight school and Dominick had already covered those, so there really wasn't much else to review.

I turned to the pair. "Thanks for your time and making this easy."

Miranda released a sly smile. "Grand gave you a hard time, huh?"

I threw my hands out. "What is it with that man?"

"If I only knew." She looked to Jaden.

"I get along good with him. Not sure what you mean."

Of course he did. I had a feeling Grand got along fine with all the workers here who didn't possess double X chromosomes.

"Good to know. Well, I'll let y'all get back to work." I turned toward the flight school. "Thanks again."

Now I just needed to put these assessments together and make the case to Daddy again.

CHAPTER TWENTY-THREE

Margaret—But do I have your vote?

THE PAST WEEK flew by in a whirlwind of flights, from Prague to Berlin to Amsterdam and London and back again through Detroit. My track currently was eastward, but if I didn't get the CEO vote, I'd been thinking about taking some western routes: Asia, maybe even Oceania.

But first I'd do everything possible to secure that vote, and the remaining cousins were in Memphis and Auburn, Alabama, so I'd finagled my flight schedule to include those two cities. The ability for pilots to pick up extra routes proved easy enough. Currently I had my sisters' votes and Rhonda's, our cousin in Miami. And since my plans fell apart when that man who will be not be named crashed our Sunday dinner, I'd have to go after my brothers' votes individually.

This also gave me a great opportunity to speak with Dominick one-on-one for the first time after his big revelation. I wanted to support him, and I would, but this decision to leave seemed a little extreme. Especially given the reasons he listed.

I missed Sunday dinner, and since the sun had set and the lights were on sparingly in the main house, I walked up on my brother's porch and knocked on the door. It was still early enough that the kids wouldn't be in the middle of their bedtime routine, so hopefully he had a couple of minutes to talk.

Dominick approached the door slowly. Because the entrance was half made of wood, half thick glass, he could easily see I was his visitor.

I stood with my back straight but tried to exude comfort in my features. Then I gave a wave.

He reached over and unlocked the door. "Hey."

"Hey. Do you have a little time to talk?"

"If this is about me leaving…"

"It's not necessarily about that, but if you have anything to say to me about it, I'm open to listening."

He studied my face, then stepped aside.

I'd abandoned my uniform at home and took a shower before heading over here, throwing on a sundress and flip-flops. I slid out of those and left them by the door with a pile of little-boy sneakers and my brother's larger ones.

He wore socks and slides which were for indoor use only. Because he had kids, Dominick enforced the no-outside-shoes-inside rule. Lisa actually started it, and while it made sense, we just didn't grow up that way.

We walked into the family room, and my nephews turned away from the board game they'd been playing to greet me. "Auntie Margaret!"

I bent over and hugged each one. "Hey, guys. What game is that?"

The youngest was missing a tooth right in front but grinned at me with that cute smile. "Survive the Earthquake. It's great."

"Oh, that sounds like…fun." And apocalyptic.

"Hey, fellas. Go upstairs to the game room so I can speak to Aunt Margaret."

My older nephew perked up. "Can we watch *Finger Family*?"

Dominick closed his eyes for a moment, then acquiesced. "Sure." They immediately stood and headed for the stairs, game completely forgotten.

Lisa never wanted them to have too much screen time, and we all fell in line behind that, respecting her wishes even though she was no longer here, including Dominick, but I wondered how much that would change now that he decided to upend all of their lives.

I wasn't here to talk about that though. "See you guys later."

Notes of "Bye" floated back down to me as they raced to the game room.

"They're getting so big." I sat on the recliner sofa and put my feet up, hoping to convey to my brother I didn't come here to fight. I only wanted a relaxed conversation.

He bent over and gathered the game pieces and board, placing them back in their box. "So, are you done with Lewis?"

I nearly choked on my own spit. "Wh-what are you talking about?"

He placed the box on the stairs, presumably to take up to the game room later, allowing my question to hang in the air. "You want something to drink? Sounds like you're choking." He already headed to the kitchen before I could respond, then returned with two glasses of water, setting one on the end table next to me.

I grabbed it up and drank greedily, stalling as much as I could. This was not the conversation I'd prepared for. When I'd had as much as I could drink, I sat the glass back down.

"So, Lewis?"

"Why do you want to talk about Lewis?"

"He's a friend and clearly misses you."

"So he told you about us?" Fury built in my stomach, roaring its way up my throat. My next words would not be pretty.

Dominick shook his head. "He did not." He took a drink of his own water, the smile evident behind the glass. "You know how the compound gossip goes around here. When I asked him about it, he basically said I'd have to ask you."

That dampened my rage considerably. "But we were careful." Meeting only at his place should have hidden anything between us.

With raised brows, my brother gave me a pointed look. "Were you? Just because he wasn't at your place doesn't mean you weren't spotted elsewhere throughout the compound. Lake strolls and intimate flights. Not to mention the way he rushed to your defense at Sunday dinner. That was a dead giveaway."

According to Meredith, Mama had her suspicions after that meal, but I didn't realize everyone had made this the centerpiece of their gossip. "An intimate flight? Really, Dominick?" I shook my head and took a sip of my water. "It wasn't like that anyway. We met on one of my London layovers a few months ago. It was supposed to be a one-time thing, then he showed up here."

"That's weird."

"Tell me about it. Apparently he moved the next day, but I didn't see him until the Women in Aviation mixer nearly three months later."

The wheels in Dominick's brain turned, evident by his scrunched forehead and unfocused gaze. "Do you think he knew who you were?"

Although Lewis withheld plenty—was still withholding, as far as I was concerned—he never actually lied, from what I could tell. "No, I think it was all a coincidence."

My brother visibly relaxed and sat back in his chair. "You never answered my question."

"We're done."

"Because I'm leaving."

He hadn't asked a question, so I let the statement hang there between us. It wasn't my brother's fault what happened, but my not wanting to see Lewis ever again had everything to do with my brother accepting a new position.

"I don't want to talk about that man. I came over to ask for your vote. You're still part of the board."

Understanding traveled over his face, and he wiped a hand over it. "I don't think I should get involved."

No, no, no, this was not happening. I'd counted on both my brothers' votes to get to nine. "What do you mean, shouldn't get involved?"

"I'm leaving. It's not for me to decide who takes over."

"Not everyone on the board works at the company. You know that. What about Rhonda, Ed, and Cedric? And their kids? All on the board, and the only time they come here is for family gatherings."

He leaned over and picked up my hand. "I'm sorry, Margaret. Until all the dust settles and folks are used to my new position, I'm going to abstain."

It was bad enough I'd lost my brother to a competitor. Now I'd lost his vote too.

I needed to recalibrate. And fast.

CHAPTER TWENTY-FOUR

Margaret—Another dreaded family meeting

A NOTHER FAMILY MEETING was called, the second one in as many weeks, but this time we met in Daddy's office. My brothers were noticeably absent—not surprising considering the meeting was about Dominick and what his leaving meant for the business, our family legacy, and the future as well as what we could do to convince him to stay. Donovan worked and wouldn't leave his office for Hawthorne Family Flying Eagles business. That was a given.

My sisters and I crammed onto the sofa in Daddy's office while Granddaddy sat in one of the comfortable chairs across from Daddy's desk and Mama took up the identical one. Although technically she didn't hold a position in the business, Dominick was her son, so excluding her was a nonstarter.

Daddy cleared his throat. "I've spoken with Dominick, and we've come up with a transition plan."

I blinked. "Wait, we're letting him go, just like that?" I snapped my fingers for emphasis.

"As you know, Margaret, Texas is a right-to-work state. He has no contract. I can't force him to stay." Daddy's stone-faced expression held no joy. Clearly this wasn't easy for him. "As I was saying, until we can find a more permanent solution, Miranda, you'll need to run the flight school in the meantime."

Miranda glanced at the ceiling, a frown on her face. "This isn't a surprise but not something I want to do."

Mama rotated in her chair and reached for Miranda's hand. "I know, honey. But it makes the most sense. You've been his number two and know the most about the ins and outs of the operation."

Granddaddy nearly choked. I guess on his own spit because he held no drink or food. "Maybe I should take over the school. I ran it before Dominick and actually know the most about it."

All heads swiveled his way, taking in his slumped posture, his walking cane leaning against the desk, and his rheumy eyes. I don't know about the rest of the room, but I couldn't imagine him working for more than ten minutes at a time. He retired over five years ago because he couldn't swing it anymore.

"I'm sure you've forgotten more than any of us will ever know, but you retired for a reason. Someone in their eighties who had given everything to this company should have a right to rest and enjoy life." Daddy, usually the voice of reason, seemed to placate his father with those words.

"Maybe you're right." Granddaddy relaxed into the chair again and half closed his eyes.

My first reaction was to tell him about himself. I hoped that was because of our rocky history and not a tell of my leadership qualities.

"Since Miranda will be full-time at the flight school, Meredith, I'll need you to spend an hour or so at the rental daily. Jaden has it covered, but he's used to sharing the responsibilities with Miranda of running the operation plus flight school. It shouldn't be too much."

Meredith's skin reddened considerably. "But I don't know anything about it at all. What am I supposed to do over there?" My sister loved the greasy pits of the repair shop, and I couldn't imagine her sitting in an office for any amount of time. If so, she could have supplanted Grand a long time ago as shop manager.

"Jaden will let you know what he needs."

My sister sat back completely deflated.

I felt for her and would gladly take her place, but I had a whole day job that didn't allow it. I could help when home though. "Hey, I could fill in on the days I'm not flying."

Meredith perked up and turned to me, a slight sheen of tears in her eyes. She mouthed *Thanks* and relaxed back into the soft cushions of the sofa.

"That's fine, but it's Meredith's responsibility. I don't want to hear that no one showed up because there was a miscommunication." Daddy looked at us over his glasses, and it felt like we were in elementary school again being scolded for wading into the lake without a chaperone.

"Okay, Daddy," Meredith and I said in unison, and we clutched each other's hands. We'd make this work, but I didn't want to. I'd rather have my brother here.

"There must be some plan we can come up with to make him stay." I threw my hand up to halt Daddy's next words. "I know he's grown and this is his decision, but it's not a great business decision for the company and I think we should talk this out. During the transition planning, did you tell him we don't have to take the improvement plan to the board? I found the money."

"It didn't change his mind. I know this is hard, but you need to let it go, Margaret. People are allowed to make their own choices, even your brother." Daddy gave me a pointed look, but not unkind.

Granddaddy just had to put his two cents in. "That may be true, but it's time for Donovan to step up. I never thought Dominick would be good for CEO because he's too soft. Donovan has an MBA and business experience, so he's primed to take over when you retire, Marshall."

My father's gaze slid to mine and back to his father just as fast. "This isn't the meeting for that. We're here to discuss transition and looks like we're done, so I'll let you get back to your day."

At that moment I realized two things. One, Daddy's vote was not mine for the taking. And two, I would be CEO over Granddaddy's cold, dead body, no matter how the vote went. As it stood now, I'd need all of our cousins to get on board with me, not just Rhonda—who honestly was low-hanging fruit, which was why I approached her first.

After I secured Donovan's vote, this would be an uphill battle.

Luckily for me, I'd never taken no for an answer before. Especially when misogyny fueled the question.

CHAPTER TWENTY-FIVE

Lewis—Persona non grata!

NOW THAT HIS sister spent most of her days at the flight school, Dominick was able to meet me for lunch away from prying family eyes. He hadn't signed all his onboarding paperwork yet, and I wanted to know why. I didn't want to put pressure on him either in case something was amiss. Coercion could very well backfire.

I drove to the seafood spot he recommended, but stayed in the car since I was nearly twenty minutes early. I couldn't sit in my house another moment because without Margaret, the loneliness had seeped back in. I wasn't sure how it happened, but I'd somehow allowed myself to get too comfortable with having her around.

A whole podcast had finished and the next was in queue when Dominick drove up. He got out of his car but appeared to sleepwalk to the door.

I hopped out to greet him before he walked into the restaurant. "All right, wait up."

He turned. "Hey, man. I didn't see you." Not a surprise considering he hadn't looked around. Someone could have blown up the car next to his and I doubted he would have noticed.

"Doing okay?" We walked through the door and gave

our name at the hostess stand. Looked like there was a ten-minute wait.

Dominick accepted the pager from the hostess, and we sat on one of the outside benches. Late October in Southeast Texas brought a mixed bag of weather. Today the air had cooled considerably, although not enough for a jacket. Dominick wore a long-sleeved casual shirt, suitable for the office.

I nudged him. "Did you hear me, mate?"

He turned a dazed expression on me. "Did you say something?"

This wasn't good. I swallowed the lump in my throat. "I was wondering how you are."

He nodded. "Oh, I'm okay. What about you?"

"Fine, thanks." I studied his profile. It was difficult to say, but I thought he looked more distracted than anything else. "You only have a few days left until your last at Hawthorne. I know you wanted to take about a week to get settled before starting, but HR mentioned you hadn't filled out your paperwork yet." Paperwork wouldn't hold him if he really didn't want to be at Gibson. He could leave at any time, but not filling it out was a problem.

He grabbed the back of his neck and rubbed. "Yeah, I'll get to it. Just trying to tie up loose ends at the school before I leave. I don't want to dump everything in Miranda's lap. Especially since she didn't ask for any of this."

It went against my best interests, but none of this sat right with me. "Hey, are you having second thoughts?" Before he could answer, I stuck out a stilling hand. "I want you to know I value your friendship and that will remain the same even if you've changed your mind."

His head whipped around. "Nah, man. I need to make a change."

"What is the real reason you want to leave? You wanted to make improvements, and you said your father found a line item to get you the money. You have what you asked for. And please don't tell me it's because your father and Margaret adjusted your work."

He shrugged. "I don't know what you want me to say. I was tired of people second-guessing me. I need a change."

I took a deep breath to steady my thoughts. No way I bought he didn't like the oversight. It was minimal compared to what would happen at Gibson, and I had come clean with Dominick about that when he made his decision to accept the offer. There had to be something else he hadn't told me. Maybe hadn't told himself. My mind latched on to that last sentence. "You need a change. I get it now. To everyone else out there, your compound is about legacy and shared family. But your immediate family was altered, and you're wondering what kind of legacy is left for your kids with their mother gone." I placed a hand on his upper arm.

He shook off my hand. "You don't know what you're talking about." His voice cracked halfway through and his shoulders shook. Then he bent over and put his head in his hands.

I had no idea how to comfort him. I'd experienced loss in my lifetime, but nothing compared to what this man must have gone through, what he still went through every day when he looked upon his kids. His family held him together these past couple years, but maybe he didn't see it that way.

Perhaps he felt smothered. That I could understand. "What can I do to help?"

He rubbed his face and stood without looking at me. "I can't stay. See you later." He handed me the pager and walked back to the parking lot.

Between Margaret and Dominick, I couldn't help but think I'd really made a mess of things.

Now I needed to figure out what to do about it.

"HEY, BRUV." CHARLIE'S face lit up over Zoom on my laptop. I hadn't the energy to hold my mobile for a video chat, having been up most of the night before. "You look a mess."

"Thanks. Nice to see you too."

"Hey, I know it's early there, but what gives?" Worry creased his face.

I rubbed my forehead with the heel of my hand, hoping against hope I could wipe away the headache I'd develop from a lack of sleep. Hawthorne worry probably had something to do with that too. "Do you ever think about the past? Like, when we grew up?"

He narrowed his eyes. "Can you be a little more specific? A lot happened while growing up, and you were a bit older."

"That's true. I've been thinking about how I got here."

"In the States?"

"Sure. But more here as a mindset."

"Is this about Sheila?" Worry morphed into serious worry now. His face was tight with it.

"Yes. No. That's part of it. More like a symptom than the root cause."

"Explain."

Where to start? I still hadn't quite figured it out myself, but maybe Charlie could help me get there. "Before you came along, I'd travel with Mummy to Trinidad to see our granny. She died before you were born, so we didn't go anymore then. It was so different there than back at home."

Charlie nodded. "Okay, sure."

"Granny was so warm and loving and made me sugar cakes." I chuckled at the memory. "Damn, those things were so good, but so sweet. I felt very loved there, and I'm sorry you didn't get a chance to meet her."

My brother's cheeks hung low and I hated making him sad, but I needed to get through this. Get to the bottom of it once and for all.

"She was so different than Nana."

He snorted. "Sounds like it."

Our English grandparents were as English as you got. I wasn't sure what it was like when my father wanted to marry my mother, but I couldn't imagine it went over well. They never made us feel unwelcome, and if there was any controversy, our parents certainly never said, but Nana was rather formal around us all. Nothing like Granny. "I think Mum was different by the time you came along. She'd adopted the English ways, or maybe I was too young to notice she'd always been like that." I shrugged. "No, I don't believe I'm wrong. We had more servants by then, and I distinctly remember having small chores before that. Not household, but at least cleaning up after myself."

Charlie's eyebrows shot up. "Really? You cleaned your own room?"

I sighed because this was where Charlie and I diverged and why it was easy for him to follow in Father's footsteps. He'd lived his whole life with everything our name afforded. But I remembered. "Yes, little brother, I cleaned up my own room. My bathroom too. Just like I do now."

I sat with my thoughts a moment. Mum had changed. She'd never been as warm as Granny, but she was more loving before. Our mother loved us, I knew that in my bones. But she didn't show it as much anymore.

"Charlie, do you know the last time I talked with Mum?"

"I'm guessing it's been a while because every time I see her, she asks if I've heard from you."

I couldn't hide the surprise on my face.

"What's with you, bruv? Of course she asks about you."

"I didn't realize. I haven't spoken with her since I told her I'd made it safely." I gestured to my mobile. "She's emailed a couple times, but I..." I what? I had some sort of latent anger? Why? "I blame her for Sheila."

"Oh man. That's fucked up."

It was because I don't think Mum knew what Sheila was after when she set us up. Still. "I suppose so, and I've only just realized it. There's so much spinning around in my head. I thought Sheila was serious about us. She'd as much said it, but she played me, brother. She was never interested in a relationship." I huffed to myself because Margaret popped in my head then.

"What? What did you just think about?"

I signed. In for a penny, right? I wanted this conversation, so no use bowing out now. "Margaret. I was thinking Margaret is the first person since Sheila I've thought of past a casual situation. I guess the difference is that Margaret made it clear up front she didn't want anything serious."

"Sheila was after more than a romp in the sack though. Has Margaret ever given you that indication? Does she know about our family?"

"Not at all, but I couldn't see past Sheila. And yes, I'm fairly certain she knows about our family. She said she googled me."

"Ugh, not Google. I can only imagine what she read. Why didn't she just ask you? Did she say?"

My stomach sank. "I believe she got frustrated with my constant deflection." That saddened me. Thinking about how I'd been with her for no good reason. Margaret came from a legacy family of her own, and she wasn't sitting around being waited on. She fought hard for everything she had, was still fighting for what she wanted.

"Wow, you are messed up." He grimaced. "Sorry."

"No need. You're right. I've been blaming myself for being gullible and assumed everyone has an agenda and let someone slip through my fingers. Someone much better than me."

In this moment, I felt Margaret's loss acutely. I needed to explain. But my past didn't excuse what I'd done to their family, no matter how inadvertently. I wasn't forthcoming, and Margaret deserved better.

I needed to make it right.

CHAPTER TWENTY-SIX

Margaret—Booty call?

I COULDN'T BELIEVE my evening drive took me here. I had no business anywhere near here, but the car drove me here like I was on autopilot.

Knocking on the door probably wasn't the best move. After all, Lewis and I had a casual understanding and even that was gone thanks to me telling him we were done. My feelings hadn't changed, but despair had seeped into my soul with everything going wrong at the compound, and I needed that physical outlet. I needed to feel.

I sent a text instead. He might not even be here. *"In your driveway. Are you home?"*

The bubbles jumped immediately. *"Yes. Come in?"*

I didn't bother to respond but gathered my purse, phone, and keys and made my way up the short walkway to Lewis's front door.

He waited with the door open dressed in sweatpants. The outline of what I'd come for was apparent through the garment.

Before I stepped up onto the porch, I stopped to give myself one more chance to flee but couldn't make my feet turn around. "I've never seen you in sweatpants."

"Oh, right. I'd just been out for a run. The weather is a

bit more cooperative."

I looked up at the sky. Although dark now, it was clear, no clouds in sight. The temperatures were mild these days, so now was definitely the time for outdoor sports if someone was into that sort of thing. "Can I come in?"

He stood aside as I strode through the door.

I sat my purse on the couch. "How do you feel about some company tonight?"

Surprise registered on his face. "I thought we were over."

"Do you want some or not, Posh?"

He grinned and reached for me, drawing me into his arms. The embrace felt intimate. Too intimate.

I pulled back. "Let's go upstairs."

If he noticed I felt some type of way, he didn't say anything; he only followed me up the stairs. When we got to his bedroom, he cleared his throat. "Make yourself comfortable. I'll take a quick shower."

I nodded but wished he hadn't left me alone. The last thing I wanted was to think. My search for mindless sex would be thwarted if I had a moment to consider my actions.

Thankfully Lewis showered in record speed and joined me back in the bedroom before I could take my shoes off. He wore a towel slung low on his hips.

I licked my lips.

He smiled. "Let's get you naked."

"Yes, let's." Finally—that was all I wanted. To get naked with Lewis and forget everything.

I shimmied out of my pants and underwear in one fell swoop, kicking them aside, while Lewis helped me out of my blouse. I reached behind myself and unhooked my bra, allowing it to fall to the floor. I wasn't sure I've ever un-dressed so quickly in my life.

Lewis dropped the towel, and I was on him before the cloth hit the floor, rubbing myself against him, dragging my fingernails along his scalp and through his curly hair.

He trailed kisses up and down my neck, then licked the shell of my ear.

"Perfect, Posh."

The warm air from his exhale breezed my ear. "I'm Posh again?"

I snickered, then slid my hands around his neck. "Kiss me."

He did, and all thoughts of votes, family troubles, and legacies flew out my head. Just as I'd hoped. He plundered my mouth with urgency, and I met him stroke for stroke with my tongue, relishing the taste of him, some sort of protein drink if I had to guess. Strawberry.

I pressed into him harder, couldn't get enough of his soft skin on mine. I'd missed this the past couple of weeks. I'd missed him, but I would examine that later when I laid in my cold bed. For now, all I wanted was to fuse myself with him and not think. "Condom?"

"Are you in a hurry, love?" He laid me on the bed and ran his tongue up the inside of my leg, from my foot to my thigh, then worshipped my apex until I writhed in pleasure, pulling against the sheets. As much as I tried to pull away, to scoot up the bed running from the pleasure, he wouldn't allow it. "Do you want me to stop?"

"No," I breathed, unable to string together any words. My orgasm hit me with a sharp twinge then sweet release, pulsing deep within my core.

Lewis laid his head on my stomach, matching my quick breaths. He reached up to stroke my chin with his thumb, and I fell into the connected movement. Then I noticed his tattoo. I'd seen it before many times, but not recently because it was located on his inner forearm in a place not readily seen. Now I studied it as Lewis stroked my neck—a tattoo of a hand shaking a snake head shaped as a hand with the snake biting the hand. This wasn't some frivolous drunken mistake; it was an intentional message. But what?

He cupped my neck and licked and kissed up my body, paying special attention to my breasts. My back arched in response on its own volition, and thoughts of that tattoo flew out of my brain along with the rest of my troubles. I'd come all the way down from my orgasm and wanted him inside me. "Condom?"

He chuckled against my neck. "Condom."

The anticipation of coming together while he rolled on the rubber spiked my pulse and my breathing sped up again, completely turned on. I came here to forget everything and allow the pleasure of our bodies to distract me, but I couldn't help thinking that there was more to all of this. Thoughts of Lewis were never far from my mind even when I blamed him for some of my troubles. I continued to be drawn to him, but I couldn't let this interfere with what I needed to accomplish.

When our bodies joined, I couldn't get enough of him, pulling him closer, deeper, grinding together at a frantic pace until we both came.

I lay there panting while Lewis rubbed small circles on

my stomach until we both calmed.

"Thanks for being flexible. You have no idea how much I needed that." I sat up to put my clothes back on.

Lewis's touch fell away and he grew perfectly still.

I looked at him over my shoulder. "What?"

"That's it?"

"What else is there?"

Did he think we were back on? I needed to get out of here with a quickness before I hurt his feelings. Nothing had changed.

CHAPTER TWENTY-SEVEN

Lewis — Feeling a little used over here

"SO YOU JUST came over for sex?" I could barely hold eye contact with her.

"Is that not what we've doing for the past few weeks? What am I missing?"

She was right, of course, but this time the booty call felt different. I couldn't help but feel used. I sat up, putting my back to her. "That's a really good question." I'd just worked through some feelings about my past, reconciling Mum's indifference and Sheila's utter betrayal, then Margaret came over and ripped my heart from my chest. I sighed. I hadn't realized she had that much power over me until now.

I looked down at my tattoo. It was supposed to be a reminder, but somehow I'd forgotten. Somehow I'd thought Margaret was different. Somehow I'd thought maybe it was okay to lower my guard. What a fool.

"What does the tattoo mean?"

I turned away from it, thoroughly disgusted with myself. "It's supposed to be a reminder that people are snakes and can't be trusted." When I first got it, it symbolized that a woman couldn't be trusted, but Margaret wouldn't take too kindly to that. After all this, I still cared about what she thought.

She came around the bed, half dressed in her underwear, and sat next to me. "Is that what you think I am? A snake?"

I rubbed my face, trying to think. It was so hard with her soft skin pressed against my thigh, her floral scent enveloping my whole being. "No, but I'm feeling very vulnerable right now." I surprised myself with the admission, and my stomach tightened in annoyance. I hadn't meant to reveal that.

"Do you think you were a snake when you stole my brother away?" She said it so calmly, almost a whisper.

I swung my gaze to her. "You think I committed some sort of thievery with Dominick? That he didn't make up his own mind?"

"With your encouragement."

"I'm a recruiter, Margaret. Dominick is a great asset that perhaps you've been underutilizing. Or, at the very least, allowing him to spin his wheels. He has so much to offer based on a track record of turning your school around."

She shook her head. "Do you really not think we appreciate him? Or know what he brings to the table? My father relies on Dominick a lot. He's the only one to hold a director position. Everyone else is a manager or below, except Daddy. And that includes my sisters who work there full-time."

"I don't know what to tell you. I put a deal in front of him, and he took it. He's a great asset for Gibson."

"Okay, and you feel perfectly fine sleeping with me while luring my own brother away from our family business. Not just any ole family business, but one that has a hundred-year-old legacy that he was proud of before you came along."

I snorted and searched the floor for my briefs. If I had to have this conversation, I'd do it with some dignity. "Maybe you should talk to your brother about what's really going on inside his head. I doubt it has anything to do with the actual job or the business." I pulled on my sweatpants and stood.

Margaret remained seated on the bed and looked up at me, her expression unreadable. "What if you thought Charlie was in crisis and I manipulated his feelings behind your back? How would you feel?"

I blew out a harsh breath, utterly sick of this comparison. "That's not what happened with Dominick. But if Charlie was in crisis and you helped him, I'd be chuffed. Good on you or whoever could get through to him."

She stretched her eyes at me. Just because she didn't like my answer didn't make it any less accurate.

"Unlike me, Charlie's had good friends and healthy relationships. I can't imagine him ever in that position." He also had Father's full support, something I'd never quite managed.

She frowned, but in a way that showed sympathy.

Pity was the last thing I wanted from Margaret. "I'm fine." I hated how loose my tongue had become around her.

"Sure, Lewis. There's a story there. And hey, listen, you don't have to tell me about it. But whatever it is will continue to put a wedge between us. So when you ask me if I came over here for sex only, the answer is absolutely. What else can there be until you open up to me?" She stood then and gathered her clothes, leaving the room.

A few minutes later, the front door opened and closed.

I was alone again, but this time I had more thoughts running through my head to keep me unsettled.

I hadn't felt this much despair in quite some time.

CHAPTER TWENTY-EIGHT

Margaret—Tainted legacy

TWO MORE DAYS until Dominick officially left for what he thought of as greener pastures. Chana planned a going-away party, but none of our hearts were in it. We'd stand tall and be supportive no matter how much it tore each of us up inside.

I pad through the house with my coffee and head out to my cherished wraparound porch to clear my head. I'd been unsettled ever since my visit to Lewis the night before. About so many things, but mostly because he seemed on the verge of finally giving me something more than a surface level of his prior life and his current feelings.

There wasn't a doubt in my mind that his feelings for me had grown as much as mine for him, but I'd never let him hurt me. And trying to love someone who hid themselves completely was a quick flight to wounded feelings.

So I sat on my porch swing and gently rocked as I sipped my coffee, trying, and mostly failing, to get my thoughts in order. There was so much to tackle, and I needed to move my feelings for Lewis to the bottom of the list. I had acquired eight vote promises for my bid for CEO and saw no path to the nine I needed. Out of the five cousins, I'd secured both female cousin votes as expected but only one of the males', a cousin in my generation. The two older men, Daddy's first cousins, wanted Daddy to stay on and guide the company through Dominick's transition and replacement. They didn't believe it could be done by September.

I huffed and shook my head. Thanksgiving would be awkward this year.

Since Dominick wouldn't budge on his abstention vote, my only hope was Daddy, so I bit the bullet and called him.

He answered on the first ring. "Hi, baby. Everything okay?"

I could imagine why he asked that considering I only called when I traveled. At the moment, the distance between the two of us wasn't more than a hundred feet, so I could've just walked over and spoke with him.

An in-person talk would only break my heart because I already knew deep down Daddy would be a *no* vote. I needed to hear it from him, but not face-to-face.

I took a sip of my coffee, then stiffened my back. "I'm okay, Daddy. I need to know how you'll vote if I bring my bid as CEO and overturn the charter that doesn't allow for it."

He was quiet, not even his breathing audible through the phone.

"Daddy? Do you not think a woman should be CEO just because it's been that way for a hundred years, back before women were allowed to do much?"

"Of course not, Margaret. I'm all for changing the charter."

I let that hang between us and took another sip of my coffee. The caffeine was probably a bad choice, but it did empower me to just get this out. "You're just not all for me being CEO." No sense asking the question. His decision was apparent.

He sighed this time. "I believe you're very capable, Margaret. You'd make an excellent CEO."

"But?"

"Yes. *But* I don't believe you actually want it. You think it's your duty, and that breaks my heart. You're thriving in your career. Why would you want to give that up?"

Tears welled in my eyes, and I cleared my throat to hide the hurt. "What about family and legacy?"

"That sounds like obligation, not passion. This family isn't going anywhere if you continue your trajectory. Just like the business will continue without Dominick if he truly wants to go."

I took a couple of deep breaths. "So you're a *no* vote?"

"I'm a *no* vote. But I love and support you, Margaret. I hope you know that. Just not in this."

"I think you're wrong, but I appreciate you telling me up front. I'll talk to you later." I hung up before he could respond and put down my coffee so I could rock myself until comforted. It would probably take all day, or maybe all week, but I'd get through this.

I only needed one vote. I wouldn't give up. Throwing in the towel wasn't in my nature.

My phone buzzed and I figured it was Daddy calling back, but when I checked the name, you could have bought me with a penny.

Seeing Lewis's name on my screen made me feel some type of way. I just hadn't figured out what. *"I dug up some information you may be interested in."*

That was weird. The only information I cared about that Lewis could dig up would be about himself. Other than that, he could kick rocks. *"What about?"*

"It's about that great-uncle you told me about."

Okay, backtrack time. That sentence definitely caught my attention. *"Tell me."*

"Can I call you? It would be easier."

"Sure."

The phone buzzed in my hand. A generic contact picture with it. We hadn't had a real relationship, no cute pictures to add. "Hello?"

"Hi. Sorry to bother, but I thought you might want to know."

"You said you have information about my mystery uncle?"

"I don't know if you recall, but you told me a bit about him and said you'd not been able to find much about his history or what happened to him."

"Of course I recall, Lewis. It's one of the great mysteries of our family. What did you learn?"

"He was dishonorably discharged from the Airmen."

I gasped.

I FOUND GRANDDADDY in the library of the main house, wrapped up with a large tome, seated in one of the big comfy chairs that absolutely enveloped you. Chana found those armchairs a couple of years ago, and now anyone who wanted to be alone with their thoughts or needed some quiet space in the house to read had the perfect setup.

"Can I interrupt?" I sat across from him, willing my face to remain neutral. I didn't want to give away the big reveal too soon. Besides, it was past time my grandfather and I had a good old-fashioned tête-à-tête.

He pulled his glasses down his nose and peered at me above the lenses. "What's this about?"

I often wondered how I got saddled with such a curmudgeonly grandfather. Mama's folks died before I was born, so I never got to know them. This man's wife, my loving grandmother, had been gone too long. While she was here, she tempered Granddaddy some, but his countenance always leaned toward grumpy.

While my bestie's grandfather took her to ball games, taught her how to ride horses, and hold crawfish boils, I got stuck with this grouchy pants clutching the last vestiges of the patriarchy with all his might.

"It's about the vote, Granddaddy, and your outdated ideas. I'd love to drag you into the twenty-first century, if you would let me." I sat back in my chair and allowed it to suck me into its pleathery depths.

He placed his book on the table beside him and straightened his back as much as he could, then glared me down, spoiling for a fight.

I maintained my stare. After all, I had an ace in the hole, and I relished every minute of this.

"My grandfather knew what he was doing when he and my father founded this place. They had a very specific vision for the future. I don't think even they could imagine what it's turned into under my and your father's guidance."

"What about your uncle's vision?"

He narrowed his eyes. "It was in line with the rest of his family."

Oh, this was going to be absolutely delicious. I had no intention of springing my findings on him now. I wanted to savor this as long as possible. "Even if that's true, do you think they could imagine what the world would be like today? When they built this place and started that crop-dusting business, could they imagine our technological leaps? The simulators we use at the flight school? Computers?" I sat forward again because I was just getting started. "How about the civil rights movement of the sixties? Your father was around for that, but not your grandfather. I wonder if he ever thought it possible his descendants would be generals in the Air Force when his sons were only allowed to escort pilots into combat."

"They were great intellects and could probably imagine all those things."

"Even women making decisions for themselves? Being able to own their own homes or have credit in their names? Leading companies?" I rose my eyebrows in question.

"Neither you nor your sisters will ever run Hawthorne Family Flying Eagles. You may as well get that through that thick skull of yours, girl."

My blood boiled, but I kept my breathing steady. I knew his views already, but to hear that blatant declaration drop from his mouth was too much.

"I wonder what would be worse for the Hawthorne Family Flying Eagles's legacy: a Hawthorne woman leading the company or a Hawthorne founder who was dishonorably discharged from the Airmen for desertion?" I sat back again and let the words drip into his ears, dropping my imaginary mic.

His eyes grew to a disproportionate size. He sputtered his words, spittle flying everywhere. "You sh-shut up right now, goddammit. You don't know what the hell you're talking about." His voice swelled louder than I'd ever heard it. If anyone thought this man was feeble, they were getting played. "Goddamn you!"

"You already said that, Granddaddy. You should probably calm down before you have a stroke or something." His ailments were few, stroke or heart condition not among them.

"What in the world is going on in here?" Mama ran in with Aunt Deborah hot on her heels.

"Your insolent daughter is in here lying through her teeth."

I crossed my legs and sat back to watch the show.

Mama gave Granddaddy a death stare. "All I hear is you in here cursing up a storm." She turned to me. "What happened, Margaret?"

"I simply asked Granddaddy for his vote."

He seethed in his chair, whistles of air rushing in and out of his mouth.

I sat up then and leaned forward. "I can't remember what you said. Do I have your vote?" It was showtime. Now would be the moment when I found out if I overplayed my hand. I bit the inside of my mouth to keep myself from saying anything else.

Mama turned to him. "Is that what all this is about?" Then she rotated to Aunt Deborah with outstretched hands. "What do you make of this?"

Aunt Deborah, always the onlooker, keeping keen observations. "I think we should ask Isaac the question again. What will your vote be? For or against changing the charter to allow Hawthorne women to lead?"

All three of our gazes landed on a defeated Granddaddy. He spit out through gritted teeth, "I vote yes."

Mama turned to me with surprise written all over her face.

I shrugged and stood. "Great. That makes the nine I need."

I strolled out of the library without a glance back.

CHAPTER TWENTY-NINE

Lewis—Would you like some tepid tea along with that rejection?

I GRABBED A metal chair under the pavilion in the middle of Market Street out in the Woodlands and watched kids play in the adjoining grass, waiting for Dominick to show up. He called this get-together, and since he hadn't filled out the paperwork to start work in less than a week, I guessed this wasn't some sort of casual hang.

My watch confirmed he was about ten minutes late. I kicked myself for not stopping by the coffee shop I passed while I had the chance walking here from the HEB parking lot. The chai was crud there, but I could get some sort of black tea to give me an afternoon caffeine boost.

The kids provided some entertainment, but I quickly bored and glanced around at the shops and restaurants all around on both sides of the lanes that bracketed this make-shift park. A movie theater advertised the latest thriller I wouldn't mind seeing. The whole area flexed a mellow vibe, and I made plans in my head to come out here again when I could enjoy it. I wondered for a moment if this place drew in Margaret, then quickly banished the thought from my mind. Margaret made it clear she wasn't keen on hanging out with me unless it was in the bedroom.

With two cups and a small pastry bag in hand, Dominick walked up the couple small steps to where I'd camped out. "Sorry I'm late, man. I got stuck in the line." He handed one cup to me.

"Ah, what's this?"

He had a sheepish expression and shrugged ever so slightly. "English breakfast tea. I know it's not breakfast time, but…" Then he opened the bag. "Blueberry scone?"

Yeah, this was definitely not good news. "Thanks." I took one of the *scones* and viewed it in puzzlement, then took a nibble. It wasn't like anything we had at home.

I sat back and chewed, watching Dominick as he glanced around, his gaze landing anywhere but on me. Finally, his chest expanding and deflated as if taking a deep breath, he looked my way. "You mentioned you were running away from your past, that Texas is a new start."

I nodded, not sure where this was going. "That's right."

"Is it something you want to talk about? Can you tell me about it, I mean?"

I studied him a long minute. Now I understood. I ran, and he was undecided if that was the move for him. "Okay. I don't normally talk about this, but I will with you." He seemed to be at a crossroads. Perhaps my story would push him one way or the other. "Let me finish this tea first."

The drink had grown slightly tepid. The coffee shop wasn't too far, which told me he must have been shoring up his resolve for some time before deciding to take the walk over to where we were now. I downed it in one continuous swallow and placed the cup on the table near the half-bitten pastry, the monstrosity completely forgotten.

Dominick's gaze grew wary.

"As often these things do, my sad story begins with a woman. A very beautiful and smart woman. An heiress, or so I thought, introduced to me by my mother who'd met her at one of her charity functions." I waved my hand around, unsure of which philanthropic event but also realizing it didn't matter. Sheila had lied her way in no matter.

Dominick tilted his head. "Go on."

"Sheila." Saying her name out loud still gave me chills but also a thrill. "She was adventurous but also down to earth. She spent money like water, and it wasn't until later I realized that most of that money was mine. We traveled…everywhere, staying in the best hotels and participating in the most exclusive excursions. And our physical intimacy…" I'd leave that to Dominick's imagination, but Sheila was adventurous there too, sometimes to my discomfort.

"She sounds fun. What happened?"

I shrugged. "She led me on. She said she wanted a forever relationship, and after six months, we were engaged." I shook my head, still in disbelief. "My mother was heavily involved with wedding planning, the news splashed over society pages and rags alike. While out with Mum, at some fancy designer salon for the wedding dresses, Sheila mentioned her wish to join the financial sector. We all believed she had a London School of Economics degree but had been busy in the public sector. She used a family name well known to Mum."

Dominick was rapt, leaning into me so far I could reach out and touch his face without straightening my arm. "I'm guessing all that was a lie."

"It was. Her story began to unravel when Mum rang one of the family members to arrange an engagement brunch and found they'd never heard of her. She'd already set Sheila up with a position, secured by Father, and my parents were too embarrassed to let the contact know they'd been taken in. No matter because word got out quickly, and what ended up on all those newspapers was me, jilted and taken advantage of. Not to mention cuckolded because here's the kicker: Sheila already had another bloke."

Dominick's eyes bulged. "She had a boyfriend?"

"No, mate. A husband actually."

"So all that time, her husband didn't care she was screwing you all over the world?"

"I've not met the man, so I don't know what he minded or did not mind. I only know that Sheila used me, my money, and my family connections to advance her career. That's really all she was after." I breathed, allowing myself to grieve for a moment at the loss of my trust and ability to see the good in people. In women. "Everyone has an agenda."

He sat back and stared at me. "Not what I expected. Not at all. I can see why you'd want to get away from London, but why here?"

"Because I'd worked as a recruiter, but that was something to pass the time. After Sheila, I turned my back on the family money and connections for good and looked for similar positions as far away as I could find. The American tabloids care nothing of me, and I'm glad about it."

"You were wronged. She should have been the one to leave."

"She was a nobody until Mum and Father turned her into a somebody. She relished the tabloid fodder, and I was happy to leave it to her." I closed my eyes a moment, staving off the tension building there. "I allowed the situation to damage my relationship with my parents; I blamed them completely. Not just for Sheila, but for their fortune and family name to make me a target in the first place."

Dominick stared at the ground and laced his hands together in his lap. "Sometimes family can be a lot. Too much."

And here was where we worked our way back to his situation. "Yes, that's true. Sometimes they can be your saving grace."

His head popped up. "What are you saying?"

"You know what I'm saying, Dominick. I'm giving you an out to stay with your family. That's what you want."

He heaved a sigh, nearly a cry. "I'm so sorry."

I pat him on the back. "No worries. I'll make it right with Gibson." There were others on the list, though none with the experience and background of Dominick. One of them would do. The truth was I should have gone in that direction from the beginning. If I had, I wouldn't have made such a mess of whatever this thing was between me and Margaret.

My shoulders relaxed, and I sat back in my hard chair. I was almost relieved at Dominick's turnabout.

The man appeared ten years younger. He grinned. "What about my sister?"

I closed my eyes again. "That is a lost cause, I'm afraid."

He shook his head. "Despite it all, you really care about her. Now's not the time to give up…mate."

I loved the man's optimism, but even I understood it was too late.

CHAPTER THIRTY

Margaret—What have we here?

JAYMES'S FEET HUNG over the arm of the sofa as she languidly popped into her mouth one grape after another. "Fire that thing up." She nodded at the laptop sitting on my coffee table.

I chewed on my lip, still undecided. "This isn't how I operate. I prefer to realize a person in real time."

She gave me the side eye of the century. "Don't act like you've never ever searched a potential boyfriend before. Don't forget who you're talking to." She swung her feet to the floor and sat forward. "Besides, you've given him ample time to come clean."

I nodded. It was time to stop playing around and search out what Lewis was really about. He'd hinted at some sort of past transgressions, and whatever those were clearly affected how he moved through the world now. I opened the computer and placed it on my lap, justifying my actions by telling myself if it lived on the internet, it wasn't an invasion of privacy. It was time to dig deeper.

"Here we go." Jaymes rubbed her hands together.

Last time I did a high-level search on the name *Watson-Grosvenor*, which highlighted immense family wealth. This time, I typed Lewis's name into the search field.

The gasp that escaped Jaymes's mouth reflected my own internal reaction.

Flashy pictures of a slightly younger Lewis and an exquisite woman splashed across my screen. The first headline read FAKE SOCIALITE CUCKOLDS PRESTIGIOUS HEIR. Other stories followed, mostly related, but some promised details of the whirlwind romance orchestrated by his duped mother.

"Lewis being fooled and dumped so spectacularly was not on my bingo card." Jaymes blew out a breath but kept her gaze glued to the screen.

I didn't know what I expected, but this wasn't even on my radar. I searched for the most reputable news source and opened that article first, raptured by every word. When I finished, I sat back and caught my breath.

My friend picked up where I left off and clicked through several articles.

I watched, stunned, my skin crawling from the invasion but my heart aching for what Lewis apparently went through. No wonder he was so closed off and cautious. From what I read, this woman fooled his mother into thinking she ran in their social circle. Which, ew, that was a thing to be vetted. Once she'd endeared herself, Lewis's mother pushed them together, although it seemed Lewis was definitely a willing participant. He even proposed, and it didn't seem coerced in any way. Then again, I was on the outside looking, reading rags to find out about someone I cared about.

"Do you think Lewis proposed on his own volition, or did the mother have something to do with it?"

Jaymes jumped. "I forgot you were even here." She tore her gaze away from the computer screen.

"It's literally my house. Where else would I be?"

She shook her head, the corners of her mouth turned down. "I don't know, Mags. Seems like some pressure from the mother, but I've met Lewis. He doesn't appear like the type to allow anyone to push him to make a decision."

A snort escaped my mouth even though I tried so hard to capture the foul sound in my throat. "I agree with you on that one. But he also seems so…" I searched my brain for the words to describe my impression of Lewis so far. "He seems worldly. Not easily duped."

"We are all fools in love." She chuckled. "At least that's what Charlotte from *Pride and Prejudice* said."

That actually rang true. And probably why Lewis picked up his life and moved halfway around the world. Equal probability was that this very public humiliation and private betrayal was the reason for our easy no-strings night in London, followed by discomfort when we saw each other again. Lewis and entanglements didn't match. At least not anymore. "It's all really a shame. I hate that for him."

She closed the computer and sat back, knocking her thigh into mine. "Explains a lot though."

"Indeed it does." I thought about our interactions over the past few weeks. It was true that I laid the ground rules in the beginning, but now that I gave it some thought, Lewis was poised to do the same. I just didn't give him the chance first. I hadn't missed the look of relief in his eyes when I proposed a casual involvement.

I also saw the signs when we became closer. Reluctant, yes. But an inner turmoil presented itself the few times after. There was something on his mind in the afterglow of our times together. Like he wanted to let himself go but constantly reminded himself that hurt lay that way.

Again, Jaymes startled when I snapped my fingers.

I narrowed my eyes. "You aren't living right."

"All these sudden movements and stuff. I'm deep in thought about all this." She waved her hand in the general direction of the laptop. "Why'd you snap your finger?"

Because I remembered something when reminiscing about Lewis's inner thoughts. There was a very physical declaration. "Lewis has a tattoo on his forearm. It's like a snake with a hand for a head. I don't know, it's like a combination snake head and human hand. Anyway, another hand shakes this snake hand. This is a cold reminder for Lewis."

"That's pretty deep. But seriously, after all that drama in England, seems like he wouldn't need a reminder. If something like that happened to me, it would be fresh in my mind every day." She twisted her lips to the side of her face.

That was the thing. I thought Lewis needed that reminder because maybe wariness went against his normal personality. Then again, maybe it was wishful thinking on my part.

"Do you think Dominick knows?"

My gaze snapped to hers. "I wonder." Then I dismissed the thought. Why did it matter? My brother's last day at the flight school, the final hours where our legacy meant something to him, was here. "It doesn't matter. Dominick is leaving." A deep sadness settle in my bones.

At that moment, learning about Lewis's misery floated from my head.

All that remained was the fact that Lewis stole my brother from me.

I couldn't let that stand.

CHAPTER THIRTY-ONE

Margaret — Confrontation, forgiveness? I can barely tell anymore.

I WASN'T SURE we'd ever had such an eventful Sunday dinner. And that was really saying something.

My bite of meat loaf hovered less than an inch away from my mouth when Dominick stood. Him having something to say wasn't unexpected, considering his tenure at the flight school was over and this was Sunday dinner, a perfect time to give a going-away speech or whatever. As usual, the entire family assembled to fill our stomachs and catch up on the week's activities.

The meat loaf set on my plate again, and I looked at it forlornly, the perfect forkful of meat and mashed potatoes, perfectly hot and inviting. It would be cool by the time I got to it again, if I even felt like eating it after Dominick said his piece.

Miranda's eyes stayed downcast, and she picked at her food. Running the flight school, along with spending all her time there, hadn't been in her plans, and although she would support our brother any way she could, it was obvious she struggled with the additional responsibility.

Dominick's sons yelled from the other room, and we all turned our attention that way until we heard one of them laugh and the other complain of his brother's rudeness. We'd learned long ago to allow them to eat in the kitchen under Chana's supervision considering family meals could go left at the drop of a hat. Nobody wanted them witnessing family members at odds. We tried to make this a safe space for them, even when Lisa was alive.

Many of us chuckled and turned our attention back to Dominick.

He glanced around the table and bit his bottom lip. "I'm not sure where to begin."

"Take your time, baby." Mama gave him a sympathetic smile, her eyes glistening. We'd all miss having Dominick around on the daily, but probably our mother would most of all. Especially if he ended up moving the boys away.

"Thanks, Mama." He sat back down and picked up his napkins, twisting it through his fingers. "Losing Lisa was…devastating."

Murmurs of agreement rose around the table, everyone's attention rapt on my brother.

"I've been mostly going through the motions emotionally, not really examining my feelings or fully realizing my grief." He dabbed at his eyes with the napkins, and Daddy slung an arm around his shoulders.

I didn't believe any of us really internalized the void Lisa left. We soldiered on, putting on brave faces for Dominick and his children.

"Then I met a new friend, one who helped me recognize I moved through the world on autopilot, not allowing anyone too close or having thoughts that ran too deep." He glanced at me.

My stomach tightened. Surely he hadn't meant Lewis.

Daddy's eyebrows drew together, and he allowed his arm to drop back to his side. "What friend?"

"I know what you're thinking, Daddy." He looked around. "All of you are thinking. That Lewis came into my life and manipulated my feelings, providing the pathway for me to leave. But that's not true." He chuckled. "Well, mostly not true. He did recruit me. That had always been his intentions. But he appealed to my business sense of wanting to have more autonomy and make the improvements I deemed necessary. But that wasn't my reason for wanting to leave."

Mama reached across the table and squeezed his hand, understanding lighting her eyes. "Tell us."

He shrugged, a grim smile creasing his face. "I wanted to run. Run away from all the memories where Lisa and I started our relationship. And our family. Away from everything that caused me pain. Somehow I thought that was here." He waved around at the room and our family. "But it was here." He placed a hand over his heart.

Tears streamed down my face, but I didn't move to wipe them away. I needed this cleansing.

He beat his chest once. "I can't run away from my heart. The hurt and memories and love will be there no matter where I go. I was stupid to think otherwise."

Daddy cleared his throat, clearly choked up. "Not stupid, son. You lost a lot, but I hope you know we'll always be here. We'll always have your back whether you're here or not, have a place for you and the kids whether you're here or not." He swallowed hard. "Of course, we'd rather you stayed."

"Really, Daddy? Is that even an option?"

"You better believe it is." Miranda perked up for the first time in days, a wide smile covering her face. "Your desk hasn't been touched."

My baby sister's outburst provided some well-needed levity. Everyone but Granddaddy wiped their eyes and laughed.

Granddaddy hadn't had much to say since I confronted him with his uncle's impropriety. His relative silence hadn't seemed to bother anyone. Not hearing misogynist patriarchal speech spewing from his mouth had been a boon for me.

Daddy's hand joined Mama's, and they both squeezed Dominick's. "Yes, of course. If that's what you want, we'd be happy to have you back. Is that what you want?"

Dominick bit back a smile. "Before I answer, I want to ensure you know that Lewis is a dear friend and even if I don't go to Gibson's, he'll still be my buddy."

No sounds came from anyone.

"I hope nobody's holding harsh feelings because he'll be around a lot. He got me back into golf, and I intend to take full advantage." His gaze slid my way with raised brows. "Matter of fact, he should be here in the next half hour or so."

I held my tongue. With what I'd put together about Lewis's past and now knowing he'd convinced Dominick he was leaving for the wrong reasons, despite that being a ding against his own interests, my heart had softened considerably. I schooled my face though, not wanting to give anything away to my brother.

Daddy's expression wasn't exactly inviting, but he didn't

say anything either.

Finally Mama spoke up. "If you're happier having him around, the rest of us will fall in line. Won't we?"

More eyes fell on me, but I didn't give them the satisfaction of reacting. Mama might have thought she knew what was going on between me and Lewis, but I wouldn't give her guesses any confirmation. Instead I picked up my fork and choked down the now lukewarm meat loaf, willing myself not to show my displeasure.

Donovan elbowed me.

"Stop, you little pest." I kept my voice low, but since no one else spoke, the whole table probably heard me.

My baby brother only laughed, clearly entertained by my irritation.

"I said, won't we?"

A chorus of "Of course, Mama" and "Yes, ma'am," and "Yes" sounded around the table.

She turned back to Dominick and smiled, eyes glistening again for a different reason. Happy tears threatened to fall. "I think we're all in agreement. Now, what's your decision?"

"Yes, I want to come back."

Daddy slapped him on the back, and Mama clapped her hands together.

Miranda stood and threw her arms around him from the back. "Thank you."

All was right in the Hawthorne family again. At least for today.

Now I just needed to intercept Lewis and figure us out.

CHANA WATCHED ME from over her glasses as she typed away on her tablet, a deep groove carved between her eyebrows.

I put my finger against my lips, then continued piling high the to-go container with succulent meat loaf, creamy garlic mashed potatoes, spiced green beans, Parmesan-crusted carrots, and tender buttermilk biscuits. I picked up a separate container for the slice of pecan pie. It wasn't unusual for me to pack up a to-go container, but this amount of food was way over the top to feed only me. Chana's unmatched loyalty to Mama never faltered, steadfast through and through, but hopefully she wouldn't mention this inconsistency. Depending on my next step, I would tell them all about my feelings for Lewis soon enough.

First I needed to speak to the man myself, and since Dominick said he should arrive soon, my chance loomed on the horizon. I stared at the pie. Did Lewis even have a sweet tooth? A lump formed in my throat at the thought of rejection. He hadn't shared anything with me, so I only knew what I'd observed. If he still couldn't open up to me after I told him what I'd discovered about his past, then hope was nil.

I needed lids. Looking around, none lay about, and my breathing got tense. Nervousness. Something new for me to contend with. Chana placed a hand on mine, and I startled. Then she slid the lids my way, concern creasing her face.

"Thank you." I closed my eyes a moment, then packed up the food and headed home. I hurried with every task because time decided not to be my friend this evening. My goal: drop off the food at my house, double back, intercept

Lewis before he could go to Dominick's door. I'd already cleared it with my brother. Officially, Dominick knew about me and Lewis, but nobody else in the family did. My intent to keep it that way until we had an understanding probably made me a fool.

It only took one person looking out a window to spoil my evening's plans.

Fast walking home was not high on my list of favorites, but if I ran, no doubt I'd tumble and the food would decorate the pathway from the main house to mine. Wild animals lurked in the forest close by, and I certainly didn't want to give them a reason to visit. We had a raccoon problem several years ago, so we took measures to ensure nothing remained outside to interest them. That did the trick, thankfully.

After depositing the food on my kitchen counter, I raced back to Dominick's.

Lewis's car already rested outside my brother's house, turned off and empty inside.

Shit.

What to do now? If he went to the main house next door, that was the end of all my machinations. No way could I navigate my family and remove him without too many people having something to say. I'd face them later but needed to speak to Lewis first.

I texted Dominick. *"Where is he?"*

Dots bounced immediately. *"On my porch."*

I slid my phone into the back pocket of my jeans and hurried to Dominick's house, rounding it to get to the back porch.

As promised, the two of them sat, beers in hand, talking under the porch light as the sun set behind them.

At first Lewis didn't see me approach. Dominick slid his gaze to me one too many times, and Lewis rotated, meeting my stare head-on.

He blinked.

Once I'd taken a couple of deep breaths to untangle the knots in my stomach, I trudged over to the steps that led up to the porch. My slick hands glided down the handrail, and I couldn't help but laugh at myself. I hadn't felt this keyed up about anyone in a very long time.

Lewis watched me the entire way, his face an indecipherable mask, green gaze completely neutral.

"Hey." I spoke to the two of them.

Dominick sucked his lips into his mouth, obviously biting back a laugh. He had a bit of fun at my agitation. Hopefully Lewis hadn't read me so easily.

"Sorry. What's going on?"

I couldn't blame Lewis for the confusion. Neither of us had contacted the other since he told me the secret my ancestors, including Granddaddy, had tried so hard to conceal. So many happenings since we last spoke. I wanted to share all that had transpired when I used his information but also everything else that occurred including what I found out about his family. I had no doubt Dominick filled him in already on his decision to stay at Hawthorne, but I wondered about his part in it.

"I know you came out here for Dominick, but I wanted to talk with you, if you're open to that."

"Sure, of course." He looked at my brother.

Dominick stood, and Lewis followed suit. "I'll see you later, man." Then my brother unlatched the screen door and walked inside.

"Everything all right?"

I nodded. "Can we talk at my house?"

He quirked an eyebrow. "I thought that was off-limits."

We'd see how the night played out before I made any declarations. "This way." I led him behind Miranda's house—still dark inside, thankfully—and didn't cross over to mine until we arrived at the end of the circular road. No guarantees our movement went unnoticed, but at this point I really didn't care.

Inside, Lewis took in the downstairs rooms, whatever fell into his line of sight. Then he smiled. "This is very you." He nodded to himself.

I didn't ask him what he meant because I curated my surroundings to my taste. Unlike Lewis's tepid town house. Of course, I'd had years to do it.

I gestured at the couch, and Lewis sat but I remained standing, holding myself back from pacing. "I need to know one thing."

He sat forward. "What's that?"

"How do you feel about me?" An unfair question, but the query tumbled out of my mouth before I could stop it. Nothing about our past interactions indicated he had anything other than sexual attraction to me, but I willed myself to look past any insecurities and confronted the situation head-on. Sort of.

"What's brought this on, then?"

I huffed a laugh. If I thought I'd get away with requesting him to express his feelings first, I'd misjudged the man entirely. A long shot surely, but the alternative racked my nerves too much. Rejection hadn't scared me; I'd faced it too often before. To become a commercial airline pilot, I'd faced rejection at every juncture. Rules were made up on the fly to hold me back. I persisted until I met my goal, the patriarchy be damned.

I took a deep breath and swallowed my pride. "So much has happened behind the scenes. I realized early on what you were doing with Dominick. It was shady."

"It was, yes, but I can explain."

"You can if you want, but I think I understand. You had a job to do, and it was nothing more than a twist of fate that we shared that evening in London months before. You actually beat me here since you left the next day, so it's not like you followed me." I snorted, a terrible pain-in-the-ass reaction when my emotions ran high. "That sounded better in my head. Of course you didn't follow me here."

He smiled and reached for my hand, leading me to sit by him on the couch. "No, these plans were in the works weeks before I met you. You know, at first, I thought maybe you knew about the whole scheme and had come to London to thwart me in some way."

I rolled my eyes. As if. He probably felt the same at my outlandish accusations. "That's...interesting."

"Right. I quickly put that out of my mind. It was obviously happenstance. Serendipity, if you will."

I nodded, probably a little too aggressively. "Exactly that. But..." I raised an eyebrow.

"Either I should have said something about my intentions with your brother or not pursued a…situationship with you."

I tapped my nose. "Got it in one. Kind of shitty, in my opinion. Which put me in a bit of a conundrum. You see, although I suspected what you were up to, I still entered into that…what did you call it, a situationship? So yeah, there's that."

"And then?" A coy smile broke through his otherwise serious demeanor.

I huffed a laugh. "And then there were things that began to change my opinion of you. Like the valuable information you gave me."

His eyebrows pulled together. "Oh, about your uncle, then? Did that prove useful?"

An understatement. "Yes, very useful. You've met my grandfather. He can be…"

"Yes, I have many feelings where he's concerned."

"Right. And you just met the man. Imagine my adult life constantly trying to gain his respect and always coming up short simply because I wasn't born male." I shook my head and took a couple breaths. This wasn't the time to get my back up about Granddaddy. At some point, I needed to exercise some emotional intelligence where the man was concerned. "Well, I'm not happy with myself, but I used what you told me to convince him that he'd have to stomach a woman in charge of our family business or I'd expose the information you gave me." Heat crept onto my face at the admission.

"Oh, I see." His expression remained neutral, but I imagine his feelings lined up with my own.

"It was rash, and I feel bad now. That secret is not something I would ever expose. It's not just me I have to think about. My whole family would be affected. Everything we've built on the back of our ancestor's reputations." I looked up at the ceiling, blinking back tears. "But I made Granddaddy believe I would. It pains me that he believed it so easily. I knew he didn't think much of me, but…" What else was there to say?

He turned to me and offered a small smile. "Listen, what's done is done. You did what you felt was right at the time. Maybe it was rash, but you can't beat yourself up about it."

Lewis didn't know me well if he hadn't realized I was my harshest critic. "Yeah. Well, I wanted to properly thank you for what you did even if I regret using the details now. I'm still glad I finally know the big mystery, and I think everyone in the family should know too. When the dust settles, I plan to have a long talk with my father." My thoughts circled back to Lewis not really knowing me. And me not knowing him.

"What's the matter? Your face is broadcasting something serious, but I'm not sure what."

I placed my head in my hands and squeezed my eyes shut. "I don't really know you." I looked up then. "But I know enough that I really want to explore something more with you."

He steepled his hands together. "When you say you don't really know me, I don't understand what that means exactly." Although he said the words, his tone relayed he knew exactly what I meant.

I screwed my lips to the side. "Bullshit. You do know. Let me ask you a question."

His whole body tensed with the mere notion of a query coming his way.

"Is there anything personal in your town house? A photo, evidence of a hobby, tchotchkes you enjoy?"

"Tchotchke?"

"You know, souvenirs or little thingies that you like."

"Ah, bits and bobs." His bones relaxed. "As a matter of fact, there is. You've never been in my office slash guest bedroom, but next time you're over…" He briefly closed his eyes. "I mean, if you decide to come over again, I'll show you."

I gave him a shy smile. "I'd like that. I want to know you, Lewis. More than what I can find online."

He stiffened, and I instantly knew what I said wouldn't be accepted in the spirit I'd gone looking for.

I couldn't come up with anything to get me out of this kettle, so I waited for the backlash.

CHAPTER THIRTY-TWO

Lewis—Lifting a weight off my shoulders

I SUPPOSED NAIVETE on my part led to this. If Margaret brought me here to tell me she wanted more than the fumbling relationship we've settled for so far, I should have guessed she searched me out online. I couldn't exactly blame her considering how closed off I'd intentionally made myself. In all honesty, her wanting more hadn't occurred to me, even as much as I wished for it. I needed to decide if I wanted to pursue something real with Margaret or hide behind my ongoing shame and hypervigilance in protecting myself.

My stomach took this opportunity to growl rather loudly. "Sorry."

"No, I'm sorry." She stood and walked to the kitchen. Plates rattled, and soon the microwave started. She came back in. "Let's move this to the kitchen table. I brought you food from the main house."

I sighed, grateful for her forethought. "Clever girl, er, woman." Somehow I didn't think calling her a girl would go over well.

She grinned, a knowing glance, then back to her chore. "Dominick announced to the entire family you would be coming around today and in the future because of your friendship." For some reason, I imagined quotes around the word *friendship*.

"Do you not think we're friends?"

She frowned in thought. "I guess it's the same as with us. Dominick can't actually know about the real you to call you a friend."

I understood where she came from with this, but I was of two minds. Should I remain quiet on the subject and allow her to assume I had a surface relationship with her brother? Or come clean because I'd shared a lot with Dominick but hadn't with her? Either option didn't bode well for me, but I'd brought this upon myself and the time had passed for me to remain clammed up. At least if I really wanted to pursue something meaningful with Margaret.

I cleared my throat. "About that. You mentioned you looked me up online. Did a deep dive, did you?"

"Matter of fact, I did." Resistance colored her face, her mouth set in a strong line, and her eyes narrowed.

"Fair. So you know all about Sheila from the popular press?"

She nodded, her expression softening.

Ah, pity. Not exactly what a man looked for from a woman he wanted to pursue. "I've told Dominick about her, but please don't feel like that's a slight to you. He needed my story in order to put his in perspective."

The wheels turned behind her eyes and her throat worked before turning at the sound of the microwave ding. She silently placed food on two plates and set one in front of me while going back for something else.

The smells that hit my nose were divine—savory meat

loaf and potatoes. My stomach warmed at the thought. "Thank you."

She returned with a much smaller plate for herself and another with a slice of pecan pie on it.

"Pudding. Brilliant." With all the amazing food before me, I'd temporarily forgotten about our weighty conversation. I put my fork down. "Sorry. Have I hurt you?"

She smiled. "No. Yes. I mean…I thought about it, and I can see how that would have helped Dominick. I'm grateful for that. And for what you sacrificed."

"That's rather magnanimous of you. Considering." Maybe this chat wouldn't go so terribly after all. Margaret appeared open to my explanations. "As for the sacrifice, please do not give me too much credit. Yes, it's true, Dominick was a huge catch, but there are, as the saying goes, more fish in the sea. I've already set my sights on someone else." I lifted my fork again and relished the perfect meat-and-potato combination. I followed that with the most succulent scone I've ever consumed. "Nirvana. Shit, these are delicious."

"Looks like my brother is king at those as well." She relayed her feelings loud and clear. She wasn't happy with me favoring her brother more than her.

Time to set the record straight. I set down my fork again. "I care for you, Margaret. And I want to see where this can go if we both put our full effort into it. You asked me how I feel about you, and there it is."

She eyed me with skepticism. "I want that too, but I'm not sure I want to put my heart out there considering how cautious you've been." She shrugged. "What can I say? I usually don't do caution. I run at everything full speed, and if we decide to do this, my method may overwhelm you."

Margaret at full speed turned me on. My trousers suddenly tightened in the general area of my lap. I pulled my napkin up to ensure I covered the evidence. I didn't want Margaret to think I only had my mind on one thing. The one thing we'd already excelled at quite well. "I can handle full speed, I assure you."

"Why should I believe that, Lewis?"

She had a point. I'd done nothing to belie her summation of my character. "I was swept up in Sheila's web. I vowed to never allow that to happen again. I've already let down my guard with you more than you know. More than with anyone else who's come since." More than true considering I'd not seen anyone more than once. I woke up with Margaret on my mind. I could tell the difference.

"So you're asking me to trust you." That skeptical expression remained on her face, but her eyes softened just a bit.

"I suppose I am." Hopefully she thought I could be worthy of her chance. "I realize it's a big ask, and I honestly can't make any promises, but I can say that I'll give my all and open up to you. That I can say. You may not like who I really am—"

She placed a finger over my mouth, then kissed the finger, our lips so close together.

That bit buoyed me, and I smiled under her finger.

She leaned back and took a bite of her food. "You should probably eat up. You're going to need your strength soon."

I ate like my life depended on it.

CHAPTER THIRTY-THREE

Margaret—Maybe I was wrong?

I SPENT A languid Monday morning catching up on my reading, relaxing on my couch. Tomorrow I'd fly out to Boston, but today was slow, my body recovering from the night spent with Lewis. There would be plenty of family confrontations at some point and I still had plenty to unpack where he was concerned, but I'd worry about that later.

First a late lunch with my bestie, then dinner with Lewis. My flight wasn't until midday, so I had time to spend a portion of the night with him but still needed to return home at a decent hour. I never played with my sleep before working.

Before leaving the house, I reached into the entryway closet and pulled out a light sweater. Early November brought on unpredictable weather, and I refused to be caught unawares.

We picked a spot nearer Jaymes's job, so it took me about twenty-five minutes to arrive.

Jaymes stood outside the restaurant, phone pressed to her ear, an animated conversation clearly taking place.

I stepped out of the car, and her face registered alarm.

She ended the call and pasted a smile on her face.

"I know you don't think that fake smile will work. We've

known each other too long for me to be fooled." I stepped up to where she stood. "What's going on?"

"I don't really want to talk about it. Plus we're here to talk about your new relationship." There were unspoken quotes around *new*. So her discomfort was relationship based apparently. Which was really odd since she hadn't mentioned dating anyone since Kelvin, and they'd broken up several months before.

I respected my friend's boundaries though. "Okay. Let's at least order first."

She visibly relaxed. "Sounds like a plan."

We sat at one of the round tables for four since the lunch crowd had mostly dwindled. No sense cramming together at one of the small square tables for two if they had the space. I picked up takeout from here often but hadn't sat inside in a while.

Whatever had bothered Jaymes before, she'd clearly let it go. My bestie relaxed into her seat and picked up her menu, shimmying her shoulders every time she read a tasty dish. "Everything is so good here."

Agreed 100 percent, but I tended to stick with the orange chicken and we could share the special lo mein and some shrimp fried rice. That is, if my friend wanted to share. I wasn't used to her keeping tight-lipped with me. "For real, for real."

"Hmm, I think I'll go with the Mongolian beef this time. Share some lo mein and rice?"

That made me relax. We were back on solid ground. "Yes, absolutely."

Once the waiter took our order, Jaymes turned her gaze

on me. "So, the vote is coming up soon."

A statement, not a question. She knew full good and well it was. "Yes."

"And you have the votes?"

Again, this wasn't news. "Uh-huh."

She picked up a chopstick and tapped it on her plate.

"You have something to say, so say it."

She inhaled a fortifying breath. "Here's the thing. And don't be mad, but I've spoken with a couple of your siblings."

The hackles rose on my neck. Obviously Jaymes grew up around my family, spending time after school and most summer days at the compound while her parents worked. She had separate relationships with my siblings outside ours, but the fact that she prefaced this whole thing asking me not to be mad spoke to a conspiracy. "About?"

"See, you're already mad."

I released an exasperated sigh. "I'm not mad, but I am concerned. Spill."

"Let me ask you a question first. How much do you love flying on a scale from one to ten?"

"Eleven." What did that have to do with anything? The news escaped—I loved my job. I cracked my neck. "Where's this going?"

Tears welled in her eyes and she grasped my hand. "You've done so much. Overcome so much. We're all so proud of you. You make a difference, Mags."

I blinked back my own tears.

"You've grown accustomed to the fight. You refuse to be leveled just because you're a Black woman, something that carries two strikes in a lot of places." She nodded her head several times and squeezed my hand like her life depended on it. "You've risen to the highest order in your profession. Not just risen, but shined so bright. And you love it. God knows you do. So why?"

She slowly worked up to her point. I internalized her words and understood what they meant. "Because I don't know how to turn away from a fight."

"Yeah, exactly. Even if it's a fight for something you don't really want. You don't want someone to tell you no and have it based strictly on your race or, in this case, your sex."

"Yes, that's true. But this is my family legacy. Am I supposed to let this fight go because it's inconvenient? I won't stop until a woman is installed as CEO."

She closed her eyes a moment, then stared at me hard. "How do you feel about essentially blackmailing your flesh and blood?"

I didn't need to ask what she meant. What I'd done had been weighing on my conscious after I'd come down from the high of winning against Granddaddy. "I don't feel good about it."

"I know you too well. We've been friends a long time."

"Wait, you didn't mention that to whichever of my siblings you spoke to…?"

She shook her head in a hurry. "Of course not. I would never betray your trust like that. But I think they deserve to know. It's their legacy too."

I placed my head in my hands, then rubbed my eyes. My heart felt heavy, and for the first time in as long as I could remember, I wasn't sure what to do.

CHAPTER THIRTY-FOUR

Lewis—Hullo, sunshine

A T MARGARET'S REQUEST, I ordered takeaway from one of her favorite restaurants instead of keeping the reservations I'd made. She had a lot on her mind and wasn't up to going out.

I could understand that. Spending time with her exceeded any need to be out and about. Plus my excitement to show her the guest room only increased since we'd first talked of it the night before.

I answered the ring at the door and opened it to a smiling Margaret. "Hullo, sunshine."

"Hello, Posh." She stepped through the door and wrapped her arms around my neck.

Hearing her playful nickname made my heart sing.

But then small shivers shook from her against my chest.

I stepped back and studied her. "What wrong, love?" Maybe she'd changed her mind about us. My stomach dropped.

"My family and this stupid vote." She dug in her purse and pulled out a tissue, then swiped it under her nose and eyes. She stuck the used item back inside her purse, joining several balled-up tissues already there. She'd been suffering awhile now.

I led her into the living room, food forgotten on the kitchen counter. "How can I help?"

She sniffed. "I guess if you could just listen? And maybe offer some advice, if you have any."

"Of course." I sat back on the sofa and dragged her back against me, tucking her under my arm until she readied herself to talk.

We sat like that several minutes. She cried some more, and I got up to get her a glass of water.

After a few deep gulps of water, Margaret wiped her eyes once again, then cleared her throat. "I'm still sick over blackmailing my grandfather with that information you gave me. Now I feel more than terrible, even though it worked."

I opened my mouth, but she raised her hand.

"Let me get this out. I have enough votes to install me as CEO when Daddy retires next September, but I don't want it. What's wrong with me, Lewis?" She took another drink.

I remained quiet, no matter that she'd asked me a question. I guessed rhetorical.

"I love flying. I love what I've accomplished the past decade. I love my family too though, and we can't stay stuck in the past. But every time I think of dropping out of contention or telling the rest of my family about our great-uncle and his transgressions, I feel sick."

So much churned within her and my heart broke. I had thoughts too but would only share if she really wanted to hear them. I had enough family dysfunction and negative experiences to fill a book, and while I hadn't made the best decisions always, I understood where I went wrong. I owed my parents a call and planned to communicate with them as soon as Margaret left later. It would be early there, but they'd be up ready to begin their day.

But first I wanted to help the woman who trusted me with this heavy conundrum.

"You can talk now. What should I do, Lewis?"

I chuckled and brushed a kiss against her temple. "Oh, love. I couldn't presume to give you that kind of advice, to tell you what to do, but I do have thoughts."

She nodded. "I'm listening."

"I'll tell you about me and see if you can apply it to your situation. Every family has secrets. You know the big mess with Sheila, but before that, there was Mum and her decision to turn her back on her culture. I'd been lucky enough to know my grandmother, and we visited Trinidad and Tobago often. I have so many fond memories, but my brother never knew her or any of our family there. After my grandmother died, something inside Mum died too. She didn't want to talk about anything to do with Trinidad and Tobago or her family there. She fully embraced being English like Father." I shrugged because all of this was conjecture on my part, but that was how I saw it through my young eyes.

"That's not something I found when I first researched your family. She really has kept it hidden."

"I'm not sure it's intentional, but it just is now. Anytime Charlie would ask her a question, she'd shut him right down. I learned to talk to him alone and answered whatever I knew. It's important to embrace family legacy, no matter what it is. At least, that's how I feel. Otherwise it tears you up inside and everyone who's related to it. Mum became sick, and I truly believe it's because of everything she's buried down deep inside."

Margaret placed a hand on my chest. "I'm so sorry."

I patted her hand and lifted it to my lips. "She's better now."

"I'm glad. So what you're saying is that I should tell the family about our uncle and founder's dishonorable discharge."

I shake my head. "I'm not saying anything. I just told you a story about my family."

"Yeah. Keeping family secrets is a disease. I see that. What about the other thing?"

"Here's where I'll give you my expertise as an aviation recruiter." I smiled and winked at her. "You can hold a vote to abolish the nonsense of a male heir without actually being the one to take the job."

She sat up as if the idea never occurred to her. "I...hadn't thought of that." The astonished look on her face was almost comical if she hadn't been balling her eyes out just a few minutes before.

"Sometimes when you're in the thick of things, it's difficult to see the solution right in front of your face." I dip my head to capture her gaze. "I understand that more than most."

"Thank you, Lewis."

The relief on her face was more than I needed by way of appreciation.

I only wanted to please her.

A scary thought.

CHAPTER THIRTY-FIVE

Margaret—I've got this in the bag

I COULD PRACTICALLY see the weight rising up from my shoulders and floating away. I would withdraw the blackmail information against Granddaddy and instead appeal to everyone to vote for the right outcome. Granddaddy's vote would be lost, but hopefully that gained me Daddy's vote for sure. And since Dominick was back, no need for him to abstain. Daddy wasn't against a woman taking over the reins—just this woman, who he knew didn't really want it. My father, endlessly trying to protect his children from themselves.

My father, a very wise man.

Telling the family about the black mark on the Hawthorne legacy would be a bit more difficult to manage. Hopefully when everyone had their fill of turkey, dressing, and all the fixings, they'd be satiated and ready to receive the truth. I had a couple of weeks to figure it all out.

Lewis stood and reached out for my hand. "Follow me upstairs."

I waggled my eyebrows. "What about dinner?"

He closed his eyes and shook his head. "I want to show you something."

I opened my mouth to make a crass joke, but he held a

hand up.

"Before you take that thought to its natural conclusion, I'm speaking of something in the guest bedroom."

I wasn't sure what to think. Then again, he did mention a hobby or knickknacks or something in the guest bedroom. "Okay." I took his proffered hand and followed him up the single staircase.

Before he opened the door on the other end of the hallway from his bedroom, he paused and bit his lip. "I do have a hobby. It's not that big of a deal, but it is a big deal for me to share it with anyone." He swung the door open and appeared to hold his breath.

I walked through and took in my surroundings. Framed maps adorned the walls and where space allowed, floating shelves held a number of bound books. I perused the titles—all seemed to reference more maps and charts, but some contained zoology and botany. Although the display impressed me, I didn't quite understand. "What am I looking at, exactly? You collect maps and other stuff?"

He smiled and dislodged the tome I held, placing it back on the shelf. "Careful, that's a first edition."

"Of maps?"

"Atlases. I collect atlases."

"Oh. That's…really interesting." I still didn't know what to make of his collection, but his hobby did interest me. Probably because it interested him and I desperately wanted to know him on a deeper level. "Why?"

He laughed and dragged me to the full-size bed pushed against the wall opposite his desk. "Let's say I fancy myself a lifelong student. I love history, and maps teach us so much not only about a particular place but the history and culture too. Even politics and religion."

Of course I knew a lot about maps. I had to for my job but hadn't thought about them in a historical context. As the family historian, maybe I could use maps to put more color to our family history. "That's actually pretty cool, Lewis." My heart expanded at the thought of him sharing something so personal with me.

When I didn't think I had any tears left, water filled my eyes again. This was Lewis opening up to me, the one thing I'd wanted for so long.

"Sorry. Are you okay? Did I say something wrong?"

I hurried to put him at ease, shaking my head and reaching for his hands. "Not at all. I seem to be a ball of unprotected nerves today. I'm just really touched."

He pulled me into his chest, resting his chin on top of my head, and squeezed.

I sunk into the warmth of his body, cherishing the closeness, the safety of his arms. Today had been a day. Honestly, the past couple of weeks had been a roller coaster, but tonight for the first time in a while, pieces were clicking into place. "Thank you."

He kissed the top of my head. "Thank you."

No explanation needed.

He clutched me one last time, then moved to stand. "Are you hungry?"

I checked in with my stomach. Waves of a slow rumble indicated that I was indeed hungry.

"I think I have my answer. Come on, then."

He didn't need to tell me twice.

CHAPTER THIRTY-SIX

Lewis—Mummy and Father, quite the pair

I WATCHED MARGARET sleep, then checked my watch. Although she'd set an alarm for midnight, I was too antsy to sleep knowing I needed to call Mum and Father before they started their day. I'd put this off for so long, and now that I'd made up my mind, I needed to execute. Otherwise thinking about anything else today would be impossible.

After making my way to the guest room, I pressed the button to video chat Mum's mobile. The sun wouldn't quite be up yet, but my parents should. They might've still been relaxing in bed before the time drove Father into action, but they'd be awake.

Proper etiquette worked against me, but anxiousness wouldn't let me go. I should've given them a heads-up before intruding into their bedroom, but as Mum answered, bleary eyed and concerned, I realized my mistake too late.

"Hiya, Mum."

"Lewis? Baby, is that you?" She squinted into the screen, then reached for her glasses from the night table.

Father moved into view, his body filling the lens. His state of half dress would've been comical if not for the worried expression on his face. "Did something happen?"

"No, no. Sorry. I wanted to catch you before you leave

for work. I need to talk with you both."

Mum took the device back and made room for them both to be in frame. "You're not unwell, right? Not injured?"

No matter I hadn't returned any of her calls in weeks and distanced myself from them many months before I moved, her primary concern for my health and well-being came through loud and clear.

I cleared the lump from my throat. "Yes, I'm well. I'm calling to apologize for being such an arse these past few months."

Mum's features softened, and Father's eyes expanded.

I couldn't blame him for his reaction. My stubbornness wasn't exactly a family secret.

"Left you speechless, I see." I took a deep breath. "Right. I could've handled the fallout with Sheila better. And never should have blamed you, Mum. For that I apologize."

Tears sprang in Mum's eyes. "Oh, Lewis."

Father wrapped an arm around her shoulders.

Tears threatened the backs of my eyes, but I held them at bay. "I've only just realized what a scamp I've been. I hope you can forgive me."

They looked at each other, then back at the camera lens. Mum smiled. "We're so happy to hear from you, darling. That's all we care about."

Father raised his brows. "We do care about that, but maybe not the only thing. I'd like you to move back and take up your rightful place in the company."

The one thing in life I'd never be able to give my father. I'd foolishly thought maybe Charlie would be enough. My brother loved the business and was happiest when learning under Father's wing. Looked like I made a mistake.

I schooled my expression and remembered the spirit of this conversation. "I realize this is a disappointment, but I can't do that. I'm settling in here and have just integrated myself fully in my career. Besides, I'm very happy here."

Mum perked up then. "Happy? Is there someone?"

I checked behind me reflexively, ensuring Margaret hadn't wandered in. As it was, the alarm should sound any time now.

When I turned back to the camera, Mum's entire face had lit up and she clasped her hands together. "There is. Tell me all about her." Apparently Mum had forgotten all about her romantic meddling. It wasn't that I expected her to take accountability for her part in the Sheila fiasco, but I hadn't anticipated her willingness to dive back into the deep end so quickly.

"She's American." That was really all I needed to say to draw disapproval.

Surprisingly, Mum's smile didn't falter. "I expected so. You are in America, after all. Is there anything else you'd like to share?"

Margaret's alarm beeped in the other room, setting off all sorts of alarms in my head.

"I'll call you tomorrow, Mum, and tell you about her. It's midnight here, and I really should get to bed."

She chuckled and shook her head. "Is that a promise, Lewis?"

"Yes, Mum. You have my word. I have something else I'd like to discuss as well. About our Caribbean family."

Her face fell, and I hated how that made me feel. Like I'd

overstepped. That had been the problem though. I was tired of walking on eggshells around this subject. Charlie deserved to know his family. We both deserved to have them as part of our community. As I'd learned from Margaret, family legacy was more important than I'd realized. "It will be all right, Mum."

She weighed her response, the gears behind her intelligent eyes cranked away. She finally made up her mind, a resigned expression creasing her face. "All right, darling. We'll talk tomorrow."

"All right."

We had a difficult conversation left to have, but I'd made it through this one, so I liked my chances tomorrow.

Meanwhile, a beautiful, dynamic woman kept my bed warm, and I needed to give her a proper send-off.

CHAPTER THIRTY-SEVEN
Margaret—The vote!

TWO WEEKS PASSED in an instant, and the compound flurried with activity in preparation for Thanksgiving the following day. Thankfully my baby sister graciously traded assignments with me. Instead of the maddening job of coordinating transportation for upwards of sixty people who had been coming in since the weekend, I'd been placed on lodging duty. Chana had already booked a block of rooms at a local hotel, but I had to coordinate the room assignments and communicate with everyone. My shoulders shook at the memory of creating a Google Doc and only getting about ten people, mostly the younger generation, to even open the document. Even my fellow millennial cousins balked. The job ended up being more than I planned to bite off, but at least my part ended days ago.

My gut told me that Miranda hadn't realized the extent of the task I traded off to her. I overheard her in the kitchen of the main house telling Jaden she threatened to fly one of the rentals over to the big airport to pick all these people up, so tired was she coordinating all the rideshares and family members to pick up relatives. Jaden only laughed and reminded Miranda of the price to fly a private plane into the commercial airport.

I got out of there as soon as I could without her seeing me. I knew my sister's limitations, and it sounded like she had one nerve left, and it was hot and red. I didn't want that smoke.

I parted my curtains and looked out to see the activity happening. Donovan, in charge of entertainment, had set up a bouncy house in the middle of the circular drive that connected all of our houses. Well, had someone set it up. Looked like the weather would hold, so a plus for the kiddos. Several bounced around already, and it wasn't even ten in the morning yet.

I poured myself a cup of coffee and made chai from instant—not a fave of Lewis's, but beggars, choosers, and all that.

He bounded down the stairs, freshly showered and smelling like spring. "I can sniff it from here."

"If you don't want it…" I carried both cups to the front door.

He grabbed the tea from my hand without spilling any, thankfully. "I didn't say that." He pecked me on the lips. "Big day, huh?"

"Not as big as tomorrow, but yeah." I anticipated the vote would go smoothly today. Telling everyone about Great-Uncle Harrison…not so much. I opened the door with my free hand and stepped onto the porch with Lewis following close behind. After walking around the porch to the side of the house, I settled onto a cozy outdoor sofa with matching foot stools and patted the seat next to me.

We watched the children play and sipped our hot drinks.

Lewis rubbed my jean-clad thigh. "This is really the life.

It's a shame you're gone half the time."

I tilted my head and stretched my eyes. "You know what they say about absence making the heart grow fonder."

He chuckled behind his cup. "I've heard that."

My job wasn't a point of contention, but since we'd just commenced the honeymoon phase of our new relationship, any time spent apart seemed too long.

He snaked an arm around my neck and pulled me closer, then placed feather kisses along my neck.

I closed my eyes and regaled in the sensation. "You know there are children right over there."

He groaned and pulled back, easing his head back against the brick. "When do they leave?"

"I thought you've been enjoying my cousins. They taught you spades and everything."

"I still don't know what the hell a possible is. Why can't you just say if you have three or four cards that will win a hand?"

"Books."

I've never seen Lewis roll his eyes, but the look he gave me was close. "Sure, love. Books. Whatever you say."

"I don't make the rules." I laughed, then sipped more of my coffee. Although we both dressed in jeans and long-sleeved shirts, the mild weather made me rethink my outfit for the day. Then again, this was Houston, and the weather could turn on a dime.

"What's on the agenda?"

"More family will arrive today and early tomorrow, so I'll need to be on the lookout for any hotel-related problems. Hopefully none will arise. Then the vote this afternoon, which shouldn't take too long, depending on what else is on the agenda. Other than that, I've got six sweet potato and four apple pies to make. Do you want to help?"

The look on Lewis's face had me almost spilling my coffee. "I, er, don't really bake, love."

From the looks of his refrigerator, this was not a surprise. Daddy cooked, and my brothers cooked and baked—really everyone learned. Mama said being able to make yourself a meal was the least of the survival skills as far as she was concerned. I was happy I wasn't born yet when she taught Daddy because I was sure Granddaddy had plenty to say about that.

"I won't force you, but I'd love some help. You can peel an apple, right?"

He perked up considerably. "That I can do."

Relief hit me unexpectedly. It hadn't occurred to me Lewis wouldn't help, and with twenty pounds of apples to peel on top of all the crust I needed to make, I would have been sunk on my own. "Whew, I'm happy to hear it."

He patted my knee, then turned into me. "Have you decided how you'll tell everyone about...you know?"

I sighed. "I'm working on it. I told Granddaddy last night that he could vote his conscious and I wouldn't use the dishonorable discharge to silence his voice." I folded my lips together and looked askance. "I didn't exactly tell him I'd be giving that information for free tomorrow. I hinted but didn't say it out right."

Lewis grimaced. "Maybe you should have given him a heads-up."

I shrugged. "Maybe. Water under the bridge now."

For Lewis's part, he didn't mention it again. One thing that I loved about him, among many others, was that he stood by while I made my own decisions. He might add some color or give me something to think about but never out-and-out told me what I should do.

THE CONFERENCE ROOM across from Daddy's office was filled with the board members, the Hawthorne family who had voting rights. As CEO, Daddy sat at the head of the table, and as the eldest living family member, Granddaddy took up the mantle at the other end. The remainder of us sat along family lines, my siblings and me presenting a united front.

I silently counted the votes, or at least what I'd ascertained. It hadn't escaped me the furtive glances Daddy's cousin, Cedric, kept throwing his daughter, Renee. I'd secured her vote as well as Cousin Ed's son, Jerome. Considering Renee and Jerome encompassed the same generation we did, they weren't as backward thinking as their fathers. That left Cousin Rhonda in Daddy's generation. Sometimes with the older women, you really couldn't tell if they bought into the patriarchy or not. Thankfully, Rhonda didn't fall into that camp.

That only left Daddy, whose gaze hadn't met mine since we sat down. I'd been clear I wouldn't put my hat in the ring for CEO, and I knew my sweet, progressive (thanks to Mama, despite his father's upbringing) father would never vote to hold women back. Unless he held out hope

Dominick would change his mind—unlikely—or force Donovan's hand and pull him back into the fold—improbable.

It was nearly impossible to concentrate as Daddy went through the quarterly business, including the expenditures for the flight school from the line item in the budget I'd found. Dominick had already put a project plan together and started on the first item, getting bids for upgraded simulators. When we finally got around to the issue of changing the charter to include women in the line of succession, I had to wipe drool from my hand where I'd perched my head.

I laughed to myself. How did I ever think I'd be cut out for the boring business of running the Hawthorne Family Flying Eagles?

Daddy cleared his throat. "Margaret has brought new business to the board. Your motion, Margaret."

"Thank you, Chairman. I move to change paragraph sixteen of section three in the charter to include women in the line of succession."

Miranda quickly raised her hand. "I second the motion to change paragraph sixteen of section three in the charter to include women in the line of succession."

Daddy nodded. "It has been properly moved and seconded to put to a vote a change to paragraph sixteen of section three in the charter to include women in the line of succession. We'll vote one by one, aye or nay, beginning to my right."

Cousin Ed shook his head. "Nay." No surprises there.

On that side of the table, there continued to be a volley between "Ayes" and "Nays," but on our side of the table, as expected, we were a resounding "Aye." The vote had come full circle back to Daddy. We had eight for the measure and only needed his to pass.

Excitement built in my veins. We'd finally bury these embarrassing, antiquated rules that were attached to our family legacy. My lungs filled with pride.

Daddy stared at the table. "Nay."

I blinked. "What?" My head swiveled around to my siblings, past a smiling Granddaddy, and back to my traitorous father who had squared his shoulders.

I jumped up and my chair skidded back against the wall. "What do you mean, nay?" My voice rose loud and Dominick reached for my hand, but I snatched it away. "I want an explanation."

"You're out of order, Margaret. Take your seat, or you'll be removed by the sergeant of arms."

I turned my attention to Cousin Cedric, who promptly turned his gaze elsewhere. Yeah, exactly. I'd like to see him try.

Meredith stood next to me, looping her arm through mine, and shot Daddy a death stare. My sister, who'd managed to dress in presentable slacks and remove all traces of engine oil from under her nails, had never conformed to traditional gender roles. I hadn't asked her if she wanted to be CEO, just assumed her happiness tied more to the repair shop than an office.

Miranda stood and muscled past Donovan to stand on my other side. We linked arms but remained silent. Then she tugged at my arm and the three of us left the meeting, the remainder of business be damned.

I shook with anger. No, rage. There was no way I'd mis-judged my own father so terribly. He wasn't like other men in his generation. I'd never been so sure of something. At least before this meeting.

We walked, my sisters and I, until we reached Miranda's cottage at the end of the drive, right across from mine. My windows were thrown open, and I could smell the sweet potatoes I'd left to bake under Lewis's supervision. I huffed. Those spuds could burn up for all I cared right now.

How did we get here?

Meredith, Miranda, and I sat on the steps leading up to my sister's house and hugged each other, pooling our anger and resentment and astonishment but also our comfort and love and compassion for one another. We would figure this out. First item on the program was talking to Daddy. I had to know why he voted the way he did. I'd wait until tomor-row though. Hopefully once I'd slept on this, I could be more reasonable.

As for now, we didn't speak, just held on to each other with all our might. Tonight we'd commiserate.

Tomorrow we'd fight. Even if we had to burn it all down.

CHAPTER THIRTY-EIGHT

Lewis—I can do rough

A T SOME POINT I realized Margaret wasn't coming back anytime soon. I removed her sweet potatoes at the appointed time, carefully avoiding the cooling apple pies that my stomach coveted but couldn't have until tomorrow. Dinnertime came and went, so I heated up leftover salmon and rice she'd made the day before. I'd never had tinned salmon before, but the way she combined it with green onions and cooked it down before spooning over a lush bed of rice was *chef's kiss*. Also, something I could probably make for myself.

After eating, I went to the front of the house to close the drapes. Margaret and her sisters sat across the drive on the front steps of her sister's house, huddled together. I wasn't sure, but my stomach sank at the thought of the vote not going their way. She was so sure the votes were there even without her grandfather's. What could have gone wrong?

I left them be and watched the telly, some mindless programming to occupy my thoughts until she returned. Only she didn't return. I fell asleep on the couch, and when I woke, the brightness of a beach somewhere stared me in the face. I switched the device off and went back to the curtains. The women were gone, but light shone from Miranda's house.

After showering, I slipped into Margaret's queen-sized bed and relaxed in her soft bamboo sheets. I needed to get me some of these, especially for the summer because they remained so cool.

I jerked awake.

Margaret placed a hand on my shoulder. "Sorry to wake you."

My senses immediately turned up. She smelled of tequila, and her hands ran smooth as silk over my chest. "Are you tipsy?"

She shook her head. "Maybe about three hours ago, but it's worn off by now."

"I take it everything turned to shite earlier."

She placed a cool finger across my lips. "I don't want to talk about that right now. I'm all talked out. I just want to…" She sighed deeply. "Feel. Is that okay?"

I sat up and circled my hand around her neck, breathing her in. "More than okay." Then I kissed her as tenderly as possible.

She responded with a soft bite to my lip. "Don't be gentle with me."

Okay, so this was more than about forgetting. She wanted to obliterate the day, and I was happy to accommodate anything she needed.

I could do rough.

CHAPTER THIRTY-NINE

Margaret—I can do angry

I LOVED LEWIS because he was a man of action. A doer. And right now all I wanted was for him to do me. To make me forget not just the vote but my family and everything tied to it. Just for tonight.

He scraped his nails across my scalp and plundered my mouth with his tongue, sucking and biting, ravishing my mouth until I couldn't breathe. Then he left. Vanished.

I opened my eyes, and he stood next to the bed, his hands resting on his hips. "Take your clothes off." His rough voice barked the order, and my hands obeyed without thought. But he grew impatient, and while I slid my blouse over my head, tangling it in my hair, he yanked at my pants, pulling the fabric down in one fell swoop along with my panties.

While still struggling to unwrap the mess I'd made of my upper clothes, Lewis tugged me to the edge of the bed. Try as I might, I could not get that stupid blouse, which was tangled not only with my hair but also my bra, off me. I couldn't see him, but I could feel him everywhere. Running rough hands up my thighs until fingers reached my apex. The friction he caused was otherworldly, then he tugged a nipple into his mouth, sucking like he had the world's tastiest mint between his teeth. Without seeing the action, my body exploded with sensation.

When I finally extricated myself from my fashion mistake, Lewis raised his head. "Too much?"

Those couple of words brought my problems rushing back into my thoughts. "Shut up and fuck me. Seriously, no more talking."

He grinned and rolled on a condom, then pulled me forward by the arms and lifted me. Lifted me! And carried me to the nearest wall, slipping inside me. I lost my mind as he plunged into me, my breathing labored. Then I noticed Lewis's breathing was hard too. Maybe too hard. *Please don't tell me he's going to lose it already.*

But he didn't. He simply carried me back to the bed and threw my legs over his shoulders, picking up where he left off. If I wasn't so ravished, I would have laughed. What I took for fighting off his release was really Lewis fighting for his life holding me up against that wall. That technique was definitely something that sounded sexier than in actual practice.

He'd found his groove now that we were back on the bed, and I allowed myself to just feel. Feel the friction when the base of his erection hit me just right. Feel the slickness of our skin sliding against each other. Feel his hands, rough against my hips, pulling me against him to go deeper. I threw my arms above my head and allowed him to fill my body with delight with every stroke.

This was what I wanted. No, needed. And Lewis realized it right away, giving me everything I'd asked for. My body was straight fire, but my mind was cold as ice, locked deep away in a cave.

Lewis slid his finger over my bundle of nerves, and the touch undid me. I fell, and kept falling, until I landed safely in his arms.

CHAPTER FORTY

Margaret — Well, happy Thanksgiving

W HEN I STEPPED into my parents' house, it was with renewed conviction and no longer feeling sorry for myself. Daddy hurt me, and he'd have to answer for that. But first I made my way to the kitchen, box of apple pies in my hands, greeting extended family members I hadn't seen since the summer every few steps. Lewis would bring the sweet potato pies over once they'd cooled, which would be a while considering they were still in the oven when I headed over here. Those were meant to finish last night, but...well, shit happened.

Hopefully the dust would have settled before Lewis made his way over here. We hadn't officially come out as a couple to family, but it wasn't a secret considering how much time he'd spent at my place the past couple weeks.

I finally deposited the pies in the kitchen under Chana's careful consideration and headed for Daddy's office.

Before getting waylaid by Mama. "Happy Thanksgiving." She leaned in for me to kiss her on the cheek.

"Happy Thanksgiving, Mama. Where's Daddy?" My voice held nothing of holiday cheer.

She grabbed my hand and led me down the hallway, past the downstairs guest rooms, past their bedroom suite and into her home office. She closed the door behind her, and I flashed back to being twelve, getting a good and deserved dressing down as my hormones raged and made living with me almost impossible.

I plopped down into a chair, arms crossed, a tween again.

She perched against the desk, not dressed for dinner yet because it was still early but wearing a nice belted shirt dress in dark fuchsia, complementing her deep brown skin. Her textured hair was brushed up into a top knot. She was casual but elegant.

She fixed me with a stern expression.

I stretched my eyes. "You can't possible defend him for what he did."

She laughed, humorless, without mirth or joy. "Ever since you were a little girl, we couldn't tell you anything. That's served you well—there's no doubt, but you don't actually know everything, dear heart."

Tears sprang to my eyes unbidden. Daddy committed the ultimate betrayal, and now Mama slithered in to finish me off. "I've never known you to kick someone when they're down, yet here we are."

"Oh, Margaret. You don't even want to be CEO. Why is this so important to you?"

I blinked back the unshed tears, anger raising its ugly head. "Do you enjoy your daughters seen as second-class citizens in this family? Nothing about the way you raised me has prepared me for accepting this outcome. Maybe I don't want it now." I shrugged and glowered, my mouth scrunched into a near sneer. "Maybe I'll want it in the future. Or maybe Meredith does. Or Miranda. Both Dominick and

Donovan have turned it down with absolution. Are you expecting Jerome to uproot his life and move here? He's a sports agent, for goodness' sake." My arms flailed around of their own volition. "I think the better question is: Why isn't this more important to you, Mama?"

She winced, then her expression was almost like she was lost. Not a loss for words, but something else.

"What's really going on here?"

Mama shook her head. "Leave it alone, Margaret. For once in your life, don't push." She almost pleaded, something completely out of character.

Unfortunately, and she knew this better than anyone, giving up wasn't in my character. "Where's Daddy?"

"You know everything, Margaret. I'm sure you'll find him yourself." Mama pushed off the corner of the desk and made her way out of the office.

Everyone knew my stubbornness came from her. She never gave up without a fight. Something was very wrong.

I took my time leaving, giving her a chance to disappear and for me to gather myself.

Daddy could be anywhere, and Lord knew this compound had more acres than someone could look through in a week, so I pulled out my phone and texted him. My intention wasn't to ambush him, so giving him a heads-up that I searched for him wasn't a problem. Daddy knew me well enough that I would be seeking answers and wouldn't be put off long.

It took a few minutes, but he texted back where I could find him.

I PULLED MY golf cart up next to the one Daddy drove to get over here. I had hoped my anger would have receded by now, but as I saw my father standing next to the lake, donned in a Stetson and a long straw of hay hanging from his mouth, the hackles on my neck rose again. He was no cowboy but liked to play up the part of Texas rancher when family came in from out of town.

We did not own a single head of cattle, and the only horse gracing the property belonged to Grand, an actual former cowboy.

I checked my anger as I slid from the golf cart. Daddy playing this part had never upset me before, but after yesterday's vote, anything the man did out of character enraged me—that vote being at the top of the list.

He didn't turn as I approached, but no doubt he tracked my movement. "You know, you're not the only family member skilled in the art of blackmail."

I stopped in my tracks, mere feet from where the man I'd idolized stood. "You know about that?"

"I do now." He angled my way, gifting me with a stern expression. "What were you thinking, Margaret?"

"I was thinking that Granddaddy is a misogynistic relic who has no place making decisions that affect the Hawthorne legacy."

He huffed. "So you decided to tarnish it all on your own instead?"

I closed the remaining distance, my stomach sinking with what I'd done. This tactic deflated the indignation from me with a quickness. "It was an empty threat to force him to do the right thing for once in his life." My voice sounded small even to me.

He nodded. "I know why you did what you did, but all you did was poke the bear. And from what I understand, it wasn't an empty threat."

"Daddy." I drew in a deep breath, shaky as it was. "It was, but if you mean I intend to tell the family today, then yes. Granddaddy has bent the truth his way for far too long. Every Hawthorne deserves the truth of our ancestors."

"Judge, jury, and executioner as usual, huh, Margaret?"

That declaration took me by surprise. Was that how the family saw me? As eldest, I meted out advice, guidance, and instruction, but it wasn't arbitrary or hubris. My directions steeped in experience and offered from a place of love could be ignored at will. Often was.

"I know you're angry about the vote, but you set these wheels in motion. If you think a dishonorably discharged great-uncle is the only Hawthorne family secret..." He held up a hand. "And before you ask, no, I wasn't aware. Nor had I ever wondered or cared that deeply. Obviously there was something amiss, but I never would have thought in a million years that's what Daddy hid." He huffed. "Makes sense why there's only one statue out there. That's a dark stain."

"And you don't believe everyone has a right to know?"

"I don't see what good it'll do. What's the benefit? I only see downsides. That piece of ancient history will only harm the family legacy, and you're not exposing anything relevant."

I looked out at the lake, a larger population of ducks milling about as the colder weather set in. Plentiful were the ducks, having flown south for the upcoming winter. I usually avoided the lake during the colder months because they could become quite aggressive especially in the later winter months when they readied themselves for mating.

My opinion morphed with Daddy's sage advice. "I see where you're coming from. But what does that have to do with your vote yesterday?"

He released a mirthless laugh. "Blackmail begets blackmail. Only your grandfather doesn't bluff."

I blinked. My father, upstanding and good as he was, couldn't possibly be susceptible to such extortion. I refused to believe it. "Your own father threatened to expose you?"

"Not me. That's the beauty of it, you see. If it were me, I'd happily fall on my sword. But he didn't threaten me. And it's not ancient history. This would cause real harm if revealed."

My mind raced with possibilities. If what Daddy said was indeed true, that our family had more skeletons than I knew, it could be anything. But whatever the secret was, it would need to affect someone in our close family for him to turn his back on his daughters so solidly. "Tell me, Daddy."

He shook his head. "It's not mine to tell, sweetheart."

Tears pricked my eyes at the sentiment, all the anger drained from my body. No matter the past actions, a wedge would never be driven between us. Any of us. "So another Hawthorne secret hanging out there waiting to ambush us?"

He studied me, a piercing gaze that latched on to me and held my full attention. "Not a Hawthorne, but cherished just the same. And nothing your grandfather should have ever discovered."

My eyes grew big. Not a Hawthorne? Daddy would never say Mama wasn't a Hawthorne despite coming into it by marriage. She might not have had a vote on the board, but she was still a Hawthorne through and through.

Who was left? Chana? While my parents counted on their house manager and often considered her part of the family, I couldn't imagine a damaging secret so big it would affect Daddy's vote. Besides, what secret would she have? She'd raised Jaden right beside us, right on this compound for over twenty years. Everyone knew his father, a Black man from nearby Galveston, who moved to California and left his wife and son behind. His excuse was that their religious and racial differences were too much to navigate. I always thought that was bullshit and certainly not a mark against Chana. I'd made some really questionable choices in men before. It wasn't extortion worthy.

That left Aunt Deborah. Her son, Andrew, visited his mother often. Matter of fact, he was the only member of Mama's family here for the holiday. His father died over twenty years ago, and Aunt Deborah made the decision to move in with her only sibling. We had plenty of room, even back then when my siblings and I filled the main house and before the other houses on the circular drive had been remodeled or built. Other homes and cottages were all livable, but my aunt enjoyed the closeness of her sister when the love of her life left this plane. Andrew went off to college a couple years later at UT and stayed in Austin after graduation.

I wasn't sure what it could be, but my gut relayed something amiss with my aunt's situation. It made sense because Granddaddy, also a permanent resident of the main house, would be privy to private conversations, whether accidental or intentional. The fact that he would use that information against us didn't surprise me in the least.

I climbed off my high horse because I hadn't been any better.

WITH THE CLEAR weather, the tennis court got plenty of use, along with the basketball court behind it. I wasn't much of a fan of either, participant nor observer, but Lewis lit up like a kid going trick-or-treating on Halloween when Dominick asked him to team up for doubles against my cousins Andrew and Ed.

I sat on the sidelines, like a dutiful girlfriend—ugh, my head rotating at the back-and-forth play.

Donovan ambled up, taking a seat next to me. "You didn't want to play?"

"You know better. What about you?"

"I've begged Daddy to build at least nine holes out here, but he said the trees are too important to the environs." My brother rolled his eyes. "Whatever."

He really did live the Houston high life with his fellow oil executives. I glanced at my baby brother and laughed. "You're too funny."

Donovan checked his watch. "Still two hours until dinner. I knew I should have had a bigger breakfast."

Lewis hit the ball, and Ed groaned on the other side, watching it bounce just inside the line and nearly toppling over. He looked to me with a huge smile on his face.

I clapped and cheered despite barely catching the end of the play only because Donovan had elbowed me.

My brother leaned into me conspiratorially. "So you and the Brit, huh? How's that gone over?"

"The jury's still out. Everyone's been on their best behavior though. Mostly because they don't want to cross Dominick, who declared Lewis his best friend." I giggled and shook my head. My sisters supported my decision, but Daddy and Mama still harbored some soreness because he tried to steal away one of their own. It would take some time for them to loosen up. Granddaddy gave Lewis the evil eye, and I was tempted to ask Chana for the hamsa that hung on a bracelet at her wrist.

That man would never come around. And now that I knew he held something over Aunt Deborah's head, his opinion meant less than nothing. Not that I ever held it in high regard, but I tried to give him the benefit of the doubt considering he came from another era.

"So where's Jaymes?" Donovan appeared uninterested, but that alerted my spidey senses.

"Why do you care?"

"I don't care. Jeesh. I merely asked a question. You two are always joined at the hip."

I searched his eyes, looking for deception. There was nothing I could pin my suspicion on, but something was...off. "As you know, Jaymes has her own family. They're having Thanksgiving on the Cane River this year, so she won't be back until Sunday."

The light went out behind his eyes.

Unnoticeable, but I'd been looking for it. "Is there something going on between you two?" Probably out of left field and silly of me to think—she was ten years his senior after all, but I never put anything past anyone.

"What? Of course not. I barely know her." His protest led me to believe the opposite. Did he have a crush on my bestie? I mean, I couldn't blame him. Jaymes's beauty only matched her kindness and sense of humor, but Donovan was a playboy. He had the Houston women all aflutter, from what I'd heard.

"M'kay." I twisted my lips to the side. "If you say so."

"I say so. Damn, Margaret, you see a conspiracy everywhere you turn. Relax."

I released a sharp huff. "I hope you're not in these Houston streets telling women to relax. I'd hate for my little brother to get cut."

His shoulders shook with laughter. "I know better."

Lewis and Dominick high-fived on the court and jogged over our way.

Donovan stood and allowed Lewis to settle next to me, rivulets of sweat running down his face and arms. The temperature cooled considerably today, probably in the high fifties, but he'd worked up quite the perspiration with his and Dominick's winning play.

"Good game, huh?"

"Match, love. Your brother and I won the whole thing." He radiated self-satisfaction, which he and Dominick deserved because neither Andrew nor Ed were a joke on the courts. Andrew even played on his high school team.

I patted his wet back and grimaced. "Good for you. How about a shower before dinner?"

"But we were going to, er, hoop." He looked at Dominick for confirmation.

My brother laughed but nodded.

"Do you even know how to play basketball?"

Lewis laughed. "Not really, but Dominick promised to teach me."

I frowned at my brother.

He shrugged. "Maybe another day, Lewis. We are cutting it a little close."

Two hours later, all the tables in the dining room, kitchen, and even small tables set up in the family room for the kiddos were at capacity. Platters of roasted, smoked, and fried turkey, roast beef, gravy, and corn bread dressing sat before me. I stretched my gaze over to long tables set up with sides of bacon-wrapped green beans, macaroni and cheese, two kinds of cranberry sauce, mashed potatoes, sweet potato casserole, cranberry-and-orange rugelach, pampushky, rolls, and another table set up with desserts: my apple and sweet potato pies, along with pecan pies, 7UP and sock-it-to-me cakes, and peach cobblers.

My stomach grumbled, and I turned to Lewis next to me.

His eyes, wide as saucers, glanced this way and that, finally circling back to me. "I've not seen so much food in one place. And that's saying something with the feasts my grandmother served."

"Why do you think my brother worked you out so hard

this afternoon? He knows the deal."

The fried turkey's savory smell wafted to my nose and called my name. But we waited until the table was blessed before making our plates.

Granddaddy stood at the head of the table, supplanting Daddy just this once, as eldest member of our extended family. He'd discarded his cane and stood as straight as I've ever seen him, probably motivated by his recent ill-begotten victory.

Anger still floated through my veins, but game recognized game. He won. I lost. This round. We lived to fight another day though. And as long as I had breath in my body, I wouldn't give in until everyone had equal rights in this family.

And I'd make it my mission to thwart him in his attempt to tarnish my sweet aunt. Of that, I had no doubt.

CHAPTER FORTY-ONE

Lewis — Staying put

M Y STOMACH STILL pressed against my pajama bottoms uncomfortably, even though Thanksgiving was three days ago. Then again, my refrigerator overflowed with enough leftovers for three or four days. Not to mention another month's worth in the freezer. I found it impossible to tire of the meals because the combination ranged from lunch to dinner; such was the variety of different food available.

Even breakfast this morning would probably contain chopped roasted beef mixed with scrambled eggs. I smiled to myself and patted my stomach. I'd lead with a slice of sweet potato pie. Although I didn't grow up with this holiday, Thanksgiving was certainly one I could get behind.

I looked over at a still-sleeping Margaret and fought the urge to wake her. The last few days had been eventful for her, and although she'd accepted the strange happenings that fueled the decisions that had been made, she hadn't given up either. If I had to count, this is only the second or third full night of sleep she'd had over the past couple of weeks we'd spent together.

I'd love to credit my comfortable mattress, but if I had to guess, Margaret had more peace now that she could go back to the career she adored without the added burden of succession weighing her down. There wasn't a doubt in my mind she would fight for her sisters when the time came, but her obligation lessened.

I eased from the bed, allowing Margaret a few more minutes of respite before she returned home to send off family members until the next big holiday.

Hopefully my own family members were in proximity to each other as I kept my promise to myself, and Mum, to be present more, even from many thousands of miles away. I ambled down the hall to the guest room and closed the door as softly as possible before easing into my desk chair and balancing my mobile against my open laptop to video chat hands free.

I selected Charlie's number first. If he wasn't at our parents' house, he could add them to the chat. He didn't answer, and I frowned at my mobile, checking the time. It was early afternoon there on a sunless and rainy Sunday. I'd checked the forecast first thing once I woke up, as was my habit to do. Although I moved away from my family, I still loved and cared about them.

Thankfully my mobile rang, and I connected the call. My brother's cheerful face filled the screen. "Hi, bro."

"All right. Where are you?" Judging by the movement, Charlie walked and talked, clearly indoors.

"I'm in my flat. Just trying to get somewhere comfortable. Hold on." He continued walking, glimpses of his place flying by in the background making me dizzy.

I looked away until he found somewhere to stop.

"What's going on, bro?" His enthusiasm used to bother

me.

Now I relished in it. I supposed the saying was true: Misery really did love company.

I grinned. "Just checking in. Do you want to loop the parents in?"

"Sure. Give me a moment."

Mum's face appeared on the screen, full smile on display. "Look at my loves."

"Hi, Mum. Where's Father?"

"Out with Benedict with the golf." She almost rolled her eyes but kept the expression to herself.

Mum was never on board with *the golf* as she called it. She thought it a waste of time. This was better anyway for what I wanted to touch on. "Do you mind if we take a little time to talk about our family history? I was telling Charlie that we should plan a trip soon to visit your family."

Her face turned weary, but this had to be something expected since I'd mentioned it to her a couple weeks before. "What brought this on?"

So many things, but I was unsure how deep I wanted to go with her right away.

As it was, Charlie didn't give me a chance. "Lewis's girlfriend is her family's historian." My brother's eyes shifted, and I assumed he gave me the pointed look.

"Mummy, that's part of it, I suppose. I helped her research an ancestor who had a bit of mystery around him. She'd been looking for answers for a while but didn't have access to the same tools I was able to use. Turns out, it was a deep secret that could upset a lot of people, but she was happy to have the information to make informed decisions."

I took a deep breath, then gave the screen the kindest smile I could muster. "I just think it would be nice to reconnect with our maternal roots."

For Mum's part, she didn't shut down, but the contemplation was clear behind her eyes. "Charlie, is this something you want? You've never expressed an interest before."

He shrugged. "I guess since you never spoke of your family there, it really wasn't on my radar. But I would like to know more. I don't know any of our cousins in Trinidad and Tobago. Nor anything about the food, and Lewis can't seem to shut up about whatever sugar cakes are."

That elicited a smile from our mother. Really, who wouldn't smile about sugar cakes? "Okay, then. Let's take that trip. Send me dates that work for you, and I'll make some queries."

"Really, Mum?" I couldn't believe she'd agreed so easily. Maybe she was ready to do some healing of her own.

She only nodded.

Charlie released a smirk. "Guess what, bruv? Yesterday they were in the West End catching a show."

My eyebrows shot up. "You can't be serious. Father went to a show?"

Charlie simultaneously shook his head and nodded, laughing the entire time. "Can you believe it, bro? Things are changing around here." He bent his head to the side. "Maybe a good time for you to come back."

I looked from an expectant Mum to my wiseass brother. As much as I'd love to see these changes in person, I had no regrets moving here. I thought about Margaret, warm in my bed, and understood waking up to her was a joy, and I wanted that for as long as she'd have me.

When I moved here months ago, I couldn't be convinced that relationships weren't transactional and everyone had an agenda. Sheila had soured me on love and commitment. Mum ignoring her culture and adopting Father's only reinforced that notion. But Margaret made me realize that one terrible experience wasn't the norm. And Mum reclaiming her upbringing, although slowly with finally talking about it with Charlie, was a great reminder and step in the right direction.

Because of Margaret, I realized someone could love me instead of what they might gain from me or my family. For me that was everything.

Margaret was everything.

"Nah, Charlie. I'll visit soon, but I'm where I belong."

CHAPTER FORTY-TWO
Margaret—Ooh la la

T HE GARAGE DOOR opened, and I pulled my car inside, smiling as I noted Lewis's car already there. Weeks had passed since we made public our relationship, but this feeling of having him here and near never got old. My job energized me, but coming home to Lewis settled me in a way I didn't know I needed.

My family was my family. They were loud, always in each other's business, held high expectations but were also steady, committed, and dependable. And loyal. Even Daddy. His own father tied his hands in a way we might not ever know. His *no* vote hadn't brought him a lick of joy.

Lewis was different in ways that encouraged me outside of familial ties. He allowed me to think for myself and make my own decisions, whether great or disastrous or somewhere in between. If I asked him for advice, he'd give it, but always through his own experiences. Never telling me what I should do or feel or think.

Quite a contrast from my know-it-all family of which I was definitely a member. Shit, who was I kidding? I was the president. Proven by my need to direct my brother's life when I never wanted anyone doing the same to me. I couldn't see before where I was a problem in everything that happened with Dominick and trying to keep him here, but I could now.

A lot of that was due to how Lewis moved through the world. I tried to reflect Lewis's way of doing things back to him but sometimes fell short. Ha, most times fell short. Old habits died hard.

The first thing I noticed when I dropped off my bag in the laundry room was the smell coming from the kitchen. In the few months I'd known him, Lewis had not suddenly become a chef. Not even a decent cook, but his willingness to learn endeared me and helped my patience level. I often channeled Mama when she first met Daddy. He wasn't taught anything Granddaddy deemed women's work. That included cooking which…how stupid can you be to not want your kid to be able to have basic survival skills. He taught Daddy to catch a fish but never how to cook it.

Anyway, Lewis wasn't raised that way. His shortcomings bred from wealth and always having servants at his every whim. At least he'd unlearned most of that, as far as I could tell. Hopefully because the only cooks around here were family members and if he continued to hang around, Mama would put him to work in the kitchen even if it wasn't anything other than peeling potatoes.

I so hoped he continued to hang around.

"What smells so good in here?"

Lewis stood before the stove, clad in trousers slung low on his hips and nothing else. No shirt, no shoes. His attention laser focused on a pot, stirring its contents.

He turned off the heat and rotated my way, letting loose a goofy grin. "Vegetable soup with beef." He made quick work closing the distance between us and pulled me into a tight hug. "I missed you."

I'd only been gone since this morning, just a quick turn-around to Denver, but I'd been thinking about this moment all day. "Me too."

He released me and reached into the cabinet for bowls. "Hungry?"

"Definitely, but, uh, you cooked it?" I chuckled to myself because no matter how good it smelled, no way Lewis knew how to make something like that with such a depth of flavor as this soup hinted at.

"Meredith dropped it off this afternoon with instructions on how to reheat it when you were on your way home." He spooned a healthy amount into each bowl. "I heated it. I'm quite proud of myself."

"As you should be." I washed my hands in the clean sink and retrieved some utensils.

The oven timer went off, and Lewis pulled out some-thing wrapped in foil. "French bread." He waggled his eyebrows. "Ooh la la."

"That smells amazing. What did we do to get in my sister's good graces like this?"

He shrugged. "Gift horses, love."

"I'm definitely grateful. Besides you being here, this is the best thing I could have come home to." Frankly, I was a little surprised Meredith had time to cook this. She'd been spending more and more time at the repair shop. Something brewed over there, but my sister refused to talk about it. That was okay. Everything came out in the wash.

"Guess who has tickets?"

I batted my eyes. "I like tickets."

He chuckled. "I know you do. We've only been to one

show since I moved here. Time to change that."

After doing a little happy dance, I jumped into his arms and squeaked. "I knew I loved you for a reason." I'd missed going to the theater district in Houston. With the whole CEO fiasco, I hadn't prioritized any entertainment.

He put me down but held me close. "Sometimes I think this is all a dream and I'll awake and find myself in that same hole where I couldn't make any real connections because I thought everyone I met was disingenuous, that they all had an agenda."

I laid my head on his chest and breathed in his citrus smell, stroking his arm where he'd had his tattoo redesigned. No longer was it a hand shaking a snake hand. Now it incorporated an eagle instead of the hand, its talons gripping the snake, and I wasn't sure what to think about that. Was I the eagle who made everything better by carrying the snake away? "And then you met me."

"Well, technically, then I met Dominick, who helped open my eyes."

I leaned back and looked into his face, a devil-may-care smile parting his lips. "Seriously, Posh?"

His expression sobered, and he leaned down to capture my lips in his. A warm kiss filled with deep affection, with a promise of more later. "And then I met you. I love you, Margaret."

It seemed like a lifetime ago we met in London. I wasn't expecting a hot one-night stand to follow me home and turn into the love of my life.

Yet here we were.

The End

Acknowledgements

This book, really this entire series, came about in an unusual way. I sat on a couch across from my publisher and brainstormed. We didn't start with the Airmen, although I'd been tossing a woman airline pilot around in the back of my head for a while, but somehow talked our way there. Big appreciation to Jane who gave me so many amazing nuggets that ended up shaping this series, starting with a big, sweeping family saga. And to Meghan for being a sounding board. Of course I wanted to stick with my wonderful editor, Sinclair, who gave me the encouragement to keep going in the series after loving this book. She always gives me amazing notes to make my stories better and this one was no different.

My critique partners are so beloved and helped me tighten the first draft so much. Jamie, you really need to hang your editing shingle out because rearranging scenes and events made this story sing. Thank you, Amanda and Bianca, for your stellar insight.

Support from the Wordmaker's group and my Tule siblings keep me going. I appreciate your reassurance and inspiration always.

And thank you, dearest reader, for giving FLY BY NIGHT a chance.

More Books by Kelly Cain

Secret Ties Series

Book 1: *A Kiss From the Past*
Book 2: *Two Sides of a Secret*
Book 3: *The Key to Forever*

The Everheart Brothers of Texas Series

Book 1: *An Acquired Taste*
Book 2: *A Tasty Dish*
Book 3: *Tastes So Sweet*

Available now at your favorite online retailer!

About the Author

Kelly Cain is a native Northern Californian but has spent the last couple of decades in Texas. Consequently, most of her books are set somewhere between those two locations. She writes Black, Blewish, and multicultural romance with determined women directing their own fates, and the swoon-worthy men who adore them.

She loves reading most genres but please don't ask her to pick just one. When she isn't reading or writing, Kelly is most likely using a genealogy site to research her extended family, where she found out about her own adoption and Jewish roots. Or cooking/baking something delightful. She has two adult daughters, and a granddaughter.

Thank you for reading

Fly By Night

If you enjoyed this book, you can find more from all our great authors at TulePublishing.com, or from your favorite online retailer.

TULE
PUBLISHING